One Golden Summer

by Clare Lydon
& TB Markinson

custard
books

First Edition June 2020
Published by Custard Books
Copyright © 2020 Clare Lydon & TB Markinson
ISBN: 978-1-912019-79-3

Cover Design: Victoria Cooper
Copy Editor: Claire Jarrett
Typesetting: Adrian McLaughlin

Find out more: www.clarelydon.co.uk
Find out more: www.lesbianromancesbytbm.com

Acknowledgements

While this book has two authors, there are always amazing groups of people behind the scenes who assist during every stage, including after we hit the publish button.

We would especially like to thank our ARC teams. Not only do we appreciate your enthusiasm for sticking your hands in the air to read advance copies, but your eagle eyes spotted some pesky typos.

Also, we appreciate all lesfic reviewers and bloggers. The time you dedicate to lift up LGBTQ+ stories is fantastic and so very much needed.

Lastly, we'd like to give a special shoutout to the listeners of our Lesbians Who Write podcast. You have been with us since the very beginning, listening to the ups and downs of *One Golden Summer* and providing us with encouragement and support that helped us get the book over the finish line. It really does mean the world to us both.

Chapter 1

Kirsty McBride looked up at her shop sign: 'Wine Time' stared back at her. It had seemed so jaunty when she'd named it ten years ago. Now, it just needed repainting. The windows could do with a shine, too. But if you tilted your head and squinted in the right light (after dark), it'd do. Sort of. Up above, the seagulls squawked as they did every day by the Kent coast, and this fresh mid-June morning was no exception. Sandy Cove's High Street was so close to the sea Kirsty could almost taste the salt on her tongue.

Kirsty's commute to work was from the flat above. Short, sweet, and environmentally friendly.

She glanced down at her feet. The pavements were pristine after an early morning clean from the council. Plus, she'd remembered to put shoes on. Twice last week, she'd come down in her slippers and had to go back upstairs. Helena had taken the piss mercilessly.

"What's the verdict?"

Kirsty turned to where Donald from Donald's Menswear was shouting from across the road. She stepped back as the number 340 bus drove past along the High Street, sending a barrage of diesel fumes up her nose. Not the best breakfast.

Three more cars buzzed by in succession before she could speak. Or rather, shout. Donald was hard of hearing.

"About what?" Her voice broke when she spoke. She hadn't had her first coffee yet.

"The sign!" Donald was wearing his brown cardigan again. He wasn't exactly an advert for fashion.

"It'll do." Kirsty gave him a grin. Compared to Donald's sign, hers was positively vibrant. Donald was closing up in three weeks to enjoy his retirement and seemed keen to spend most of his final days on the street shouting at people over the traffic. He gave her a double thumbs up, then turned and went back into his shop.

Kirsty did the same. Her business partner, Helena, sat behind the counter, leafing through a copy of *Homes & Gardens* magazine that she got on subscription. When she heard the door, Helena looked up, her dark hair framing her angular face. The radio was playing a summery song that Kirsty recalled from her teenage years. Something about being head over heels. She'd been exactly that at age 17 with Tracey Staples, right about when this song came out. It hadn't been reciprocated.

"We need to paint the front of the shop and touch up the sign."

Helena held up the magazine, her index finger pressed into the image of a door. "We could paint it this colour." She twisted the magazine towards her face. "Elephant's Breath, apparently. Sort of stone-coloured?"

"I was thinking something winey. Perhaps a claret? Maybe an accent of sauvignon blanc inside?" Kirsty dropped her phone on the counter and stood beside her friend. The spice of Helena's Opium perfume tickled her nose.

"I do like a nice sauvignon blanc."

Kirsty gave her a grin. "I know. How was the one you took home last night?"

"Divine. Hugh loved it. He cooked a gorgeous seabass to go with it. We should employ him as our chef; he's that good."

"You're a little biased, seeing as he's your husband."

Helena put the magazine down and picked up her mug of coffee. "All true, I am." She paused, tilting her head. "Can we afford a paint job?"

Kirsty twisted on the ball of her foot and sat down at the large wooden tasting table that was the star of the space. It was surrounded by walls of dark wooden shelves lined with bottles of wine from all over the world. A wine library. If you were going to sit a wine exam, it would be the perfect place to study. "If any of my side ventures take off, perhaps. Plan a few more weddings, birthdays, anniversaries. We've got the team-building wine tasting tonight. That could lead to a whole new cash stream." Wine sales were steady, but rents were rising. They needed to diversify. Getting online sales up and running would help so much. It'd been on Kirsty's to-do list forever.

"How many are coming later?"

"Around 30, so we might have to move the table back."

Robbie Williams came on the radio. Helena hated him. True to form, she turned him off with a scowl. She walked over to the table and sat down opposite Kirsty, drumming the tips of her fingers on the varnished, solid oak. "As well as weddings, birthdays and all that jazz, you remember what I went to a few months ago?"

Kirsty furrowed her brow. "Rehab?"

"Shut your face." Helena gave her a look. "A divorce party. Hugh's friend. Ironically, it was like a bloody wedding. Could be something to look into."

Kirsty folded her arms and sat back. "Aren't they for the rich and famous? I never had one when I got divorced." She'd just drunk wine, eaten too much cheese and played Whitney Houston non-stop like you were meant to.

"They weren't so big seven years ago. Now, they're all the rage." Helena shrugged. "Plus, we're in the right age bracket. Our forties. It's when life disillusionment truly sets in. I read a study the other day that the most miserable age is 47."

"It passed me by in the blink of an eye." Kirsty could barely remember how she felt last week, never mind two years ago. She and Helena were both 49 now. The big five-oh looming next year.

"Me, too. No bloody time to be miserable with a business, husband and a teenage son." Helena paused. "But if we need to raise more income, it could be another string to our bow. I'm full-time now, so we can expand our side gigs. If they take off, Anton can be roped into helping out. We're in this together, partner." Helena said the last bit like she was John Wayne.

Kirsty couldn't help but smile. "Divorce parties." She picked up her phone and typed it into her notes app.

You never knew.

It could become a thing.

* * *

Kirsty knocked on the door to her parents' cottage and stood back to admire the outside. Ian and Ruth would never wait until their house needed painting: they were proactive about such things. The freshly painted New England-style white boards shone even in the early evening light. Dad had offered to come and paint the shop. Kirsty had resisted so far, because even though he looked young for his age and was handy with a paintbrush, he was still in his early 70s. Plus, she wanted to be able to sort out her own life and not have to rely on her parents.

The door opened and her mum greeted her with a customary hug. "There's my gorgeous girl who needs a haircut!" Her mum squeezed, then held Kirsty at arm's length. "Do you need me to call Simon for an appointment?" She ushered her into the hallway.

Kirsty shook her head. "I can make my own hair appointments, thank you."

"Okay!" Mum gave her a pointed look. "You look less tired than you did the other day, though, so that's good."

Visiting her parents was rarely an uplifting experience for Kirsty's ego.

The smell of roasting meat coated the air, along with an underlying sweetness. Shortbread? Apple pie? Kirsty would find out soon enough. Her mum didn't care it was over 70 degrees outside. She loved a roast dinner any time of the year, not giving in to summer salads easily.

Kirsty walked through to the lounge. Her dad was in his favourite armchair, doing his daily crossword puzzle. He'd recently declared *The Guardian's* "too easy," and had moved on to *The Times*.

"How's it going, Dad?"

He looked up, giving her a smile. "I'm stuck, so that's good, right? But you're just the person. One down. Californian grape derived from the same origin as primitivo. Nine letters."

"Zinfandel." She sat on the sofa opposite.

Dad snapped his fingers. "I knew you could help!" His eyes landed on the bottle of red she was still holding.

Kirsty put it on the floor beside her.

"Anything good?" Dad asked, as Mum sat on the sofa beside her.

"Chilean merlot. Solid."

"Wonderful. It'll go well with the lamb we're having." Mum patted Kirsty's knee.

"Your hair looks nice, too." Dad pointed a finger. "Shiny."

Kirsty gave her mum a triumphant smile.

She ignored it. "Talking of wine, how are things at the shop? Has Helena been up to any mischief of late?"

Kirsty's smile didn't last long. "Helena is just fine. *More than fine.* She was in before me today. You should see her plans for the festival table."

Her mum's eyes narrowed. "I'm just uneasy, after what happened."

"That was two years ago, so give her a break. She wants the business to succeed, just like I do."

They'd been over this. Her mum's dislike of Helena stemmed from their friendship at school, where Helena had been something of a hell-raiser. She'd done her time in London's financial district, before coming back and investing in Wine Time when Kirsty's ex, Anna, had taken her money out. Yes, there had been an incident two years ago where Helena had done a wine deal that sounded too good to be true. It had been, and had blown a hole in their profits, but she'd made amends since.

Kirsty put an arm around her mum. "I'm a big girl who can book her own hair appointments and look after her own business, okay? Without Helena, the shop wouldn't have survived my divorce or the downturn. Plus, she had some good ideas today for getting new business, so give her a break, okay?"

Her mum gave her a look, but also a tacit nod of understanding.

Kirsty already needed a drink.

Her dad put down the paper. "Come through to the kitchen, and we'll get the wine open." Kirsty and her mum followed.

Her parents had recently had their kitchen redone, and it looked fabulous. Kirsty would be lying if she said she didn't have kitchen envy. Her parents had an island, fancy bar stools, sleek white counter-tops and cobalt-blue units. Stepping into it was a far cry from her kitchen's shabby-chic look.

Her dad pulled the cork on the wine with a satisfying pop, and Mum lined up some glasses. Not the posh ones. It was only Thursday, after all.

Her parents shared a kiss before he poured. They were cute. Everyone told Kirsty that. They were the relationship she'd tried so hard to emulate, but had failed with quite some panache. It was a constant source of dismay for her mother.

"Stop being so adorable, you two." Kirsty took the offered glass from her dad and swirled her wine around, breathing in the bouquet. She took a sip and let it sit in her senses, smiling as she did. Wine always made her happy. In an instant, her muscles went from tense to relaxed.

"You'll find *your* adorable, too. You just have to get out there again and look." Her mum tapped her watch. "Time's ticking on, and it's been too long since Anna. Don't waste your best years; that's my advice."

Kirsty couldn't help her eye roll. "We've touched on Helena, the shop, and now my lack of a relationship. I've told you already I'm open to meeting someone, but I can't just magic a woman out of thin air."

"You wouldn't even meet up with Shirley's niece."

Her mum had been trying to set her up with her best friend's niece for weeks. Kirsty knew four women who'd slept with said niece, so she wasn't about to go there.

"Can we move on to a topic that won't wind me up, please?" Kirsty swallowed down a sigh with another sip of wine.

Her dad bumped her mum's hip. "Leave her alone, Ruth. And your mother's just looking out for you, that's all. We both want the best for you."

"Just saying," Mum added.

"Keep your *just saying* to yourself." But Kirsty couldn't stay mad at her parents for long. They were always on her side.

She took a deep breath and decided to start again. "Were you at the festival meeting this morning? I couldn't make it."

Sandy Cove's annual Oyster Festival was taking place in five weeks. It drew crowds from near and far, and was a big deal for the local economy. Kirsty had wine and oyster tastings planned, along with a couple of other events at the harbour.

Her dad nodded. "It's all systems go. As well as the parade, there's going to be a music stage, an art trail and of course, the oyster eating competition." He paused. "Are you planning on eating one this year?"

Kirsty shuddered. "I know I'm a Sandy Cove native, but that's a step too far. You know my feelings on oysters. Nice to look at, terrible to eat. However, I am looking forward to the festival putting a boost in trade."

"It might bring a flock of new women to town, too," Mum added, a glint in her eye.

She was incorrigible, wasn't she?

Chapter 2

Saffron Oliver pirouetted through a group of chattering tourists exiting Holland Park onto Kensington High Street, complicating her path to the café for her appointment.

A child collided into her legs, nearly causing Saffron to topple over. How could the boy, who was half of her five-eleven frame, pack such a wallop? The crash didn't faze the child, who gleefully bounded away. Saffron shoved her obnoxiously large sunglasses back into place and whisked a lock of blond hair behind her ear. No one attached to the wild child apologised or even noticed the incident, too busy arguing in Italian accompanied by frantic arm movements. Saffron ducked out of the way and released a sigh of relief.

She slipped into the café, groaning when she spied the bustling crowd. Why oh why did Pearl always arrange to meet in one of London's hot spots?

"Oh my God. It's you!" A woman snapped a photo of Saffron on her iPhone, her fingers flying over the screen. No doubt posting it online without a moment's thought to Saffron's right to privacy.

Saffron tucked her head down, hoping she could complete the remaining ten steps without—

Another woman excitedly asked, "Can I get a photo with you?"

Saffron tamped down the urge to shout no. "Of course. Give me your phone. I'll snap it for us." She'd learned it was best to be in control as much as possible when taking pictures in the wild. Otherwise, she risked having an unflattering shot floating in the ether, resulting in seemingly endless mockery on social media and talk shows. Saffron Oliver was never allowed to have a bad moment or even a normal one. No, the thirty-two-year-old actress had to be picture perfect even on a stifling hot day in June after a restless night of sleep.

"There you go." Saffron returned the phone with a wide grin, and pivoted in such a way to make it nearly impossible for another person to ask for a selfie without coming across as overly pushy. It'd taken her years to develop this manoeuvre after allowing one or two fans to get a photo so she seemed gracious, when she really desired to be left alone.

Taking a seat across from Pearl, Saffron folded her arms, irked by the elation on her agent's face. She always wanted all eyes on Saffron. "Explain why I had to meet you here during a rush on cold drinks because it's bloody hot."

"Speaking of bloody hot, those jeans look amazing on you. Like the designer painted them on." Pearl pretended to put a finger on Saffron, pulling it back as if on fire.

Saffron inhaled deeply, shoving her glasses on top of her head.

"Even if you aren't happy to see me, I'm glad you're here. I've missed spoiling my top client." Pearl scooted Saffron's drink over. "Got your favourite."

Saffron sucked on the straw, the iced caramel macchiato

satiating her thirst, but not her annoyance. "If you really wanted to spoil me, you'd let me enjoy my respite between shoots."

Pearl's eyes lit up like a slot machine. "I've got good news. No, great news."

"My next movie fell through, and I can take six months off, not just one or two?" Inwardly, Saffron did her happy dance, but outwardly, she remained stoic because Pearl had the habit of stamping out all hope for a peaceful life.

"Yes and no."

"I'm not following." Saffron eyed her agent's glee with a healthy dose of caution.

"I was able to get you out of that indie project that in all likelihood would be a box office snooze and highly unlikely to garner any nominations, so what's the point, really?" Pearl hitched a shoulder. "Instead, James Thorpe has advanced the production schedule for the next great thing that will have all your fans screaming with joy. We're talking serious cash." Pearl let the script land on the tabletop with an emphatic thud.

Saffron read the working title: *Girl Racer 3*. Pinching her eyes shut, she bit down on the insides of both of her cheeks. Luckily for her, a barista fired up a machine, the sound drowning out a helpless whimper.

"Isn't it exciting?" Pearl squirmed in her seat like a child unwrapping birthday gifts.

"Considering I've been in the first two, not so exciting." Saffron flicked the pages, imagining tossing it into a fire one page at a time.

"Don't undersell yourself. You're the Racer Girl." Pearl loved to change the wording to make it seem Saffron was the only stunning female astride a motorbike, when the cast included many babes on bikes to pull men and women into the cinema to watch an action flick starring mostly chicks. "It's your megastar status that's made the third film a possibility, and trust me when I say this. I'm going to put the screws to them. We're talking eight figures."

"I don't need more money." If she had to do a movie, Saffron would have preferred the indie option, but even that wasn't all that appealing, since Saffron suspected she had been offered the job solely for her celebrity status, not because they thought her perfect for the role.

"Of course, you do. Everyone needs more money. Do you have a fever from this heat? Should I call your doctor?" Pearl lowered her head to inspect Saffron, not in a joking way. Sharks had more humanity than Pearl, who hunted for any money-making scheme, no matter the humiliation for Saffron.

"I don't have a fever. I just want some time to relax." Saffron glanced away, her gaze landing on an abstract painting of Holland Park, the name of the local artist and price printed below the frame.

"I'll book you a day at the spa." Pearl added with charitable gravitas, "A full day."

"I don't think a day will cut it," Saffron scoffed.

"Do you need a weekend retreat? Where did Stevie go for two days of pampering?" Pearl rapped her fingers on the table. "I'll have my assistant look into it. We'll get you the rest you need. Don't you worry."

Saffron reached for Pearl's hand to steady the finger tapping. "You don't understand. I don't want to be pampered for a couple of days. I want to go away for a month."

"A month!"

"At least. Two would be even better." If Saffron had it her way, she'd be gone until September. Could she dare for longer?

"That's simply not possible. Not at all." Pearl pressed a finger onto the table, whitening the tip.

"It has to be because I've booked a place in a quiet seaside town."

"Which one?" Pearl had her phone handy to log the details.

"I'm not telling you, otherwise I won't get a moment's peace." It wasn't like Saffron would be able to stay hidden no matter where she went, but she preferred making things as hard as possible for her demanding agent who had no boundaries.

"What about the movie?"

"What about it?" Saffron sipped her drink, avoiding Pearl's hardening stare.

"It can't proceed without your blessing."

"I'm sure the world will survive without another movie about illegal street racing."

"What's bugging you?" Pearl folded her arms over her chest.

"I told you. I need a break. I've been in the biz for too long. I can't even go out for a coffee without people wanting to take a photo with me." Saffron leaned close to Pearl and spoke as quietly as possible to only be heard by the agent. "I'm tired of always having to be the glamorous star. It's exhausting."

"Do we need to get you a trainer to work on those muscles? Cindy has a facial fitness expert she can't stop raving about. I heard she's turned down working with Angie, but I know I can get you in. No one will have the guts to say no to the hottest actress on the market." Pearl reached for her phone.

"No. I don't need any more trainers." Saffron pressed her palms together to avoid the temptation to scream. Instead she said in a monotone voice, "How can I get you to understand?"

"What?" Pearl blinked rapidly as if trying to swat away Saffron's words.

"That I need rest. Not two days at a spa. A real break. Away from facial trainers, makeup artists, cameras, fans, sets, and..." Saffron tapped the title page of the script.

"You don't have to read it. I have. It's perfect." Pearl repositioned in her seat. "What if I can convince them to push back the start date for filming? Will you commit then?"

"I can't agree to make a film I haven't read the script for. That's something I've never done, and I don't plan on starting now." Saffron massaged her brow.

"Okay, fine. Take it with you. I'm sure I can clear your schedule for a week or so."

Saffron shook her hands in the air, the fingers curling with rage, before sitting on them to avoid someone catching her in the act. The paps would have a field day with that. "You're not listening. No one ever listens to me." Her chin trembled, and she had to shut down her emotions before uncontrollable tears fell from her eyes. Once again, she stared at the artwork.

"That's rich, coming from Hollywood's hardest working actress. You were in three movies last year. Everyone on the planet was listening." Pearl tossed her head back, smiling smugly.

"No, they were watching me say someone else's words. That's not the same thing." No one knew the real Saffron, not even those closest to her. She'd become an amalgamation of all the characters she'd played, and even Saffron couldn't remember if caramel macchiato was actually her favourite drink or if it was Amanda's, the American TV character she'd played for ten years on a hit sitcom that made her a household name, before she made the leap to film at the ripe old age of 25.

Pearl let out an anguished sigh. "Two weeks."

"This isn't a negotiation. I'm going away for at least one month, maybe two."

"What will you do? You haven't taken time off like that since I've known you."

"Exactly!" The tension behind her eyes made the lids heavy with sleep. "I want to know what it feels like to be human again, not a commodity."

"No one treats you that way." Pearl pursed her lips.

"Hey, Saffron. I prefer you without clothes." A teenage boy made a crude gesture and ran out of the café with two giggling friends, none of them old enough to shave.

"You were saying?" Saffron waved for Pearl to mount her next line of attack.

"If I agree to this—"

"You seem to think you have a say—"

"Let me finish." Pearl gave Saffron her steely agent glare typically reserved for negotiations with media moguls. "Go away to this magical town by the sea, but take the script with you. I'll give them the straight arm"—Pearl held out her own arm, with her palm out in a protective manner—"long enough for you to have the time you need to come back, refreshed and better. How does that sound?"

Pretty good, aside from the coming back bit. "I can live

with that." It wasn't like Saffron had a choice. This was the movie business. If you were hot at the box office, everyone wanted a piece of you.

"Will you please tell me where you're going. You've probably told Michelle, who's only your assistant, not your pit bull in the ring getting you the respect you deserve." Pearl hooked her thumb, jabbing it at her own chest, proud of her tenacity.

Michelle had arranged the house in Sandy Cove, but Saffron knew not to share that with Pearl, who hated Michelle for not betraying Saffron, even though Pearl badgered the assistant non-stop. "Not a chance in hell. I don't need you sabotaging my holiday."

"I wouldn't dream of doing such a thing." Pearl batted her lashes as innocently as possible.

"Yes, you would. Like the time you scheduled a magazine spread after my appendix burst."

"That issue was about women juggling work and the stress of everyday life."

"Please." Saffron gazed at the exit, wanting this exchange to end. "That was a medical emergency, not me trying to figure out how to find the time to shop for groceries and pick up the kids."

"You don't have kids."

"You're missing the point."

Pearl heaved a sigh. "I don't understand why you still get upset about it. It was ages ago."

"You had a makeup artist and photographer in the recovery room." Saffron stiffened in her chair, her stomach twisting into knots.

"Argue all you want. That's one of the most visited articles on the internet, and millions of people wished you well."

"Because that was the most important aspect of me nearly dying."

"Dramatic, much?"

Saffron circled a finger in front of her face. "Actor, remember."

"I do. The question is, do you?" Her stare intensified in hopes of subduing Saffron into submission. It usually worked in the past.

"What does that mean?" Saffron steadied her breathing, not wanting to wilt. She needed this time away, or she feared she'd break beyond repair.

"You want to run off, leaving the opportunity of a lifetime on the table." Pearl pointedly looked at the script.

"I know you don't understand or believe me when I say there's more to life than another *Girl Racer*." There just had to be.

"Like what?"

"I don't know. That's what I need to discover. If I don't do this, I won't make it." Saffron hadn't wanted to say that out loud, but Pearl wasn't getting it.

"Why can't you find yourself, or whatever you need to do, staying put in London, where I can find you?" Pearl's voice lost some of its harshness, offering a ray of light.

"Because I don't want to be found by you." Try as she might, Saffron couldn't disguise the anger in her tone or rigid shoulders. More proof she was on the brink, because she'd always been able to keep her feelings in check when it came to Pearl.

"Who do you want to be found by?" Pearl mocked, her gaze flicking upwards.

"Time will tell."

Chapter 3

Kirsty was putting the finishing touches to a supplier email when a customer came in. She recognised her from previous visits. Stylish clothes, platinum hair. Plus, she knew her wines. Most of Kirsty's walk-in clientele had a maximum budget of £10. But this woman always hovered over the more expensive shelves. The wines told Kirsty she either knew her grapes, or just liked the finer things in life. Or possibly both.

"Can I help you?" Kirsty checked she was wearing shoes, not slippers. Score.

She walked over to the customer. "That's a lovely wine right there." Kirsty pointed at the Primitivo Reserva, from a vineyard in Puglia that she'd visited years ago with Anna. It seemed like another lifetime.

"I read about it in the latest edition of *Decanter* magazine. Have you had a run on it?"

Kirsty shook her head. "Maybe if we were in Surrey or Bucks. I don't think *Decanter's* widely read around here."

"It is by me." The woman held out a hand. "I'm Ginger. I've recently moved here. Yours is my favourite shop on the High Street, so we should be on first-name terms."

Her hand was ice cold, but Kirsty didn't flinch. "Kirsty, good to meet you." She glanced at her watch, then around the shop. It was 3pm on a Wednesday, and she was due a break. "I was just about to put the kettle on. Do you fancy a coffee?"

Ginger's face spelled surprise. "That would be lovely."

Kirsty pulled out a chair for Ginger. Five minutes later, she came back with two steaming mugs of coffee. "I can't do iced coffee, even in this hot weather."

"I only drink hot coffee, water, or red wine. Those three things." Ginger took her mug with a word of thanks.

"No white wine at all?"

Ginger shook her head. "My ex hated it, so by association, so did I." She paused. "Perhaps that's a reason I should start drinking it though, right?"

Kirsty didn't respond. That one was very much up to Ginger.

"I love the wine selection here. Are you the buyer?"

Kirsty nodded. "Co-owner, shop girl, buyer, marketer. Although the final one is my downfall, but I'm working on it." She paused. "You said you just moved here?"

Ginger gave her a slow nod. "I have. Got one of those lovely seafront cottages by the Poseidon Inn."

Kirsty let out a low whistle. "Prime real estate. You definitely need expensive wine to go with that address."

Ginger cackled. "My sister would say the same." She leaned forward conspiratorially. "The truth is, I'm not loaded. I'm recently divorced, and our place sold for more than we thought. Hence, I've bought a nice house and am treating myself to some good wine. I deserve it." She paused, annoyance crossing her face. "I need to stop saying *we* and *our*, don't I? Old habits." She shook her head.

Kirsty got it. It'd taken her a good few years to stop the habit herself after she'd discovered Anna wasn't adhering to her marriage vows in the same way she was. "If you've only just got divorced, I think you're allowed a little time."

Ginger sipped her coffee. "I need to shake myself out of the habit soon. I want to slap myself every time I do it."

"I got divorced seven years ago, so I know what you're going through. If it helps, it does get better." However, Kirsty wouldn't go through those initial stages of divorce again for anyone. The pain and devastation of realising your happily ever after had just come to an abrupt end had been almost too much to bear.

Ginger sighed, before looking Kirsty in the eye. "It does, sort of. I'm still a little out of sorts, unpacking boxes, marvelling at the speed of change. Our house had only been on the market for two weeks when it sold. One minute we were arguing about who got the Charles Eames chair; the next, it's sitting in my new lounge, but Dave isn't."

"At least you got the chair."

"That's what my sister told me. Still, I wanted a fresh start after Dave said he was leaving. You can't get fresher than moving 100 miles to a town I barely know."

"That's a brave move." At least Kirsty had the loving embrace of her community to fall back on. Anna had left, but she hadn't gone far enough. Just five miles down the coast to Honey Bay. They still ran into each other on occasion. She held up her mug. "Consider your first friend in town made. We divorcees have to stick together."

"I'll drink to that." Ginger took a sip, before putting her mug on the table. "Actually, I had meant to come in here on business. I run my own web agency, and I've got the contract for the town website. My job is to put Sandy Cove on the map and make it more of a destination for the whole country, not just London. I'm a web developer but I'm working with some freelance content staff, and I thought I could run some features on local businesses for a start."

Kirsty liked the sound of that. "Great idea. Only, don't look at our website." She winced. Due to financial constraints, she'd set it up herself with a little help from Helena's son, Anton. However, it still needed a lot of work. "We don't even have online sales set up. Please don't judge."

Ginger snorted. "Since my life turned upside down, I've been trying to leave my judgement by the side of the road. But if you want, when I have more time, we could have a look at it over a bottle of wine, and I could give you my professional advice. Seeing as we're friends now." She gave her a piercing grin that somehow looked familiar.

Kirsty beamed right back. "You're on. Our website needs all the help it can get. Professional or otherwise."

A few moments passed as Ginger took in her surroundings. Kirsty followed her gaze. Shelves of wine from all around the world, along with a stand of spirits nearer the till, and a more upmarket selection behind the counter. She also had a range of fancy crisps and chocolates, as well as a fridge full of cheese to accompany her wines. That particular addition had gone down a storm as soon as she'd introduced it a year ago.

"You haven't thought about having a divorce party?" Kirsty's conversation with Helena came flooding back.

Ginger quirked one carefully styled dark brow. Was that the original colour of her hair? "Do normal people have those?"

Kirsty nodded. "Apparently they do. My business partner went to one that was like a wedding. She's been to a few. It's quite popular in your 40s."

Ginger let out another cackle. "So are golf and running, but you won't catch me doing either." She finished her coffee. "Although, maybe it is what I need. A public commitment to a completely fresh start."

"If you need help, I run a party planning business on the side, too. So far, I've mainly done birthdays and anniversaries, but I'm thinking of branching out." She paused, snagging Ginger's piercing blue gaze. Another jolt of recognition. Kirsty ignored it. "But this is not a hard sell. Just a thought."

Ginger stared at her for a few long moments. "It would be a brilliant 'fuck you' to Dave, wouldn't it? With his 'I'm just not feeling it anymore' attitude after 15 years of marriage?"

Wow. Fifteen years. Kirsty's marriage had blown up at the archetypal seven-year itch. But 15 years? She couldn't imagine it.

"It could also be a great way of introducing yourself to the community. Embed yourself in the town. Give them free booze and a disco, and I'm sure you'd have a ton of friends for life."

Ginger cupped the back of her neck with her right palm. "It would also be a fabulous way to show my old friends where I'm living. Show off my new home. Show them Ginger is back and ready to party."

"It certainly would be." Kirsty got up, grabbing both mugs. "Have a think about it, and let me know."

Ginger got up, too, picking up two bottles of the primitivo from the shelf. "I'll do that."

Kirsty keyed in the purchase on her card machine, then offered it to Ginger. She inserted her card and entered her pin, placing her wallet on the counter.

Kirsty glanced down. She was no label aficionado, but even she knew the wallet was Gucci. Wine selection wasn't the only area where Ginger was seriously flashing her cash.

"You need a bag?"

Ginger shook her head, producing a rolled-up carrier from her handbag. "The more I think about this idea, the more I like it. Plus, if I invite all my mates, you could have a few new clients on your hands. If our 20s were the time of weddings, our 40s are when we're all breaking up."

Kirsty smiled. "You're preaching to the choir. I was 42 when I split with my wife." At least now, when she said it, the words just felt like words. No emotion attached. It had taken a lot of work to get to that place.

"If you split seven years ago, that means you're 49?" Ginger's eyes widened.

"So the calendar tells me." Fifty next year. She had no idea how it had happened.

"You look incredible." She gestured to Kirsty with her hand. "Smooth skin, and you're in fabulous shape." She peered closer. "Not a grey hair in sight! I would have said you're younger than me, and I'm 42." Ginger slumped, leaning her hip on the counter. "What is it about getting divorced at 42?" She didn't wait for an answer, pointing a finger in Kirsty's direction. "You're my role model from now on. You've come through it, and you seem happy." She stared at Kirsty. "Are you happy?" Panic danced around her eyes.

Kirsty recalled asking something similar in the early days

when she never thought that would be possible again. This answer was crucial for Ginger. She wasn't going to lie.

"I am. It's taken me a while, but now I can talk about it like it happened to someone else. Like Anna was just somebody I used to know."

Ginger nodded. "Have you met someone since?"

Kirsty stalled, then shook her head. "Nobody who counts. But then, maybe I wasn't ready. I'm open to meeting someone now. Give it time, and you will be, too."

Ginger scrunched up her face and put her wallet in her handbag. "I'm not looking to meet a man anytime soon. I want to enjoy being single for a while and settle in here. Starting with a banger of a party." She held out her hand, and Kirsty shook it. "Lovely to meet you, and thanks for the coffee and the wine. I'll be in touch."

The shop door closed, and Kirsty allowed herself a smile. Her first possible divorce party booking and website help. Business might be looking up.

Chapter 4

Saffron killed the car's engine in the assigned parking space of her new home. For the month, at least, although she'd booked the place for two, ever the optimist. But the thought of crossing the threshold of yet another temporary residence filled her with loneliness. The soul-sucking type that made her wonder what was the point to anything. She could have stayed with her sister, but Saffron had opted not to so she could have some alone time to figure out her life. Had she made a mistake?

Not the best start to her holiday, and Saffron was fully aware it'd been her idea to take time off in Sandy Cove. It'd sounded like the perfect solution to snap her out of her blasé attitude of late. Now that her plan was in motion, she couldn't ditch the sensation of drowning in angst, unwilling to dig deep to yank herself out.

She reached for the script on the passenger seat, not to give the movie a chance, but to appraise the sketch she'd drawn on the back at lunch. A woman gazing out over the sea, done like the retro ads of the twenties when people were giddy about the end of the war, not knowing the depression and WWII were right around the corner. In the sketch, the woman on the page stood forlornly, yet Saffron remembered a whimsical lightness as her pencil flew over the paper, not a thought going through her head. Just the action and a sense of purpose.

Saffron tossed the script into her shoulder bag and got out of the car, not wanting to haul her luggage inside. Maybe a walk along the beach would knock the cobwebs out. As soon as she was in motion, her brain whipped into hyper speed. The rest and relaxation explanation she'd given Pearl was only part of the reason she'd chosen Sandy Cove.

On the promenade, she kept the water on her right-hand side, focusing on the water's edge, a few white sailboats bobbing on the surface. At the periphery of her vision, there was a red and white striped lighthouse. A slight breeze wrapped around her flesh and ushered goosebumps to life, despite the sultriness in the air.

Her mind flitted to her sister, who was going through a trying time after divorcing a man Saffron had liked. No. Saffron loved him like the brother she'd never had and couldn't process the two of them splitting up. The majority of Saffron's relationships hadn't lasted beyond the *shiny new object* phase, but it had given her hope that her sister had found her Prince Charming. Surely that meant Saffron could find her princess. But had the possibility evaporated in a puff of smoke the moment she pursued acting when she was fifteen? And, if love wasn't enough to bind her sister and husband, what chance did Saffron have for a happy ever after?

She spied an artist standing outside one of the front row pastel-coloured beach huts on a grassy slope leading up from the water. The woman had a paintbrush behind her ear while she gripped another with her hand, making sweeping strokes on the canvas. From her angle, Saffron only spied blue and black paint, and it was easy to guess the artist was under a creative spell. There was much to capture. The rolling waves of the sea lapping against the pebbled beach. Two yellow labs sprinting after a tennis ball. A toddler wobbling between mother and father, exploring the shore. Everyone existing independently of each other, all the while providing the painter a cohesive scene.

Saffron studied the woman, the way her hand moved, how she squinted with one eye to soak in the details, and then dove back to work. Saffron admired the artist's easy-going vibe and the ghost of a smile on her lips, and instinctively understood the painter knew this was what she'd been born to do. What would it be like to do what one loved every day, creating art for others to admire? Not such commercial projects like *Girl Racer*.

Her buzzing phone zapped Saffron out of her daze, and when she read the name of her agent on her device, she clicked the decline button and pocketed it, cursing the swirling sensation of bile rising in the back of her throat.

After taking one last sweeping look at the beach, Saffron headed towards the High Street to locate the café for her meet-up. Wading through the people strolling here and there with not much purpose aside from window shopping, Saffron entered The Perfect Cup, pleasantly surprised it was also part bookshop. She'd been meaning to pick up something to read. Anything as long as it wasn't that bloody script.

"Can I help you?" There was a spark of recognition on the woman's face.

Saffron lowered her gaze to the menu on the counter and picked the first drink on the list. "Cinnamon dolce frozen coffee."

"Your name?" The woman's hand shook as she held a pen to the plastic cup.

Saffron's mind went blank, unable to conjure up her usual plausible fake name, so she blurted the blandest name she could think of. "Pam."

"Pam?" the woman parroted, her eyes wandering to the magazine rack with Saffron's image blazing on three of the covers.

"Yep."

"Okay." The woman scrawled the three letters, set it to the side for her co-worker, and finalised the transaction.

Saffron tapped her card, her head tucked down.

"I'll bring it out to you, P-pam."

Mumbling a thank-you, Saffron selected a table close to the counter, putting her right in the line of fire, but there wasn't much that could be done since no other table was free. Someone had left a hardcover book they'd opted not to buy, and she cracked it open, holding it face level in an attempt to avoid detection. Peering over the top to scope out the scene, her shoulders sagged, as she spied two women browsing the books on a table, whispering behind furtive hands. Evidently, her Pam ruse had miserably failed.

A woman in her sixties entered the shop and nearly gasped when her eyes landed on Saffron. So much for thinking people who flocked to Sandy Cove weren't the *Girl Racer* types but more into art communes that cobbled masterpieces out of flotsam that washed onto the beach. Where did she have to go to be anonymous? A cave? Deserted island?

The door opened, and Ginger, her sister, waltzed to the counter to order, along with a woman Saffron had never laid her eyes on.

Ginger, not clocking Saffron yet, ordered.

The woman with striking cheek bones, an adorable button nose, and a brilliant smile that warmed Saffron's insides, followed suit, and then let her gaze wander, quickly locking onto Saffron, her eyes widening with recognition. "Don't look now, but"—the woman, ignoring her own admonishment, goggled over her shoulder—"but Saffron Oliver is right behind us."

"Are you sure?" Ginger's voice was playful, probably for Saffron's benefit.

The brunette turned back around. "I can't believe it. Saffron Frigging Oliver is right there. I could touch her."

Ginger edged closer to the woman. "I take it you're a fan."

"I might have a tiny crush on her. It's even possible I've imagined what it would be like to take off her biker leathers." She fanned herself, seemingly oblivious to how near she stood to Saffron. She stole another furtive glance at Saffron. Did the woman think Saffron was blind or deaf?

"You should introduce yourself." Ginger still avoided making eye contact with Saffron, instead focusing on paying the barista.

"Are you mad? She's a superstar. Also a lesbian icon. I mean, what the fuck is she doing *here*?"

Saffron wasn't sure what to make of the situation. Should she get up and let the woman know Ginger was goading her? Stop the brunette from even more awkwardness?

"I'm serious. You should waltz up to Ms Oliver and ask her out. What's the worst that can happen?" Ginger posed innocently.

"How long have you got?"

"I'll do it for you."

The woman shook her head. "No! I wouldn't know what to say."

"I would. I've known her all my life. She's my sister." Ginger flicked her fingers in a hello gesture to Saffron.

The woman pulled back as if cold water had been dumped over her head. "She's *what*?"

"My sister. Let me introduce you." Ginger hooked an arm through the woman's, her hand on a hip.

"Oh, no. I can't. Not after…" The woman's face went up in flames, and Saffron wouldn't be surprised if smoke started to billow out of her ears. "This is so embarrassing." Now, the brunette looked everywhere but in Saffron's direction, although the tips of the woman's ears deepened to a dark purplish colour.

"Don't be silly. She's really quite down to earth." Ginger tightened her grip on the woman's arm.

The dark-haired beauty's legs didn't budge, causing Ginger to implore Saffron with those kind blue eyes. "Come on, Sis; tell her you don't bite."

Saffron was about to speak, but the barista bellowed, "Pam!"

What happened to bringing it to me?

Saffron rose to retrieve her drink. With each step, another chunk of her dignity cracked away. Mumbling a thank-you to the barista, Saffron flipped back around, with all eyes on her. She slinked back to her seat, wanting to hide behind the book again, but it was useless now.

Ginger, shaking her head and still chuckling, guided the woman to the empty seat at the table, and then Ginger hooked a chair with her foot and yanked it over. "Let's start over. Kirsty, meet my baby sister, Saffron."

Kirsty dipped her head, seeming as though she hadn't regained her voice after jamming her foot down her throat.

Not that Saffron was the super sophisticated woman she'd played to a hilt on more occasions than she could count. Real life had a way of crashing through the thin veneer of perfection, leaving Saffron to wonder if everyone was gutted to learn first-hand she wasn't the Hollywood goddess her inner circle made her out to be.

Ginger looked to Saffron and then her friend, a devious, playful glint in Ginger's blue eyes.

Saffron shot her sister, who loved to ruffle feathers, a silent plea for Ginger to strike a normal chord.

Ginger moved her head to the left so Kirsty couldn't witness Ginger sticking her tongue out at Saffron the curmudgeon and then launched into her news. "Kirsty is trying to convince me to throw a divorce party. She owns a wine shop, but is branching out into party planning. Isn't that grand?"

"A what party?" Saffron had trouble speaking, given she never considered Ginger would want something like that.

"Divorce party."

Saffron swallowed. "I thought you said everything had been as amicable as possible between you and Dave."

"It has been, aside from him saying he didn't see us

together in our golden years, and he wanted to be free to find the right one. That still stings." Ginger patted her heart.

"I'm sure it does, but remember, the party isn't about him." Kirsty met Ginger's eyes, flashing her a confident smile. "The party is about you proclaiming no matter what, you'll be fine and it gives you the opportunity to embrace your independence with open arms."

"I like the sound of that. Not an end, but a rebirth." Saffron turned to her sister. "I think it's a great idea."

"You don't think it's petty?" Ginger craned her neck, taking note of Saffron's drink. "You hate whipped cream." Her crinkled nose relaxed, and she grinned. "Did you panic again?"

Saffron shoved the drink over to her sister. "You know me so well."

"It's amazing how simple things trip you up."

"I'm not used to getting my own drinks." Saffron shrugged, knowing how bad that sounded. "Now, about this party. I want to pay for it."

"I can't let—"

"Don't argue." Saffron shook a finger in the air. "The guilt of missing your wedding has been eating away at me. No TV show is worth more than you."

"Turns out you made the wisest decision, because the marriage didn't stick, but your career hasn't let up." Ginger slapped her hands together, her right one zooming off into space to demonstrate.

Saffron placed a hand on her sister's. "Let me help by paying for the party. No expense spared. Please. It'll mean the world to me."

"I don't know, Saff. I'm not the type to make a big to-do out of things." Ginger tugged on her earlobe, dropping her eyes to avoid Saffron's pleading expression.

"Let's turn over a new leaf together." She lowered her head to gaze into Ginger's eyes. "Don't say no."

"Fine, but I don't want anything super posh. I mean it."

"You can have whatever you want."

Ginger finally took a sip of the drink. "It tastes like cinnamon ice cream goodness. Yum." She turned to Kirsty. "You should get one."

"Where are my manners?" Saffron rose. "Would you like one, Kristy? You two did order, right? It's taking ages."

The brunette's face crumpled. "It's Kirsty."

"Oh, right, soz." Now why had Saffron slipped into flippant millennial speak for sorry when she only did that over text? As if getting the woman's name wrong didn't matter at all, when in truth, unease strangled Saffron's vocal cords.

Kirsty bristled even more. "I'm fine with a simple coffee."

"You need one of these. Usually, I'm like you and prefer something plainer, but this is like drinking dessert." Ginger smacked her lips.

Kirsty gazed longingly at the drink, finally nodding in agreement.

Pleased to see the brilliant smile back in place, Saffron headed for the counter. While changing the orders, she glimpsed out of the corner of her eye, Kirsty rising with a phone to her ear, meandering to the other side of the store, her fingers running over the top of some magazines.

After paying, Saffron returned to her seat and nudged

her sister's foot with her own under the table. "How are you doing, really?"

"Remarkably well despite a few wobbles here and there." Ginger stretched her arms overhead. "Coming here was the best decision I've made. This place is freeing. The hustle and bustle of London made me feel trapped, and I constantly bumped into friends who knew us as a couple or kept wandering by the places we spent time together."

Kirsty dropped a stack of magazines on the table. "These will give us some party ideas."

Right on top was one featuring Saffron, as if declaring loud and clear the woman's true intentions. "Is this the real reason why you want to plan my sister's party?"

Kirsty took a step back. "What do you mean?"

Saffron knocked the magazine off the pile. "To use my name to boost your business."

"Saffie!" Ginger's hand flew to her mouth, using the nickname from their childhood when Ginger thought her sister was acting like a brat.

Undeterred, Saffron stared at Kirsty, noticing how her grey eyes had more sparkle than her smile.

"In case you didn't get the memo, I didn't know you were Ginger's sister until moments ago." Kirsty pointed towards the till, where the embarrassing scene had played out.

"So you say." Saffron snorted, having dealt with these types most of her life. "Or were you putting on a show to con both of us?"

"What exactly are you accusing me of?" Kirsty jutted out a hip, placing a hand on it, drawing Saffron's eyes to her spectacular curves.

Ignoring her increased heartbeat and the kindness in Kirsty's grey eyes, Saffron stayed the course, her voice losing some of its steam. "You wouldn't be the first to go through someone close to me to get what you want, all the while pretending to be a supportive friend."

"Who do you think you are?" A vein in Kirsty's neck bulged.

"Saffron Oliver, the lesbian icon." She waved a hand in the air. "Those are your words, not mine."

"What happened to Pam? Is that your real name instead of the silly stage name?" Kirsty blew a raspberry.

Saffron's eyes darted upwards, seeking the calming sensation she'd had by the waterfront, but her patience had dried up. After years in the Hollywood scene, Saffron was wary of anyone who seemed too good to be true. Turning her back on the beautiful woman, Saffron said, "Ginger, let me plan this party. I've rented a place on the water, and I'm in dire need of a distraction. Your party will be the talk of Sandy Cove—no, all of Britain. Butlers in the Buff. You'll be carried in, Cleopatra style—"

"Whoa, there! I love you. I do." Ginger paused before digging in. "But I don't want a Hollywood type party. If I do this, I want something my speed, not yours."

"You think I'm the Hollywood type?" Saffron flinched.

"Not when it comes to your own life. I know for a fact you hate being noticed. Yet, when it comes to those you love, you struggle with your impulse control."

"I'll keep myself in check, I promise." Saffron bounced up and down in her seat, pressing her palms together. "I can do this."

"Tell you what. Why don't the two of you work together?

Because Kirsty isn't using me to get to you. She agreed to plan this party before you entered the picture. You need to learn not everyone wants to use you."

"But—"

"It's okay. I don't need to be part of the planning, and I would never get between sisters." Kirsty started to step away, but Ginger yanked her back.

"You're going to be part of this, and you, dear sister, are going to help, not take over. I need my new friend and sister right now, more than ever." The pleading in Ginger's tone was genuine.

Saffron met Kirsty's eyes. "Okay."

"Fine," Kirsty managed through gritted teeth, but from the rising and falling of her chest, she wasn't thrilled with Saffron taking part.

Saffron had a hard time removing her focus from Kirsty's breasts, upset with herself for the sudden interest in what lay beneath the fabric.

"Well, this is off to a fantabulous start." Ginger laughed. "Hopefully, it won't crash and burn like my marriage." Her expression turned serious. "Can you two agree to be cordial?"

Saffron offered her most charming smile. "Absolutely."

"I know we didn't get off on the right foot, but I think you'll find most in Sandy Cove stick to their own business, myself included." Kirsty offered an apologetic smile.

Ginger bobbed her head in agreement, but pointed to one of the covers with Saffron posing with Echo Black. "Tell me about your *Girl Racer* co-star."

"Nothing to tell." Saffron's eyes darted to Kirsty, who had sunk back into her chair.

"That's not what the tabloids are saying." Ginger made goo-goo eyes.

"Who do you believe? Your own sister or people who peddle rubbish?"

"Touchy!" Ginger looked to Kirsty. "Maybe we should start a matchmaking business, because my sister has terrible luck with women. But who am I to say anything? You two are planning my divorce party. Isn't this a strange world we now live in?"

Saffron met Kirsty's eyes, this time seeing not a conniving woman, but something else that could be even more dangerous. Whatever it was, Saffron couldn't trust it. Swearing to tread carefully to avoid getting hurt, she leaned back in her chair, feeling more secure staying silent. No matter how pretty the words or the messenger, people were all the same in the end. No one wanted Saffron for who she was, just for what she could do for them. Kirsty may not be using Ginger to get to Saffron, but the woman could still be trouble.

Chapter 5

Kirsty scanned the wine aisle in her local Sainsbury's, taking note of her competition. Wine Time couldn't hope to compete with their pricing, but what they had on the big supermarkets was a better selection as well as personal service. Their weekly wine tastings were gaining in popularity, and she hoped to add more. Kirsty put her basket of food through the self-checkout, slung her reusable bag on her shoulder, and headed back out into the sunshine.

After being in the air-conditioned supermarket, the outside warmth smothered her. The summer was shaping up to be a good one, which was fabulous news for Sandy Cove's tourism. Kirsty had already started to see the boost in their sales from the Down-From-London weekend crowds. She passed The Croissant bakery, its window decorated with Union Jack bunting and pastries in the shape of fishing boats and oysters. The windows of Threadless, the town's haberdashery, were adorned with knitted waves, along with shipwrecked sewing machines. Meanwhile, the post office had gone to town with the fishy theme, complete with sand, shells, fake oysters, and rocks. Kirsty was late getting to Wine Time's festival display, and the competition was already heating up.

She walked past Nick's News, pleased to see they hadn't decorated yet either. She wasn't the only slacker in town. However, their window did have a selection of magazines. On two of the front covers, Saffron Oliver's face stared back at her—or rather, her *Girl Racer* alter ego did. She was dressed in miles of tight black leather, her hair impossibly golden, her eyes arrestingly blue. Now she knew why she'd recognised Ginger's gaze: it was a carbon copy of Saffron's.

Kirsty had seen the *Girl Racer* films like every other lesbian with a pulse, and Saffron's stare had stayed with her. Kirsty even had a dream where Saffron pulled up on her bike and told her to hop on. Just thinking of her dream, where Kirsty had straddled her bike and locked her arms around Saffron's waist, sent heat to Kirsty's cheeks and a rush between her legs. She closed her eyes and steadied her breathing.

She'd made such an idiot of herself yesterday. Why hadn't Ginger told her who her sister was? Of course Kirsty had a thing for her: she didn't know one lesbian who didn't. However, they all might think twice if they met her. Saffron had proved herself to be self-centred and obnoxious. What was it they said? Never meet your heroes. Saffron Oliver had demonstrated the cliché was totally correct.

Kirsty shook her head and turned to carry on walking back to her flat. However, when she looked up, Saffron was walking towards her.

Shit.

Her mind scrambled to fully obliterate her recent thoughts, but it wasn't easy.

Did she have time to look down or cross the road before they made eye contact?

Too late. Saffron gave her a brief wave.

Kirsty gave her a reluctant smile.

Saffron's blond hair had that effortless style about it as it danced on her shoulders. Did movie stars use different hair products as opposed to mere mortals? Kirsty could ask her. But she'd probably get a snappy response. She wished she'd never mentioned the divorce party to Ginger now. How could the sisters be so different?

Remember, she was an idiot to you yesterday. She is far from the image she portrays.

Saffron came to a stop in front of her, giving Kirsty a half-smile. "Just the person I was hoping to bump into."

Those were not the words Kirsty had expected to hear. She wouldn't have been surprised if Saffron had crossed the road to avoid her. Yes, they'd told Ginger they'd work together, but Kirsty was fully expecting Saffron to sack her any minute. It might be for the best.

"I wanted to apologise for yesterday. We got off on the wrong foot, and that's my fault."

Kirsty glimpsed her reflection in Saffron's aviator sunglasses just before Saffron took them off. She tried really hard not to be flummoxed by looking the object of her sex dreams in the face, but it was pretty distracting. If anything, Saffron was more gorgeous in real life than on-screen.

It didn't change the fact she'd been an arsehole, though.

"I'm sorry I accused you of using me for your business. I don't trust many people because every time I do, they betray me. In fact, I wouldn't be surprised if the paparazzi didn't turn up soon as I'm sure somebody's already told them I'm here."

Saffron's baby blues were so mesmerising, they were verging on criminal. "Maybe that's true in your world, but this is Sandy Cove. We look after our own here, and Ginger counts as that now. You're her sister, so you do, too. I won't tell a soul you're here, okay?"

As if to demonstrate the small-town feel, Shelley from 'Seaside Surprise!' gift shop walked by. She gave Saffron a smile, then tapped Kirsty on the arm. "We had that bottle of red last night with dinner. It was delicious and went so well with the steak." She didn't wait for a reply, just carried on walking.

Saffron stared after her. "I guess this isn't what I'm used to. But I'm hoping to relax into my stay here. It would be good not to have enemies so soon. What do you say? Can we start again?"

Kirsty pursed her lips. "You're going to play nicely and not throw your rattle out of your pram?" She couldn't quite believe she was saying that to Saffron Oliver, but she was.

"I promise. And if I do, you can tell me to stop being a tit. Okay?"

That made Kirsty laugh. Maybe there was hope yet for the movie star. "You're on. I look forward to calling you a tit in the not too distant future." She shifted her shopping bag up her shoulder.

Saffron held out a hand. "Can I carry that for you?"

She was chivalrous, too. Nobody had been chivalrous to Kirsty in quite a while. "I don't have far to go, but thanks for offering." Were her cheeks as hot as the sun, now? "Which way were you walking?"

Saffron shrugged. "I don't have plans, so I'll walk wherever you're going. That's what friends do, right?"

Kirsty nodded towards her flat, and Saffron fell into step beside her.

"What do you think of the divorce party idea? Now you know it has nothing to do with you and everything to do with Ginger."

Saffron put her shades back on and glanced Kirsty's way. "Any excuse for a party is a good one. And I do understand the reason behind it. Like I said, my experience with people lately has been a challenge."

"Hence you're hiding out here?"

Saffron nodded. "Something like that."

"Maybe you're mixing with the wrong people."

"You might be right."

They crossed the High Street together, Saffron tripping on the kerb and nearly face-planting on the pavement. It took everything Kirsty had not to laugh, but she kept it in.

"I look forward to your ideas anyway, and I promise to keep you up-to-date when you head home. Is home in London?"

Saffron nodded. "It is. But I've rented my place here till beyond the Oyster Festival. I'm not going anywhere for a while."

"You can do that? I read somewhere you were due to start filming for the next *Girl Racer* movie soon." Kirsty's cheeks flared at her own words. She didn't want to sound like she was keeping track of Saffron's life, but she'd looked at the *Girl Racer* Instagram account this morning. Just to get an update on her new sort-of client.

Maybe she should stop doing that now Saffron Oliver was her new sort-of friend.

Yep, even thinking that was still totally weird.

"I've got the script, but they can't start filming without me. I haven't signed on the dotted line yet either. Don't believe everything you read in the press."

"I'll try to remember that."

A young woman with a toddler and pram walked towards them. She was the daughter of one of Kirsty's mum's friends. Tilly? Tracey? Kirsty couldn't quite remember. The woman greeted her as she walked by.

"You know, there are a few things that are different here from London." They resumed their walk, Wine Time coming into view. "First, not everyone knows who I am, which is so refreshing. Second, you all walk *so* slowly."

Kirsty shook her head. "What's the rush? It's called strolling, you should try it sometime. It's meditative. You're not in London anymore."

"I'm well aware. Another thing is you seem to know *everyone*."

"That's what happens when you live somewhere your whole life. There are upsides and downsides." Kirsty couldn't sneeze in Sandy Cove without it getting back to her parents.

"But you *know* people. I don't even know my neighbours."

Kirsty snorted. "I married mine."

"That's taking it a step too far."

"It clearly was, as she left me."

"I'm sorry to hear that."

"Don't be. I'm over it." As much as she'd ever be. "Her loss, as everyone here keeps telling me." Telling her parents had been the worst, because she'd felt like she was letting them down. Although, telling a movie star you were crap at love was currently running a pretty close second. Particularly one

45

who was rumoured to be involved with her gorgeous co-star, Echo Black. Therefore, she was very much a love ambassador to boot.

They drew up outside Wine Time. "This is me. My empire. Well, mine and my business partner's." Kirsty dropped her shopping at her feet. Her shoulder would have a red mark.

Saffron glanced up at her sign.

"I really need to get the name touched up." Seeing it through fresh eyes made Kirsty painfully aware of that. "It's on my to-do list."

However, Kirsty didn't have time to dwell as the shop door opened and Helena came out, eyes wide, phone in hand. Oh gawd, she was going to be embarrassing, wasn't she? She gave Kirsty a look, then stuck out a hand to Saffron.

"Hi, a real pleasure to meet you. Saffron Oliver," Helena said, just in case Saffron needed to be reminded of her name. "I just want you to know, I'm a *huge* fan. Love the whole *Girl Racer* thing. Girl power and all of that." Helena let go of Saffron's hand and punched the air.

Kirsty winced. "This is my very enthusiastic business partner, Helena."

Saffron removed her sunglasses again, before turning the full force of her megawatt smile on Helena. "Lovely to meet you, too." She punched the air with slightly less ferocity. "Doing my bit for girl power."

Helena fumbled with her phone, stabbing it nervously. "Do you mind if I take a photo for our wall of fame? We don't get Hollywood superstars in Sandy Cove very often."

Kirsty stepped in, putting a hand on Helena's arm. "We don't have a wall of fame."

"We could start one." Helena's tone was indignant.

"No photos." Kirsty gave her a look. "Saffron's here on a break, and we should respect that."

Helena threw her a scowl.

Saffron rubbed her hands together. "How about this? No photo for your non-existent wall of fame, but I will definitely come in and buy some wine. I only have a bottle of gin in my house, and it would love some company."

Helena clapped her hands. "We've got some fantastic selections for all budgets. Yours will be slightly higher than most I expect."

Kirsty rolled her eyes. She'd have to tell Helena to rein it in.

Saffron let out a whistle when she walked into the shop. "This is a gorgeous place." She ran a hand over the tasting table, before walking along the shelves, reading some of the tasting notes handwritten by Kirsty, hanging on strings around the necks of the wines. "I love the personal touch. 'Overtones of peach'. Yum." Saffron looked up. "Peaches are my favourite."

Saffron's gaze settled on Kirsty.

Kirsty went to speak, but no words came out. She cleared her throat, as heat flushed her cheeks.

Tongue-tied in front of a movie star?

Get a grip.

"It's from a lovely producer in the South of France. It's got a slight pettiance and excellent body." Kirsty had gone into wine-pro mode. That was good.

Saffron took a bottle from the shelf. "I'll have to try it now." She paused, never taking her eyes from Kirsty.

Something fluttered in Kirsty's chest. She ignored it.

Repeat after me.

I will not get a crush on a movie star.

"Even better, how about you pick a box of wine for me? You're clearly the expert. I like full-bodied reds and interesting whites. Fizz, too. Surprise me."

"I can do that," Kirsty said. "Do you have a budget?"

"I trust you not to fleece me."

"That from the woman who trusts nobody. Quite an accolade." Kirsty pulled her shoulders back. She was almost back on solid ground. Her body no longer betraying her. Back to being a grown-up doing her professional job. "We offer delivery, so I can drop it round tomorrow. Did you say you were staying at the Beachcomber house?"

"I love that one! Always wanted to have a look inside," Helena said, phone back in hand.

Saffron turned.

Helena raised her phone.

"Put it down!" Kirsty mouthed.

Helena did as she was told, busying herself behind the counter.

"Yep, the Beachcomber. Are you sure? I can pick it up."

Kirsty shook her head. "I have a few other deliveries to do, so I'll add you to the list." She pulled out her phone. "Give me your number and I'll message first to check you're in."

Saffron walked over, took Kirsty's phone, and keyed in her digits.

She smelled insanely good. Movie star-good. And now, Kirsty had Saffron Oliver's number. She was going to try not to fixate on that.

"There you go." Saffron flashed her million-dollar smile.

"No selling my number to the tabloids. I haven't seen any paparazzi yet, which is a minor miracle."

"We're going to keep it that way, aren't we, Helena?" Kirsty narrowed her eyes in Helena's direction.

Her business partner nodded, her tone resigned. "I never even met you," she told Saffron.

Chapter 6

Saffron paced in front of the windows looking out over the water, the selling point of the house and the original reason why she'd jumped at the chance to rent it.

She'd pictured herself sitting in a cosy chair, book in hand, sipping a glass of wine, allowing her mind and body to recoup from the business of being Saffron Oliver, Hollywood star. Fame and celebrity weren't what they were cracked up to be, but the problem was, no one learned the brutal truth until it was too late to switch course, saving one's sanity.

Since her teenage years, Saffron couldn't trust most people she came into contact with, aside from her sister and Michelle, her assistant. She had to pay the latter an obscene amount of money to keep Michelle loyal, but there was the niggling fear that everyone had their price. Even one of her exes had betrayed her, although the woman hadn't had the integrity to own up to her treachery.

Why then, was Saffron pacing, with her eyes glued to the promenade, not the peaceful waves lapping the pebbled beach, in hopes of spying Kirsty, who'd texted saying she'd be by within the hour? What good would come from fostering a friendship with a total stranger? One who had no clue what it meant to be associated with a celebrity, even on a basic level. The paparazzi hadn't converged on Sandy Cove yet, but it was only a matter of time. Her photo had appeared on people's social media accounts, logging her location in Sandy Cove. Pearl had taken a screenshot, with the message: *Never knew oyster town was magical.* It wasn't clever, but it did drive home the real message: Pearl had found Saffron.

Once the locusts descended, would Kirsty be able to handle the deluge? Having cameras stuck in her face? Invasive questions? The temptation of financial payments to spill the tiniest details, like what wine did Saffron pair with seafood?

Contemplating getting to know Kirsty was sheer madness. Saffron's head understood that.

The knock on the front door portended trouble for Saffron, because her pulse quickened and her stomach did a swoop like a flock of seagulls descending on the fresh catch of the day.

This was bad. So very bad.

After one final look in the mirror to ensure she looked better than okay, Saffron swung the door open to see Kirsty astride an old-fashioned three-wheeled bike.

"Oh my God, that's amazing." Saffron walked down her steps to the promenade and craned around Kirsty to see the antique wooden storage box, bold white block letters spelling Wine Time and the shop's number, secured between the back two wheels. "Where did you find this masterpiece?"

Kirsty's cheeks turned an adorable pink. "It used to sit outside a chocolate shop on the High Street, so when they closed, I bought it and restored it just enough to make it ridable but kept its old-world charm."

"Do you need help getting it inside?" Saffron shoved up her sleeves, ready to be put to work.

"Nope. Yours is the last delivery." Kirsty lifted the lid, the hinges protesting, and hefted a large box onto one of her shoulders, the sleeve of her T-shirt rolling back to reveal a toned bicep. "Where do you want me? Er… I mean the wine?"

"Let me help." Saffron tried to take the box, knowing it contained twelve bottles and wasn't light by any stretch of the imagination, but Kirsty twirled away evading help, the bottles inside clinking.

"When I say delivery, I mean full-service. Point me to the kitchen."

Saffron did. "Are you sure about the cart? No one will take it?"

"It has my shop's name and number on the sides and back. Where would anyone go without every local knowing they'd nicked it from me?"

Saffron looked up and down the beach before climbing her wooden steps and clicking the door shut with trepidation. "It's hard for me to wrap my head around leaving something outside in plain view, trusting no one will steal it. Don't you have a bike lock or something?" She followed Kirsty to the kitchen.

"This isn't London. You need to start accepting we do things differently here." Kirsty bent her knees and placed the box on the granite counter-top.

Saffron snapped her fingers with both hands in an attempt to act normal and like she hadn't been ogling Kirsty. "It just seems so abnormal."

"I think always worrying someone is going to hurt you isn't normal or a decent way to live."

Saffron let those words sink in. Could she ever adjust to the Sandy Cove way?

Kirsty seemed to notice the surroundings for the first time and let out an appreciative whistle. "I've always wanted to see the inside of this place. This kitchen is to die for." Kirsty's eyes panned the gourmet set-up with all the sparkling chrome. She moved closer to the glass door. "And, the view of the sea from the private garden is incredible. I could sit here for hours, drinking coffee."

"Not wine? I'd assumed with a shop named Wine Time, it was, well, always time for it." Saffron leaned against the island.

Kirsty's face split into a dazzling grin. "Between you and me, I try to drink it only in the evening."

"Scandalous!"

"Remember, that's not common knowledge and could wreck my rep." She jiggled her brows playfully.

"Is it hard being surrounded by exquisite wine all day and not sampling the goods?" Saffron mimed taking a naughty sip, her mind not exactly on wine.

"It's just part of the job, really. Like you being surrounded by beautiful people. I'm sure you're able to not lick—" Kirsty's hand flew to her mouth. "I really have no idea why that particular example came to mind."

Saffron laughed. "We have signs on every set. Do not lick the actors."

"Can I nosey around?" Kirsty looked past Saffron.

"By all means." Saffron led them to the sitting area. "I keep meaning to buy a book and some wine to spend my evenings with. Thanks to you, I can tick wine off the shopping list."

She made a large check mark in the air, wondering why she couldn't stop from acting punch-drunk.

"I love the stone fireplace. A pity you won't be able to use it while you're here."

"Can't win them all." An image of Kirsty in front of the fire, the reflection of the flames in those eyes—Saffron swallowed.

"Maybe you can strip down and—"

"Lie on a bearskin rug, ready for my naked photo shoot?" Saffron raised one eyebrow.

"Do you have a crowbar?"

"For?" Saffron enjoyed Kirsty twisting herself into knots, refreshing considering most delivered the cheesiest come-on lines with sincerity as if that would make the star swoon. Kirsty was sincere by being awkwardly real.

"To unwedge my foot out of my mouth." The blush on her cheeks deepened to a dark rose, highlighting the beauty of her facial features.

"It's quite charming being around someone who speaks their mind." Saffron couldn't quite wrap her head around why she'd been so frank.

"Glad you think so." Kirsty glanced about. "There aren't many personal touches, are there?"

"That's the curse of always staying at someone else's place. You're captive to someone else's artistic taste, which can be a blessing or a curse."

"Don't you have a home in London?"

"I do and a place in California. But even those have been decorated by other people. I'm hardly in a place long enough to crave putting my own stamp on it. Everything is usually taken care of by others, under the watchful eye of my assistant." Saffron shrugged, as the knowledge settled into her chest like a heavy stone.

"Must be nice."

"Yes and no." Saffron ran a hand over the back of a velvet couch. "It'd be nice not to feel like a stranger all of the time. Lately, I've been thinking it'd be good to plant some roots. I daydream about getting a dog, being able to go for a walk every afternoon. To not rush everywhere but to have the time to savour the normal things in life."

"It's a good thing you're here, then, because this place is the definition of slow and steady, especially when the DFLs aren't here."

"The what?"

"Down From London." Kirsty checked her wrist. "Speaking of walking, I best get going for mine."

"You don't want a glass of wine before you go? I mean, it's only fair after you lugged it here." Saffron's mind wandered back to the glimpse of bicep.

"I can't. But if you're serious about getting into a normal swing of things, why don't you take a stroll with me? I just need to return the bike to the shop, take care of some admin, and then we can walk along the seafront."

"I'd love that." Saffron gazed at Kirsty a tick too long, then dropped her eyes to the hardwood floor. "If I won't be a bother."

"I'd enjoy the company. I'll be back in two shakes." Kirsty ducked out, not giving Saffron time to back out.

Not that she would have. What was it about Kirsty that pulled Saffron in? Her charming smile? Kind eyes?

Genuineness? Or was it the adorable way the wrong words bubbled out, taking both of them by surprise?

It was invigorating to be around someone who was so normal, not afraid to speak her mind, despite the outcome, which in Saffron's biz meant damaging the brand. Yes, that was it. Normal was what Saffron had been craving for years but wasn't able to identify the need for it until this moment. Granted, their first meeting had been a clusterfuck, with Kirsty fangirling, causing Saffron to raise her walls. But, the two of them had been able to set aside the hard feelings easily. That had to say something, didn't it? But what?

Her phone buzzed, and she saw the text simply saying *outside*.

Saffron grabbed her bag, neglecting to give herself a once over in the mirror, not wanting to waste any time.

"Which way?" Kirsty asked. "Towards Branton Bay or the other side of Sandy Cove."

"I don't know. Which is better?" Saffron looked to her right and then left.

Kirsty smiled. "Depends on your definition, but if you fancy an oyster, which is a Sandy Cove must, I suggest going left."

"I don't want to break any musts of the town." Saffron fell into step with Kirsty. "I love the beach huts. So colourful and quaint."

"My parents own one close to your place."

A family passed them on their right, the adults gaping at Saffron.

She retrieved a baseball cap out of her bag, pulling it down low over her eyes.

"It must be weird to have people recognise you wherever you go?"

"I've become used to it, but it can be annoying." Saffron's words came out more bitter than she intended and they continued walking in uncomfortable silence. So much for setting aside the movie-star discomfort.

Another group of people ambled by, but Saffron turned her head away from their gaze, pretending to be taken in by the brilliant bluish-green colour of the water in the hazy afternoon light.

"Oh, look!" Saffron pointed to a bright pink hut. "They offer water sports. I've always wanted to try some."

"I kayak."

"You do?"

"Cross my heart." Kirsty acted this out, drawing Saffron's gaze to the V of the T-shirt. "I can teach you."

Saffron had to rip her eyes upwards. "I'd like that very much."

The amount of people increased as they neared the bustling harbour, a mix of families out for a stroll, their cheeks red from being out in the sun, and workers in overalls hauling in the day's catch. A man in a red forklift eased the forks into the slats of a wooden pallet where sacks filled with mussels had been placed. He steered through the crowd with expertise to a waiting truck.

"You ready for that oyster?" Kirsty gave Saffron a heart-stopping *now or never* smile.

Saffron's eyes zeroed in on the cash only sign over the takeout window. "Uh—"

"Remember, it's a Sandy Cove rule." Kirsty extended an admonishing finger in the air.

"The thing is, I don't ever carry money."

"Just like the Queen. No worries. I can spot you a fiver."
Kirsty reached into her bag and pulled one out. "Stay here."

She left Saffron standing away from the crowd, which was
sweet, because even with the hat, a few people did a double
take, looking as if they thought they knew who Saffron was
but couldn't place her.

"Here you go!" Kirsty presented her with one oyster.

"Where's yours?"

Kirsty leaned close. "The truth is I can't stand them."

"Now you tell me!" Saffron eyed the half shell. "This
would have been useful knowledge before you purchased one
just for me."

"I knew you'd back out. Besides it's—"

"Tradition. So you keep saying, but if you don't eat them,
how am I supposed to believe anything you've said?" Saffron
shook her head mockingly but grinned foolishly.

"Because I have tried them, which is why I know I don't
like them. Many others love them. There's an entire festival
dedicated to oysters." Kirsty pointed to one of the signs. "A
whole week of events to celebrate the oyster and its impact on
the town. Don't let my aversion influence you. Surely, you've
had one before, being a movie star and all that." Kirsty nudged
Saffron in the side with an elbow.

"I have, but the last time I did, I got a terrible case of food
poisoning."

"One of the selling points of the Sandy Cove Native is their
freshness, so blot that experience from your memory, tip it
back, and swallow." Kirsty acted this out, the confidence in her
eyes so damn appealing.

"I may be more trusting if you didn't just confess you aren't a fan." Saffron dramatically jiggled the shell, the shellfish moving slightly, enjoying putting on such a show, because it seemed to draw Kirsty closer as a way of offering her support.

"The longer you stare at it, the harder it will be to bite the bullet. The best thing to do is just get it over with."

"You really aren't selling this must-have Sandy Cove experience." Saffron returned the playful nudge into Kirsty's side, closing the space between them even more.

"Pretend you're on a movie set and you have to eat it."

"Right. I can do that. I mean, it's how they got me to jump out of a plane." Saffron raised the shell to her lips. "Here goes nothing."

Kirsty, open-mouthed, watched.

Saffron chomped into it once. Twice. Then swallowed.

"Well?" Kirsty's eyes goggled.

"You're right, Sandy Cove oysters are nice and fresh."

"Would you like another?" Kirsty started to fish in her wallet.

"Not today, but I do think I will have many more in the not-so-distant future. When I have money of my own. Can you add the oyster to the party bill?"

Kirsty waved the idea away. "My treat."

"No, I can't take your money. We should discuss your rate."

"Well... I do have a number in mind, but we're having such a lovely time." Kirsty's gaze swept the surroundings. "I can't talk business when there are people walking their dogs and kids getting ice cream."

"Just tell me. I'll make sure to pass it along to my assistant to arrange payment."

Kirsty handed Saffron a paper she'd pulled out of her bag.

"You've got to be kidding me." Saffron scanned the itemised list of expenditures.

"If it's too much, I can drop—"

"It's not enough. There's no way you can pull this off with this amount of money." Again, Saffron ran a finger down the figures.

"Oh, I know I can."

"But what about your time. You need to be paid for that."

"It's on there." Kirsty jabbed a slender finger at the calculation.

"At a ridiculously low rate." Saffron slapped the paper against her leg. "I can't let you work for basically nothing."

"It's what I charge."

"You need to learn how much you're worth and not sell yourself short."

Their eyes met, neither speaking, but Saffron's insides turned into a schmaltzy mush.

A child burst into tears after dropping her ice cream cone.

"Can I borrow another fiver?" Saffron asked.

"Sure."

Saffron hunched down and asked the kid. "Can I get you a new cone?"

A tear-streaked face nodded yes.

After the child's parents thanked Saffron and they went on their merry way, Kirsty studied Saffron with a quizzical expression, but didn't say a word.

"Add that fiver to the bill, in addition to the oyster." Saffron got a pen out of her bag and clicked it. "Actually, I'll add the charges." She looked up. "Shall we shake on it?"

"If you insist, but I trust you'll pay."

"I do insist. And, I'll be keeping track of all the incidentals and amending the bill accordingly." Saffron stuck out her hand.

Kirsty took it into hers.

They gazed at each other, holding on.

"Are you sure you don't want an oyster? When was the last time you ate one? Tastes change." Saffron was well aware she still held Kirsty's hand, but she was finding it difficult to let go.

"Trust me when I say I don't want one."

"You don't know what you're missing out on."

Chapter 7

Kirsty wobbled as she hit the top of the step ladder. She clutched the metal handle to steady herself. She was in the shop window, and she really didn't need to give the town a live performance of falling on her arse. Helena couldn't climb ladders due to a vertigo issue, so the job of putting up their festival bunting and posters had fallen to her. Kirsty reached up and secured the bunting over the hook she'd put up a few years ago. They used it to string their Christmas lights, too.

"How did the wine drop-off go?" Helena had drunk three cups of coffee today, which wasn't helping her Saffron-inspired mania. Kirsty was glad Sandy Cove didn't attract celebrities as a rule, just artists and writers who Helena could walk past in the street and never recognise. Movie stars, it seemed, were her Achilles heel.

Unlike Kirsty, who was taking her burgeoning friendship with Saffron Oliver totally in her stride. Particularly after Saffron had texted to say thanks for the wine, and even signed off with a kiss.

Yep. Easy breezy.

"It went fine." Kirsty wasn't giving too much away.

Somehow, she felt an allegiance to protect Saffron at all costs. Like she needed it. "I dropped the wine off; she admired our bike."

"Of course she did!"

"Then I left. The end."

She was lying to Helena.

That was new.

"Did you get a photo of her with the bike? It would be really good for business if we put that on Instagram."

Kirsty rolled her eyes as she got down. "I told you, no photos of Saffron on our website, she's here to escape that sort of attention. Also, can you drop the social media obsession? We hardly ever post anything anyway. Wasn't that meant to be Anton's job under your supervision?" They'd made grand plans to make it a regular thing, but nothing had come of it.

Helena focused on boxing up their regular restaurant orders, lugging the wine onto the counter with a grunt. "I'll get him on it. He's not doing much else during his summer holidays apart from sleeping." She smoothed the brown masking tape along the top of wine box to seal it, then wrote the name of the restaurant on the top. "Did I tell you we got a couple of new orders from people who saw the profile Ginger did of you on the town website? She's got good PR going on with that, so tell her thanks."

"You can tell her yourself. She's coming for the New Zealand wine tasting later."

Helena grinned. "Is her sister coming, too?"

Kirsty shook her head. "No, she has podcast interviews to do all evening for *Girl Racer*." Their lives really couldn't be more different, could they?

"Shame." Helena wagged a finger in Kirsty's direction. "But my spies tell me that wasn't the end of your afternoon yesterday. Hugh's friend Larry spotted you walking along the beach with Saffron."

That figured. "She just walked with me after I dropped off her order. Nothing more." Kirsty moved the ladder to the back of the shop, before leaning on the counter beside Helena. She sipped her coffee. It was cold. She made a face.

Helena took the mug without a word. She reappeared a couple of minutes later having microwaved it. It was one of her more appealing habits. Then she studied Kirsty like she was a museum exhibit. "You say nothing more has gone on, but something has." She waved a finger in front of Kirsty's face. "You look a little out of sorts. Flushed. Like you've got indigestion."

"It's a hazard of working with you."

Helena gave her a grin. "I remember that face. Confusion mixed with something else." She furrowed her brow, then put a hand on her hip. "You *like* her."

"Every woman with a pulse likes Saffron Oliver. Even the super-straight ones." Kirsty sipped her coffee. It burned her tongue, so she put it down.

"Yes, but they're not popping round to hers like you are." Helena paused. "This wouldn't be such a bad idea, you know. A lesbian romance would put the shop on the map!"

"Are you asking me to sleep with her to boost business?" She was being sarcastic, but Kirsty's body responded nevertheless, her heart pulsing on cue.

Helena smirked. "I'm not seeing this as a great hardship."

"I might start bringing earplugs to work, just so I can tune you out. Or maybe noise-cancelling headphones would be better." Kirsty walked back over to the window, concentrating on their festival poster. Was it straight? She tilted her head. Straightness wasn't her forte.

"She seems nice, though, right?"

Helena wasn't giving this up.

"I mean, lesbians don't trot around Sandy Cove every day. You get on, and she's single." Helena held out her hands like this was a done deal.

"Just because we're both lesbians doesn't mean we're going to get together. I believe I taught you this in Lesbian 101. Besides, she's in her early 30s. I'm 49. I'm hardly a catch."

"Nonsense. You're gorgeous. Youthful. You could easily pass for late 30s."

Kirsty heard that often. It didn't change her age, though. She was still *groan when she got out of a chair* years old. Although Helena wasn't wrong. She was attracted to Saffron. But she was also attracted to Fiona in the post office. She wasn't about to sleep with her.

"I do like her, though. After a dodgy start, she's proving to have a sense of humour, which is good. I'm taking her kayaking."

Helena whipped her head up at that. "Kayaking? You haven't done that since you and Anna split."

"I've done it a few times, just not quite so often. Maybe it's time I started again."

"That's how it could all start. You, Saffron, a kayak. I can see it now." Helena stared into space dreamily.

"Or me, Saffron, capsizing."

"You need to watch more romance movies."

"Or maybe you need to watch fewer. I'm nearly 50. She's a Hollywood star. I'm not dating the star of *Girl Racer*. Those kinds of things don't happen to little ol' me."

* * *

Kirsty plonked a tube of salt and vinegar Pringles on her coffee table, and grabbed a couple of wine glasses from the cupboard near the sink. The wine tasting downstairs this evening had been a real hit, and Ginger had come up to her flat for a nightcap.

Kirsty glanced around the main room of her flat: kitchen at one end, small dining table and four chairs, and a sofa big enough for three at the other. It wasn't much, but it was home, which had been the most important thing when she needed it. Moving above the shop was meant to have been a short-term affair, but it'd turned into years. Now, Kirsty was comfortable. She wouldn't rule out moving into a house with a partner, but until that day, she was happy here.

"I absolutely love your place, it's so cosy and welcoming." Ginger was standing at the fireplace, holding up a photo frame. "Is this your parents?"

Kirsty nodded. "Yep, on their wedding day. They had way more luck than either of us. Still happily married, sometimes nauseatingly so."

"Good for them. The world needs more love."

Kirsty let out a gust of laughter. "Those are not the words of someone about to plan their divorce party."

Ginger gave her a smile. "I can be bitter and twisted but still wish happiness for others. It's a skill I've perfected over the past few months."

Kirsty brought the glasses over to the sofa and popped the cork on a fresh bottle of red. "You're going to like this one," she said. "It's a grenache-tempranillo blend from Southern Spain, a little spicy with mixed berries. Plus, they sent me a free case, so I'm talking them up. I'm easily bought."

"I'll remember that." Ginger clinked her glass and took a sip. "I'm no expert, but that is pleasingly winey."

Kirsty laughed again. She'd found herself doing that a lot around Ginger. She was on her wavelength, easy to get along with. Who would have guessed they only met last week? It felt like they'd packed in a lifetime over the intervening days.

"First things first: have you narrowed down a date yet? I'm thinking after the Oyster Festival, when hotels will have more room."

Ginger nodded. "The third weekend in August. Does that work?"

Kirsty nodded. "Let me put a few feelers out. Obviously, we're in wedding season, and a lot of the bigger places will be booked up. But you never know. Let's work with that for now."

Ginger put her glass on the table and sat back. "Putting a date on it makes it so much more concrete. I've only just got divorced, but it still seems a little surreal." She rubbed her hands together. "But this is my fresh start. I just have to keep remembering that."

"Totally. A new beginning. Maybe I should have had one."

"You still could. We could make it a joint one."

Kirsty shook her head. "Seven years later is a little late. Plus, this is your big day, your moment. It's not about me."

Ginger ran a hand through her hair. "You're right. It is about me, and I should embrace that."

"Have you thought about what you might want? A dartboard with Dave's face on it? A punchbag? Stripper? I've seen some out-there ideas on the web, but I wasn't sure that was the way we wanted to go."

Ginger shook her head. "I'm not trying to shock anyone. The main thing is I want it to be on my terms. Because looking back, the last few years haven't really been. I've been giving in to what Dave wanted for a while. Not drinking white wine just because he didn't want to. Then I tried those ones from New Zealand tonight, and I loved them." She threw up her hands. "What else have I been holding back on that I should have been savouring?"

Kirsty got it. "When Anna and I broke up, one of the first things I did was buy some lilies. She was wildly allergic, and I've always loved them. Sometimes compromising for partners is a good thing. But only if the compromise is reciprocated."

Ginger nodded. "Exactly. I've pussyfooted about with my life far too much. Which is why this party is important and has to be what I want. Not what Saffron thinks or what she can afford. Which is a lot, obviously, but I don't want her to get carried away. That's your job to police. Tell her no. She's not used to that."

Kirsty gave her a salute. "On it. Saffron and I already have an understanding anyway."

Ginger turned. "Oh really?"

Heat rose to Kirsty's cheeks. "She apologised for her behaviour when we met. Told me to call her out if she did it again. I'll just add saying no to the list."

"You've seen her? I've only had one coffee. Otherwise,

she's been avoiding me. She told me she has stuff to sort with work and her personal life."

"We ran into each other on the street, and I delivered some wine to her place. Nothing major." Kirsty's skin prickled as Ginger's inquisitive gaze settled on her. "You should go round, take advantage of her veranda. It's got a glorious view."

Ginger went to say something, then stopped. She took a sip of her wine before she continued. "I'll do that. I hope she enjoys it here. She deserves happiness. I had it for a good chunk of time, until Dave went weird. Saff's never stayed still long enough for it to happen."

"She's got enough wine from my shop now to keep her still for a few days, at least." Kirsty paused. "Talking of wine, we need that for the party, too. So much to think about and only a handful of weeks to plan."

Ginger turned to her. "Am I asking too much? Should we have it in September?"

Kirsty shook her head. "Nope. It's my personal mission now to make this work." She tapped the side of her nose with her index finger. "Nobody knows Sandy Cove like I do. Well, apart from my mum, but she's on our side."

"I'm so glad I met you. In quieter moments, I've been staring out at the beach, wondering if I made the wrong decision moving here. Meeting you has completely turned it around, so thank you."

"My absolute pleasure." Kirsty meant it, too. "Plus, the profile you did on the town's website has already got us some new business, so we owe you, too. Let's talk guest list. You've said you've got friends coming. What about family? Parents? Any other siblings?"

A shadow passed over Ginger's features. "It's just me and Saff. My parents aren't with us anymore. I might invite a couple of my cousins. But I reckon about 30 people on my side, then perhaps some of the locals, which I'll look to you for."

"Leave it with me," Kirsty replied. "This party is going to be exactly the relaunch your new life deserves."

Chapter 8

Saffron sat on a bar stool at her kitchen island, doodling on the backside of one of the pages of the *Girl Racer* script, kicking her legs freely.

Her agent's name flashed on her phone.

Should she answer? Ignore?

The phone stopped ringing.

Good.

It started again.

Not good.

"Hello." Saffron attempted to sound as breezily as possible.

"Why are you ducking my calls?"

"I was on the treadmill and couldn't answer in time." Saffron closed her eyes, embarrassed by the obvious lie. Like an amateur, she hadn't even faked being out of breath.

"Were you on the treadmill for twelve hours yesterday?"

"I hadn't unpacked my phone charger until this morning."

"Uh huh." Pearl sounded as unconvinced as a parent holding a spliff while her teenager claimed she had no idea why it was in her room. "Have you read the script?"

"I have it in front of me right now." At least that much was true.

"And?"

"And, what?" Saffron smacked her forehead with her free palm.

"Can I tell them you're on board?"

"I haven't finished reading it yet."

"They're not going to wait forever." Saffron could picture Pearl's snarl looking so much like the attack dog she claimed to be.

"I completely understand if they want someone else for the role."

"They don't!" Pearl released a whoosh of air. "This production can't go on without you. Hundreds of people won't get work because of you. Is that how you want this to play in the press?"

"Gee, thanks for that guilt trip." Or was it a threat? Would Pearl stoop to that level? Would she seed stories about her own client acting like a spoiled brat to get Saffron back in line?

"It's the nature of the business. Are you holding out for more money?"

"Not at all."

"Then what's wrong? I can't help you if you don't tell me."

I hate acting!

"I'm sorry. I'll finish reading it soon. I promise."

"In the meantime, I've scheduled another podcast interview next Wednesday. Don't think of blowing it off."

Saffron made a gun with her fingers and blew her head off. "Wouldn't dream of it. I've got to run. Bye." She ended the call.

She'd hate knowing I'm sitting here, drawing on the precious script and haven't read a word. That thought put a smile on her lips.

Taking up a pencil, she eyed the sketch she'd made of Kirsty, trying to capture the way her grey eyes sparkled when she smiled. The sparkle transformed into fireworks when she tilted her head back and laughed, so carefree and beautiful.

Saffron crossed her legs.

It was foolish to let her mind wander to Kirsty, who in all probability wasn't giving Saffron a moment's thought. Why would she be interested in a Hollywood star? The tabloids were chock full of stories about the vapid Saffron Oliver. Or the mysterious and moody actress who'd recently ditched her girl squad to appear on red carpets alone. None of them could make up their minds, which suited Saffron most of the time. She didn't want anyone to know the true Saffron. Or, that had been the case until popping down to Sandy Cove.

It was no use, though. Down-to-Earth Kirsty wasn't the type to daydream about Saffron. Sure, Kirsty had confided in Ginger about stripping off Saffron's leathers, but that was before they met. Daydreaming was one thing, acting on those impulses was an entirely different matter. Besides, Saffron never had good luck in the women department. Only bad, bad, bad—

Her phone buzzed and she read the text: *Ready for a kayak session this afternoon?*

She tapped her pencil against the drawing of Kirsty, wondering if her luck was about to change.

* * *

Kirsty stood outside a bright pink beach hut with blue trim, waving both hands, making it impossible for Saffron to miss the destination.

"Did you have trouble finding the place?" Kirsty took a deep breath.

"Not at all." It'd be hard to miss Kirsty's *joie de vivre* coupled with the cheery hut. "This place is amazing." Saffron read the hand-painted sign over the door: *Toffee Cottage*.

Kirsty followed her gaze. "My parents named it that because when I was a kid, I had a serious toffee addiction."

"Do you now?"

"Not after my seventh filling. The detox wasn't fun for anyone." She couldn't maintain her pointed stare, as if daring Saffron to laugh, and broke into a wide grin.

"Poor you." Saffron tugged the collar of her shirt from her flushed skin. "Can I get the grand tour?"

"After you." Kirsty did a slight curtsy.

Saffron stepped inside, noticing it wasn't much bigger than a garden shed, but way posher like a sophisticated playhouse for grown-ups. "Oh, I love the vintage stuff, especially the beaded chandelier."

"My parents bought this place more than forty years ago for a song and most of this stuff came with it. My nana made the quilt on the daybed. You can sleep two in here comfortably, but when I was a teen, we'd put up a tent on the porch with sleeping bags, and six of us could spend the weekend all on our own, feeling like proper grown-ups. My parents liked that we weren't far from home." Kirsty wheeled about, looking out the door at the water. "This place always makes me feel at peace with the world. I can sit on the porch and watch the tide roll in and out all day and never get bored. At night, I become enthralled by the stars." Kirsty looked over her shoulder, her penetrating gaze igniting a fire inside Saffron. "This little oasis has been a part of my life since the seventies."

"It has not." Saffron took a step back.

"It has."

"There's no way you can remember spending time here in the seventies." Saffron narrowed her eyes to inspect Kirsty's face. "No way at all."

"Yet, I do. Does that shock you?" Kirsty slanted her head in such a way a wave of dark hair framed her alabaster skin and Saffron had to stifle an urge to plant her mouth on Kirsty's full and, no doubt, soft lips.

"It does. What's your secret?"

"For?"

"Looking fab."

Kirsty waggled a finger in the air. "I've already agreed to teach you how to kayak. No need for shameless flattery."

"I'm not known for being shameless."

"Is that right? What are you known for?"

Saffron couldn't tell if Kirsty was taking the piss, but opted to give her the benefit of the doubt. "That's for me to know and for you to find out." *Guh*. Was that the best she had?

"Sounds like a challenge."

"Do you like challenges?"

"Only ones that are worthwhile."

Nervous laughter escaped Saffron. "I guess time will tell if I'm worth it or not."

Kirsty's expression darkened. "You get paid how much per movie?"

Again, Saffron struggled to decipher the true meaning behind the question and pivoted. "Do your parents still live in Sandy Cove?"

Just like that, Kirsty's cloudy eyes returned to vibrant. "Yes. You might get the chance to meet them at the festival."

"That must be nice." Saffron regarded the family photos on the cheery pink wall. "When I was a kid, we used to go for beach holidays in Devon and Cornwall. Sandy Cove has the same charming character, but the beaches there were sandier. Sometimes, when I get overwhelmed, I like to close my eyes and relive the good memories with my parents at the beach." As rare as they were.

"Ginger told me they aren't around anymore." Kirsty's voice was soft and full of heartbreak.

Saffron took in a deep breath and clamped her hands together, applying enough pressure to staunch the blood flow. She'd taken great pains to bury her relationship with them. The fact she brought them up at all was troubling. "So, what's the plan? I stopped by the marina and picked up a wetsuit. I also got a swimsuit. Which should I wear?"

"I'd wear the swimsuit under the wetsuit to prevent chafing. Why don't you change first? I'll wait out here."

"What? You don't think you can control yourself from not taking a peek at the goods?" Saffron levelled her eyes onto Kirsty's, wondering if the woman would take the bait.

"Considering you're of the opinion that I'm not old enough to remember the seventies, I don't think getting naked in front of you will help me maintain that belief."

Saffron's eyes travelled up from Kirsty's feet, along the curve of her calves, past her toned thighs, continuing still upwards, staying longer over the swell of the breasts, until finally resting on those stunning eyes. "I doubt you could disappoint in any department."

"No pressure, then. Go on. Get changed so we can enjoy the wonder that is the sea." Kirsty spread her arms out wide, as if Saffron was about to experience a once in a lifetime event.

Inside the hut, Saffron undressed and slipped on a simple black one-piece the man at the shop had recommended. She attempted to slide one leg into the wetsuit, only to be met with resistance, the neoprene refusing to budge up or down. She tried the other leg, ending up with both feet stuck.

"Um... I may need help," Saffron called out.

"What?" Was the muffled reply.

Saffron hopped to the door, opening it, and keeping her body out of view. "I can't get the wetsuit past my feet."

"Did you buy K-Y?"

"Are you talking about lubricant?"

"Yes. It can help, especially with a newbie."

"Are you talking about me or the wetsuit?"

"Well, given the situation, I'd say both. Do you want me to come in and help?" It was evident Kirsty was trying not to laugh, and her tone was laced with humour.

"Please." Saffron hopped back a step to allow her to open the door wider, still keeping out of view from the people walking to and fro on the promenade.

Kirsty, with eyes closed, put out a hand. "Where's the suit?"

"On my feet. Why do you have your eyes closed?"

"You're the one who suggested I wouldn't be able to stop myself from peeking." Kirsty seemed tickled being able to toss that comment back at Saffron.

"I have a swimsuit on. It's not like I'm naked."

"Are you sure you want me to open my eyes?"

"Are you good at fumbling in the dark with another woman?" Saffron sucked in a breath, shocked by her words. These were the types of statements that could get her into hot water if leaked to the press.

Kirsty's eyes flew open, and there was a mischievous twist to her lips. "I see how this is going to be."

"At least, you can see now. For a moment, I thought we'd never leave the hut." Saffron gazed at the daybed, realising that wouldn't be a bad trade off. She glanced down at her feet. "How does this get on me?"

"One yank at a time." Kirsty's gaze roved over Saffron's nearly six-foot frame. "This could take some time. Maybe we should send out for reinforcements. Or tea. A proper British woman can't die without a final cup of tea."

"You think you're so funny. I'd like to see you get into motorbike leathers." Come to think of it, Saffron would love to witness that first-hand.

"That's an excellent point. You can put those on, but not this. Is this just a ruse to get me into the hut with you half naked?"

"I wish I could say that was the case." Saffron tried to change her footing, but wobbled, and if it weren't for Kirsty steadying Saffron, she would have crashed to the floor. "This was your idea. Help me."

"Okay, okay. Let me get to work." Kirsty leaned down, allowing Saffron to get a pleasing glimpse of cleavage.

Saffron placed a hand on top of Kirsty's warm shoulder. "Who invented these things?"

"Probably the first brothel owner." Kirsty yanked on one of the legs, nearly causing Saffron to topple over again.

"Did neoprene exist in biblical times?"

"I may remember the seventies, but not all the way back to ancient Egypt."

After much tugging, grunting, and much more tugging, the wetsuit was on Saffron.

"*Voilà!*" Kirsty put her hand up for a high five.

Saffron slapped it, her fingers curling around the hand, before letting go. "Do you need help with yours?"

"Nah. I'm a pro."

"Okay, then. I guess I'll step outside." The air whooshed out of her chest, like a balloon being speared by a knife.

On the porch, Saffron strained to hear Kirsty call out for help, but no such luck.

After a couple of minutes, Kirsty bounded out of the hut, tossing Saffron some water shoes. "Put these on while I get the kayak from the storage in the back."

"Don't you need help?"

"And risk getting sued if Hollywood's It Girl breaks a leg? After the wetsuit incident, I think it's best if I take care of the dangerous parts." She winked. "Lock up the hut for me, please." She tossed Saffron a gold-painted oyster shell that had been repurposed into a key ring.

Saffron took a seat to put on the shoes, watching Kirsty's lithe body carry the kayak to the water's edge. The woman had muscles on top of muscles. There was absolutely no way Kirsty was alive during the disco age. No way in hell. Not with a body like that. But why would she say it if it wasn't true?

"You coming?" Kirsty waved.

Depends on your definition.

Saffron locked the door and made her way over the pebbled beach to start their adventure together.

Chapter 9

"This is lovely, spending a little time with you. We hardly see you anymore since you've been planning this divorce party." Her mum walked beside Kirsty along the promenade, the warm July sunshine already buttering their backs. To their left, the sea caressed the pebble beach, not quite full of sun-worshippers yet at just gone 9am. However, the early-morning water sports crowd were out already, taking full advantage of the good weather.

"Always got time for a cup of tea at the beach hut with you. Although then I've got to meet Dolly at the Lobster Grill. It looks like she might be able to accommodate the party after she had a wedding cancellation."

Mum snorted. "At least that couple won't need a divorce party down the line, so they saved themselves a lot of money. What's this woman's name you're working for? Some kind of herb?"

"Ginger." Kirsty didn't need to look at her mum's face to know what it was doing. "She's lovely, too. I'm sure you'll meet her soon." Kirsty clutched her parents' beach towels, along with one of their bags of provisions for the day. They'd left Dad at the shop, choosing a paper and having a coffee with his friend, with instructions to "bring iced buns for elevenses." Kirsty hoped Dad understood the importance of that task, or else there'd be hell to pay.

"Is this Ginger single? Is that why you had your hair cut? It looks lovely, by the way."

Kirsty turned her head. "She's divorced, so yes she's single. But she's also straight, before you start matchmaking."

Mum gave her a look. "Shame. I'll have to tell Shirley, though. Her son just got divorced. Perhaps they'd be a good match? You remember Christian?"

She did remember Christian. He was a total gobshite and Kirsty was only surprised his divorce had taken so long. "Shall we let Ginger get used to being divorced first before we marry her off again?"

"I just want everyone to be happy."

"Not everyone's version of happiness matches yours." It's a conversation she'd had with her mum many times. Kirsty had been at her happiest over the past few years, but Mum could never fathom that. Happiness for her equalled romance. For Kirsty, happiness was a state of mind. Although, she had to admit, since meeting the Oliver sisters, her quota of happiness had increased.

"I shouldn't invite him to the summer BBQ tomorrow, then?"

"I hope you're joking."

Mum elbowed her as they walked. "Of course I am. You're coming, though? As well as Helena and Hugh?"

Kirsty nodded. "Wouldn't miss it. The annual opening of Dad's BBQ is a tradition I'd never mess with."

"He's got a new one this year. Gas. He keeps going out

and turning it on when he thinks I'm not looking. Still, it makes him happy, so who am I to judge?"

A whoop from the beach made them both turn their heads as two young girls ran into the sea, screamed at the temperature, and ran back just as fast. On their right, Saffron's Beachcomber house came into view.

Mum nodded towards it. "I heard the posh house is off the market for a while. Do you know who's renting it?"

Prickly heat tiptoed up Kirsty's spine. "Ginger's sister."

"She mustn't be short of a bob or two."

"She bought a box of wine from the shop, so she gets my vote. I took her kayaking the other day, too."

"You still remembered how to do it? That kayak has been gathering dust for a long time since Anna. But good for you."

Her mum was now the second person to point that out. Perhaps she had forgotten the things she liked to do since Anna, and the shop had taken up more and more of her time. It had been almost a five-year break from kayaking, save for a couple of solo rides here and there. But after the past couple of weeks going out on her own and with Saffron, she was back in the saddle. It felt good. Like she was returning to her true self.

Kirsty put a hand to her chest as they walked past Saffron's house. She looked up to the veranda. It was empty. Where was Saffron? Doing more movie publicity? Reading a new script? Thinking about moving back to London after her break by the sea? Something in Kirsty's chest contracted at the thought.

Watching the star of *Girl Racer* staggering about their beach hut and trying not to fall on her arse had made her smile. Kirsty was beginning to glimpse the human face of the movie star. The one the public never got to see. She'd also witnessed Saffron's long, lithe body in her wetsuit that clung to her in *all* the right places. She had the mental snapshot stored safely in her mind. Kayaking with her had been invigorating, being back in touch with nature. Saffron had woken up Kirsty's passion for getting out on the sea, not simply looking at it. Her shoulders ached after all the paddling, but it was a good ache. One that made her feel switched on, ready to jump back into living fully.

Saffron made her feel alive. Kirsty had been happy, but maybe there were levels of happiness.

In just a few short days, Saffron had made her level-up.

They arrived at Toffee Cottage, and her mum unlocked the door, bringing out the easy lounge chairs and setting up the small table on the porch. Kirsty gripped the waxed white wooden railings and stretched out her back, taking in the view. She couldn't imagine not living near the sea. It was part of who she was. She smiled up at the lighthouse, then turned to where her mum dropped a magazine on a chair.

"I need to go to the loo again." Her mum shook her head. "Don't get old. Your bladder packs up." She wandered off in the direction of the public toilets on the promenade five minutes further along the beach.

Kirsty flopped into the opposite chair and stretched out her legs. She yawned then checked her watch. Two hours before she had to meet Dolly. She might just sneak in a coffee and iced bun if her dad showed up on time. She grabbed the magazine from the other chair, then stopped when she saw the front cover. A photo of Saffron holding hands with her *Girl Racer* co-star Echo Black sat in the top corner, with the headline: *Are This Star-Studded Couple Made For Each Other?*

Kirsty sat up straight, her cheeks flushing red, a feeling of dread sinking down into her stomach. Of course, it would be naive of her to think Saffron didn't have relationships, but was she still in one? Everything she'd said indicated otherwise, but how recent was that photo? Was that why Saffron had taken a break from filming? It would make sense. Kirsty flipped to the story to find out more, telling herself it meant nothing.

She'd just met Saffron.

They lived in different worlds.

So why was it that seeing her on the pages of a magazine with another woman felt like she'd been punched in the gut?

* * *

Dad turned up just in time with a packet of Digestives.

Mum could barely hide her disgust. "Where are the iced buns?"

"They'd sold out." Dad took off his sunhat, and scratched his bald head.

"There wasn't even a cake of some sort? Have you learned nothing in our 50 years of marriage?"

Dad buried his head in his paper, clicking his pen to tackle the crossword.

Mum ate a Digestive, but her face said it was a protest biscuit.

Kirsty passed around the coffee, smiling at the normalcy of her parents' interaction. She'd never quite had that with Anna. She wanted it in her life going forward.

An image of Saffron's smile flashed into her mind, but vanished just as quickly, like one of those red dots in an eye test. Kirsty frowned at her thoughts. First, Saffron was a movie star. Second, she might be involved still.

"Kirsty!"

She stood up. All the hairs on the back of her neck did the same. Saffron's face was now grinning up at her in real life from the promenade below.

Kirsty's heart boomed.

Standing beside Saffron was Ginger, both wearing Aviator shades, black T-shirts and denim cut-off shorts like they were twins.

Kirsty waved and beckoned them up the slight incline to the hut.

"Mum, Dad, this is Ginger and Saffron. Ginger's having the divorce party I'm organising. Saffron's her sister and she's renting the Beachcomber."

They all shook hands, and Ginger and Saffron removed their sunglasses. Saffron clipped them over the neck of her T-shirt and raked a hand through her hair.

Kirsty blinked, remembering the magazine article and the way her spirits had slumped. Then again, maybe it was fake news? What had Saffron told her? *"Don't believe everything you read."*

Besides, it was pretty hard to be annoyed with Saffron when she was standing in front of her looking every inch the movie star. Kirsty should have put more make-up on this morning. Was Saffron even wearing any? Then again, she didn't need to. She had youth on her side.

Dad was still shaking Saffron's hand with his head tilted,

trying to place her. "You look familiar. Do I know you from somewhere?"

Saffron glanced at Kirsty. "You haven't told them?" Her tone was amazed.

Kirsty shook her head. "You said to keep it on the down-low, so I did."

Saffron opened her mouth, then closed it. Her lips glistened invitingly.

"Wow," she said, giving Kirsty a look that made every muscle in her body tense. "Not many people listen."

"I'm not many people."

Time stood still as Saffron stared at her for a few more seconds, before her mum's voice broke the moment.

"She told me you were Ginger's sister, but that's about it. But you do look familiar. Did you used to work at the Co-op?"

Kirsty swallowed down laughter. "She's an actor, Mum."

"Anything I would know?" Mum's face lit up.

Saffron flashed her superstar grin. "Nothing you *should* know, believe me. The *Girl Racer* movies?"

Blank stares from Kirsty's parents. "Not really our sort of thing," her mum confided. "But welcome to our little town. You're just visiting I take it?"

Saffron nodded. "A few weeks of fresh air and the sea. I'm loving it so far." She put an arm around Ginger's shoulder. "But my sister here has bought a house, so she's here for the duration."

"You're having the divorce party?" Dad picked up his paper. "You might know this clue." He picked up his pen. "Divorce, or abort. Nine letters."

"Terminate," Ginger replied almost instantaneously.

Dad checked, then gave her a grin. "Well done." He reached for his pen and filled it in.

Kirsty could have happily clunked him over the head.

"This is a fantastic beach hut," Ginger told Kirsty. "This is where you keep your kayak? Saffron was just telling me all about that. Sounds like fun."

Kirsty nodded. "We'll have to go out one day."

Ginger shook her head. "I'm strictly a look-at-the-sea girl. I'll leave that to you two." She stared out to sea. "It's so relaxing here, though. I can feel my tension seeping out of me. Like summers when we were kids in Cornwall, isn't it?"

Saffron gave her a slow nod. "Exactly that. We just need ice cream, buckets and spades, and we can recreate it properly."

"Nathan's Ice Cream Hut is just down there." Kirsty leaned over the porch and pointed along the promenade.

Saffron put her elbows on the wooden railing and leaned next to her. "Is that right?"

Saffron's lips were close to Kirsty's as she turned her face. She nodded. "Just there," Kirsty replied, her eyes dropping to Saffron's lips, then pulling away.

Too dangerous.

Kirsty might be ready for another shot at love, but not with someone who was skipping town in a few weeks. Saffron had just more or less said so to her mum. She was not a viable option for *so* many reasons.

Saffron stood back up. "Who wants a 99? On me?"

Four hands went up.

"Yes please!" Mum said, turning to Dad. "A delicious vanilla ice-cream cone with a chocolate flake in the top will make up for the iced bun disappointment."

Dad gave her a *butter wouldn't melt* grin.

Mum leaned in to Ginger and Saffron. "Nathan, who runs the ice cream hut, was Kirsty's first boyfriend when she was seven."

"Mum!" Kirsty needed to keep a leash on her mum's tongue sometimes.

Saffron turned as she jumped down to the promenade. "I'll look forward to checking out your taste in men." She gave Kirsty a wink.

Saffron was back in minutes holding five 99s, ice cream running down past both wrists.

"Take them!" Saffron held out her hands, before licking all her fingers one by one.

Kirsty gulped. She stared at the wooden slats beneath her feet and clenched her toes in her flip-flops.

Focus on your ice cream.

Nothing else.

"You know what? You two should come to our BBQ tomorrow." Mum took a bite of her chocolate flake. "Ian's cooking the best lamb chops in town, and we've never hosted a real live movie star before. Are you free?"

Ginger swirled her tongue through her ice cream, before nodding. "I'm free most nights seeing as I know nobody except the people right here, so that would be wonderful."

Saffron nodded too, her gaze falling on Kirsty. "Count me in. So long as you promise to show us some baby photos of your daughter."

Her mum needed no more invitation. "I'm sure I could rustle some up."

Chapter 10

"This is one of my favourites!" Ruth held the yellowed photo delicately by the corner. "She always had her left eye closed when in direct sunlight. Those greys of hers are super sensitive."

"Oh. My. God." Saffron, sitting at a wooden table with Ruth, leaned closer. "How adorable is she in that pink pinafore dress? Was this taken over Easter? It had to be."

Ruth nodded. "She was about three years old, so she didn't put up much of a fuss about wearing dresses. As you can see in this photo the following year, that changed drastically." She handed Saffron a photo of Kirsty in a red hoodie, with the hood up, and yellow checked trousers, holding a doll by her hair, the plastic toy carelessly touching the ground. "I'm glad she's outgrown her Rupert Bear stage."

"Her what?" Saffron scratched her cheek.

"The outfit," Ruth said, distracted by the shriek of one of the guests on the other side of the garden.

"Come now. You must remember the comic strip." Kirsty set her glass down on the table.

Saffron shook her head.

"The bear who wears a red jumper and bright yellow

checked trousers." Kirsty narrowed her eyes. "I think it's still going."

"I didn't have a typical childhood." Saffron twisted her long hair to the side to get it off her neck, the sun seeming to sear her back.

Ruth stopped trying to figure out the reason for the fuss on the other side of the garden and returned her attention, pointing at the photo. "Sadly, it was the last year for dolls."

Kirsty gave Saffron an *I'm sorry* smile, probably for the childhood comment, and then said to Ruth, "Oh please, Mum. Dolls are lame, even back then when we weren't spoiled for choice like kids are today."

"She really liked Swingball. She took great pleasure in whacking that ball for hours." Ian wore a maroon apron with *100% British Beef* printed on it, and a rainbow badge on the left strap.

Saffron nearly choked on her wine.

Ruth ignored her husband, too busy rifling through more photos. "Here's me holding Kirsty when she was only a few weeks old."

Saffron seized the photo. "Oh, look how tiny you are." She showed Kirsty.

"You're wearing checked trousers!" Kirsty waggled a finger at her mum.

"Don't blame me for the fashion in 1971."

"Mum!" Kirsty's face morphed into a livid grape colour.

Ruth laughed. "If you're just going to yell, leave us be. Or better yet, open another bottle of red to match your face."

Kirsty shook her head but followed Ruth's orders.

"She's always been a touch shy." Ruth sorted more photos from the shoebox.

Saffron gazed at Kirsty, talking to Ginger, as she uncorked a bottle. How did the woman make that task sexy as hell? Only if Kirsty turned a little more to the right, Saffron would be able to really check out her bicep.

"How'd you come up with the name Saffron?" Ruth's expression was completely judgment free.

"All the credit goes to my parents." Saffron narrowed her eyes.

"It's not a stage name?" Ruth didn't seem to believe that, like the majority of the human population.

"I wish, but no, my parents saddled me with the name and my agent loved it, so I was born Saffron Oliver and I'll have to live my entire life as a seasoning." To make matters worse, Saffron didn't even like the spice since to her it only added colour, not flavour.

"If you ask me, you lucked out in the name department. Saffron is the most expensive spice on the market, which is fitting for a movie star. Maybe they saw into the future." Ruth's smile gave the parents in question the benefit of the doubt, something Saffron never did, not even after all these years.

Saffron shifted in her seat, and a football bumped the back of her leg. She swivelled around to spy a dark-haired girl, no older than six, doing her best not to look like the guilty party. "You like football?"

The girl nodded.

Saffron looked to the left and right but didn't see any other suspects. "Who are you playing with?"

The girl proudly pointed at her chest.

Saffron hopped up. "Can I kick the ball with you?"

The girl nodded enthusiastically, and Saffron passed the ball to her, impressed by the speed it whipped back in return. The two of them drifted to the side, Saffron laughing. The girl attempted to hog the ball, dribbling circles around Saffron. She responded by placing a hand on the child's head, keeping her at arm's length, while the girl attempted to get a boot on the ball.

"You're cheating." The girl took another swipe.

"I have to. You're just too good." Saffron continued to stiff-arm the child. "Are you related to Megan Rapinoe?"

The girl broke free, swiping the ball and taking it with her across the lawn where two children her age, who'd just arrived at the party, stood. Soon enough, they fell into a game.

"Looks like you've been cruelly cut from the team." Kirsty handed Saffron a glass of wine.

"So it seems. I didn't know the local footballers were so ruthless. Thanks." Saffron took a sip. "Sandy Cove is making me soft. I'm a bit out of breath."

"We can't have that. Take a seat." Kirsty waved to a couple of seats to the side of her parents' garden.

Saffron crossed her legs, resting the glass on the arm of the chair. "You're lucky."

"What do you mean?"

"This." She waved to the guests. "Everyone here seems happy and genuine. I haven't felt this at ease in a group in I don't know how long."

"Is that the experience of all actors? Or…?"

"I think most of us have our guards up, especially after getting burned the first time."

"What happened?" Kirsty wore a sympathetic expression, with curiosity brimming underneath.

Saffron stared into the red liquid, rolling the glass between her palms, stirring the contents. "I trusted the wrong person."

"And?"

"She let me down. She says it was a mistake, but…" Saffron gave the glass one final swirl before knocking back a sip.

"You don't believe her."

"It's hard to know the truth. I'd like to, but I promised myself never to put myself in that position again."

"It sounds lonely."

Saffron stared at Kirsty's parents, Ian with his arm around Ruth's waist as he turned the meat on the grill. Ruth rested her head on his chest, turning and smiling at Helena for a photo. "It's part of my life."

"Does it have to be, though?"

Saffron didn't answer, because although she couldn't see a way around her isolation, she didn't want to say it to Kirsty of all people. "What about you?"

"What about me?" Kirsty flinched as if not expecting to be put into the hot seat. Or did she think Saffron wasn't the type to get to know someone else? Kirsty wasn't wrong, for the most part.

"Has anyone let you down?"

"My ex did."

"Right. That's probably why you got divorced. Sorry. Stupid question." Saffron shook her head as if trying to rid herself of disappointment.

"There are no such things as stupid questions."

"Isn't that just something teachers say?"

"Probably, but it sounds nice. So, ask away." Kirsty gestured she was an open book.

"If I remember correctly, she was a neighbour of yours."

"Yes. Sandy Cove is a charming place, but it's also small. She's still only five miles away, and it's not unusual for us to bump into each other."

"I'd hate to run into mine." *Unless I ran her over with my motorbike.*

"Won't you be working with her again?"

Saffron snapped her head up to look at Kirsty. "Who told you that?"

"I'm sorry. I assumed we were talking about Echo Black. I saw an article talking about the pair of you."

Saffron bristled, but forced out laughter, which more than likely was stilted, if not intimidating. "Oh, no. What I had with Echo doesn't warrant a blip on the relationship chart." For some inexplicable reason, Saffron added, "A lot of what you read in the press about me and Echo is just for show to rev box office sales." Okay, part of that was true, which didn't appease Saffron's guilt for misleading Kirsty about Echo.

"Is it hard to keep track of what's true or not?"

"It's all part of showbiz." Saffron shrugged, not wanting to waste any more effort on the backstabbing Echo Black. "What's it like having normal parents?"

Kirsty started to speak, stopped, and then stared at her parents. "I never realised how lucky I was until recently. It's funny how you can take the simplest things for granted, but when it's pointed out to you, it's like seeing it in a whole new light."

"Come on you two! It's time to eat." Ginger held her plate in the air as if they needed a visual of the sizzling lamb chops to tempt them.

Kirsty put a hand on Saffron's thigh. "To be continued."

"I've never been a fan of cliff hangers."

Kirsty gazed into Saffron's eyes as if she not only understood that to be true, but she also knew how the thought of the unknown rattled Saffron to the core.

* * *

Plates and cutlery rattled as Kirsty and Ruth started to clean up after the meal.

"Can I help?" Saffron rose to her feet, not waiting for an answer, loading her arms up with dishes to take inside.

Kirsty followed her inside, her arms also laden with plates. "Thanks for this."

"Always willing to help." Saffron stood in the kitchen, unsure where to set anything down given every surface was already overloaded. "There's not much room for anything."

Kirsty stacked her plates on top of one pile and then relieved Saffron of hers. "Not much more can be done until after the first load of dishes has finished."

"Are you sure? I don't mind washing up to help your lovely parents get a head start."

"Don't be silly. They'd never expect that of anyone, let alone a Hollywood star."

Deflated Kirsty still thought of her as movie star and not as just a person, Saffron nodded. "Right. Well, it's getting late, and I better head back to mine."

"Do you know where you're going?"

"I just need to follow the water to—"

"The biggest house."

"Even I can't mess that up." Saffron laughed, staring at her Converses finding them suddenly fascinating.

"It's hard to believe you can mess up anything."

"Trust me, I can." Saffron slowly lifted her gaze, and awkwardly offered a hand for Kirsty to shake. "Good night."

Kirsty accepted the gesture, her skin soft and warm, while she placed her other hand on Saffron's elbow. "Stay safe."

"I doubt I can get into much trouble on the way back." Saffron's mind was going into hyperdrive coming up with compromising situations to get into with Kirsty, the most appealing one involved shoving her against the wall and finally feeling what it would be like to kiss those tempting, luscious, dark-red lips. "Good night," she said again, failing to come up with any other words to express her true thoughts.

Outside, Saffron glanced back at the family home, wondering how everything would have been different if she'd had loving parents like Ruth and Ian. Would her love life not be such a wreck? Her one true contribution to any relationship worth pursuing was her ability to torpedo it because that was all she knew how to do.

A breeze kicked up, propelling Saffron along the path.

Several minutes in, she lingered at a pub facing the sea, the patrons long gone, making the tables and benches seem abandoned. The sound of the waves stilled Saffron to soak it all in. She'd craved moments just like this, when enduring endless fourteen-hour work days on the *Girl Racer* set. To have peace and quiet, allowing her the chance to think or not.

"Saffron!"

She turned to Kirsty, running towards the pub.

"You forgot your bag."

Even though Kirsty held it in her hand, Saffron reached for the absent strap on her shoulder. "Oh, thank you. I don't know where my mind is these days." She stopped herself from adding, "Since meeting you."

The security light of the pub bounced in Kirsty's grey eyes.

"What were you thinking about?" Kirsty asked.

"How this place allows me not to think?" Saffron chuckled over her honest answer. "That probably doesn't make sense."

"It does, but the way you were standing, I thought you might be—" Kirsty waved a hand in the air. "It doesn't matter. Just ignore me."

"I could never do that. Go on. What did I look like?" Saffron really wanted to know every thought Kirsty had about anything and everything.

"It's just... er... I wondered if you were thinking of your parents."

Had Kirsty been mulling over Saffron's comment about her childhood? Saffron was used to her social circles, who would have ignored the comment because that was part of her girl squad code. No questions or giving an offhand comment a moment's thought.

"Not right before you called me, no. When I left, though, I had been thinking how nice it would have been to have parents like yours."

"What were they like? Yours?" She wrapped her arms around herself, and Saffron wanted to experience being held by Kirsty.

"Not the most responsible, but what can you expect from

two adults who named their daughters Ginger and Saffron?" She tried laughing it off, adding a *what can you do* shrug.

"I know they aren't in the picture anymore, but what happened to them?"

Saffron took a seat at one of the wooden tables. "They died in a car crash years ago. They had a big night out. That was their thing. For most of my childhood, I remember them leaving Ginger and me alone every Friday night... and..." Saffron turned her face towards the water. "It's been just Ginger and me for so long now. It's why I want to do everything I can for the party. She was my sister and parents all rolled into one, and I want to let her know how much she means to me."

Kirsty sat next to Saffron. "You two are lucky to have each other."

"We are." Saffron pulled her knees up onto the bench, holding herself, resting her chin on one leg. "This looks like a nice pub."

"It's the Poseidon Inn." Kirsty grew serious. "I'm sorry about your parents."

Saffron glanced up. Her eyes became misty, and she started to look away but forced herself not to tear her gaze from those supportive greys. "It was a long time ago."

"It probably doesn't make it any easier."

"Yes and no." Saffron's bottom lip trembled, and she wanted to disappear into Kirsty's embrace.

They stared at each other, the only sound coming from the sea, and moonlight glittered on the water's surface.

Kirsty shivered.

"You're cold. We should both head home."

"Probably so." Kirsty sucked in a breath.

After some hesitation, they both got to their feet.

"I guess this is really good night, this time." Saffron didn't want it to be, but it was the only way to protect Kirsty from the inevitable Saffron torpedo.

"I guess it is. Good night, Saffron." Kirsty turned to leave.

"Um, Kirsty?"

Turning slowly, there was hopefulness in her expression. "Yes?"

"You forgot to give me my bag."

Kirsty palm-slapped her forehead. "Right. It's the reason I'm here."

Saffron wanted to ask if it was the only reason but wasn't sure how she'd respond to the answer, afraid of all the possibilities.

Chapter 11

"Are you sure you don't want to just go with an invite cut into the shape of a dagger?" Kirsty glanced down at her legs, which were whiter than she'd like. It wasn't something she normally worried about when summer rolled around. However, now she was mixing with Saffron and Ginger—both effortlessly tanned—it played on her mind. Kirsty had tried using fake tan one year, and her mum still referred to it as "the summer of orange".

"A bit too violent." Ginger adjusted her shades on the bridge of her nose. They were much needed today on Ginger's back patio, which looked over the beach. To their left, the Poseidon Inn watched over the sea beyond. To their right, stalls were setting up to sell hundreds of oysters and gallons of fizz throughout the day. Straight ahead, the tropical smell of factor 30 being applied to acres of pale British skin filled the air.

"What about a rainbow?"

Ginger let out a bark of laughter as she shifted on her padded garden chair. "Saffron's the gay one, not me." She paused. "Talking of which, we went to the Lobster Grill for dinner the other night. Fish and chips to die for."

Kirsty nodded. "Best in town."

"You weren't lying. Anyway, it didn't escape my attention she was talking a lot about you." Ginger pressed the tip of her index finger into Kirsty's knee. "I think she likes you."

Kirsty took a breath and wasn't sure what to do with it. How was she meant to react? In a typically British way, naturally. "Don't be silly. I might be gay, but I'm far too old. Plus, she's a movie star." She put a finger to her chest. "In case you missed it, I'm very much not."

"That's beside the point." Ginger cocked her head. "You get on, right?"

Kirsty nodded. She couldn't deny that.

"You don't look at her and want to vomit?"

"You've got such a way with words."

"I know. I should have been a poet." Ginger grinned. "What I mean is, Saffron scrubs up well. So do you. You get on. What's the issue? I've always wanted my sister to meet someone who's not famous, someone normal. Famous people are crazy, take my word for it. Echo Black being a case in point." Ginger gave her the trademark Oliver smile. "You, however, are the picture of normality. You'd be perfect."

Echo Black. That name again. She was very much a feature in Kirsty's life these days, even though Saffron had implied what they had was purely for movie publicity. Did Ginger know that? Kirsty went to reply, but Ginger held up a single finger in front of her.

"And don't give me that 'I'm too old' guff. There's an age gap, but Saffron has lived a million lives. She's an old soul and you're hip. Plus, she goes for older women. Always has. Echo Black isn't as young as she says she is, believe me."

Perhaps Ginger didn't know the truth. Perhaps Saffron had just confided in her. Kirsty's insides beamed at the thought. "I've just never gone for someone so much younger before."

"How old was your ex-wife?"

Kirsty sat up straighter in her chair. "Two years younger. But it wasn't the age that drove us apart. She wanted to live a bigger life than me. She wanted to travel. To go out to parties. I've never been that person. I'm far more of a homebody."

Ginger eyed her. "Did she cheat on you?"

An image of Anna on their cream sofa in their old house trying to explain away sleeping with someone else flitted through her mind. Kirsty hadn't thought about it in a while. She nodded, feeling empty. "She met someone at one of those parties, in the end."

Ginger gave her a sad smile. "I wish Dave had cheated on me, rather than just deciding he'd had enough and wanted out. It would have made it easier to take."

"It didn't feel like that at the time." Kirsty clenched her fist, then released. "In the end, I'm pleased she did it. Looking back, we weren't right for each other."

"Whereas you and Saffron could be." Ginger pressed a finger to Kirsty's arm. "I think Saffron could be a homebody, too. If she let herself. She's still figuring out who she is. She's a little late to the party."

"I don't know." Kirsty frowned. "Even if age weren't an issue, I think my lifestyle and that of a movie star aren't all that compatible."

However, when Kirsty tried to picture them together, it was surprisingly easy. Saffron in her ripped jeans that clung to her perfect bum. A casual arm around Kirsty's shoulder. Hot lips on hers. Kirsty's tongue sliding up Saffron's tanned neck, caressing her silky skin.

Kirsty shifted in her chair, then crossed her legs. She put a hand to her cheek. A tenner said she was blushing. "Anyway, enough about your sister. I'm here to discuss your party invites."

Ginger gave her a knowing look. "Have I made you all flustered? You look just like your mum when you are. Which is no bad thing, by the way. Your parents are gorgeous."

"They have their moments." Kirsty rubbed her hands together. "The invites." She grabbed her phone and showed Ginger an image. "You could have something like this? It's a fridge magnet the size of a card, and we can get it designed however we want. I've got an illustrator in mind. So now we just need to come up with something funny for the front."

Ginger studied the product, before turning to Kirsty. "A magnetic card invite. I love it." She leaned over and gave her a crushing hug before pulling away. "You're a genius. The one thing we don't want to do is let Saffron take charge of this. She gets carried away when it comes to me. She still feels guilty for not being at my wedding."

Ginger's phone lit up. "Speak of the devil. My sister is on her way."

Kirsty ignored the way her senses woke up at the mere mention of Saffron. Yes, she'd looked gorgeous at her parents' BBQ. Yes, they'd shared a moment on the beach. But Kirsty was still who she was. Could Ginger be right in what she'd said?

Kirsty stretched her arms in the air, turning her head to look for Saffron. No sign as yet. Out on the glassy sea, an impressive windsurfer was doing their thing. "It's a yes to these invites?

You don't want to go for online, as I found some fab ones there, too?" She had to get back to the matter at hand.

"Positive." Ginger's tone was final. "When Dave and I got married, we did it in a rush. Youthful impulsiveness. I was still reeling from my parents' death. Saffron was filming all the time, so I never saw her. We just upped and did it. No invites. A handful of guests." She leaned her head back to the sun. "This party is my belated wedding." As soon as it was out of her mouth, Ginger sat up. "I only just realised that when I said it out loud." She stood up, pacing her paved back patio.

"Morning all."

Kirsty turned to where Saffron was undoing Ginger's back gate, walking towards them with a pad and pencil case tucked under her arm. She was still impossibly tall, her vest top casually hanging off her broad, tanned shoulders. This morning was turning out to be a tsunami of the Oliver sisters.

Before Kirsty could reply, Ginger ran over to Saffron and grabbed her by the shoulders. "I just realised something!" She was shouting like she wanted the whole beach to hear. "This party is my wedding!"

Saffron put her things on the patio table and took Ginger in her arms. "I know, which is why I want it to be perfect," she said, her mouth beside Ginger's ear, her eyes on Kirsty. Saffron's gaze was heated.

All the blood in Kirsty's body travelled south.

Ginger promptly burst into tears.

Kirsty blinked and jumped up as Saffron steered her sister to a chair. Saffron pulled up a seat beside her, with Kirsty to Ginger's right.

Saffron and Kirsty both went to put an arm around

Ginger at the same time, only succeeding in clutching each other.

Kirsty turned her head left just as Saffron turned right.

Boom! Kirsty's heartbeat revved in her ears like a thunderclap.

Electricity crackled between them, Ginger the conductor.

Saffron held her gaze for far longer than necessary, and Kirsty only broke when it seemed a little unfair to be doing *whatever they were doing* while Ginger was having a moment. However, tell that to her libido, which was currently zigzagging around her stomach, before settling somewhere *way* lower down.

Kirsty crossed her legs again and held in a breath.

This was not her normal Thursday morning, flirting with a movie star. *Were they flirting?* She had no idea.

Ginger blew her nose with some force, which brought everyone back to the present.

Saffron removed her arm.

Kirsty cleared her throat, her thoughts in tatters. What the hell was going on? She was still on the clock here, still being paid to be Ginger's party planner.

Even if the woman paying the bills was causing her heart palpitations.

Kirsty put a hand on Ginger's thigh. She was by far the safer sister to touch. "Like Saffron says, this is going to be perfect, because we're all going to make it so."

Ginger blew her nose again. "Kirsty's sourced some brilliant fridge magnet invites, so that's sorted, too."

Saffron nodded. "Great."

"Now, we've got the date, venue, booze and invites dealt

with. Just the food and entertainment to finalise." Kirsty squeezed Ginger's knee. "We're cooking on gas."

Saffron snagged her gaze one more time. "I couldn't agree more."

* * *

Kirsty picked up her phone. "Shit, it's nearly ten. I'm opening up today. I have to run."

Ginger nodded. "Sure thing." She snapped her fingers. "I never gave you that coffee, though."

Kirsty shrugged. "I'll get one on the way back."

"I'll come with you. I need the steps. I'm buying." Ginger got up, looking towards Saffron. "You coming? Or were you heading elsewhere?"

"Right with you." Saffron picked up her pad. "You can drop me off on the way."

Ginger ran in to get her house keys and locked up. They fell into an easy step side by side, the sea a calming presence to their left. The beach was beginning to fill up with day trippers, towels and blankets spread out on the pebbles. Kirsty had always been glad they had their beach hut so she didn't have to lie on a bed of tiny rocks.

As they walked, Kirsty was hyper-aware of Saffron's arm grazing hers, making her sweat that little bit more.

"Okay, so Kirsty's invites sound good. But did I tell you I can get you some in the form of oyster shells, that smell of the sea when you open them?" Saffron had on her *I'm a genius* face.

Ginger stopped in her tracks. "Seriously? In this weather, you want me to pipe fishy smells into people's houses?"

Saffron's face fell. "It's the smell of nature!"

Kirsty bit down a laugh. Saffron was well-meaning, but Ginger knew how to put her in her place. Still, she clearly cared about her sister's party. In fact, she was far from the self-centred arsehole Kirsty had first met.

"I like Kirsty's idea better."

Saffron shut up.

They carried on walking, past the oyster stalls, then one selling beach apparel, along with soft drinks, ice creams, and sticks of rock. Kirsty's mouth watered as they passed the candyfloss machine. She'd always been partial as a kid.

"What about what you're wearing? I can help you with that, right? You need something special. Something to tell everyone you're back on the market."

Ginger snorted. "Are you sure you're not projecting? Do you need something new to tell everyone *you're* back on the market?"

Kirsty almost felt sorry for Saffron.

Saffron sighed, her pace slowing. "It's a good job you're my only sister, otherwise I might see if I could replace you." She paused, kicking a stone with her bubble-gum pink Converse. "I could get my assistant to fly you in something from Milan. Something designer. You'd look a million dollars. What do you think?"

They stopped outside The Coffee Hut, somewhere Kirsty had brought Ginger before.

"Coffee here?" Ginger asked.

Kirsty nodded.

"Hello!" Saffron waved her hand in front of Ginger's face. "Milan? Designer dress? Your sister trying to help?"

If Saffron had stamped her foot, Kirsty wouldn't have been

surprised. She could picture them as sisters when they were younger, with a similar scene playing out.

"I've already sorted a killer dress from a boutique Kirsty recommended on the High Street, so no need for Milan or anything over the top." Ginger's voice softened. "I know you mean well, but I'm doing this my way."

Saffron went to respond just as her phone rang. She checked it. Her shoulders hunched. Then she spun on her heel and walked off.

Ginger nodded towards her. "That's her agent, Pearl. Saffron needs to sack her. Pearl only has Pearl's interests at heart. Every time Saffron speaks to her, she hunches a little more. I want her to be happy, and it's not going to happen with Pearl in the picture."

They arrived at the front of the queue, and Ginger ordered three white coffees, which they took to a nearby outdoor table.

Saffron joined them after a few minutes.

"Everything okay?" Ginger asked.

Saffron put her phone on the table, along with her pad and pencil case. "Just Pearl. Movie stuff. The usual. I'd rather not talk about it." She sipped her coffee. "Back to your party and the dress I won't be buying you. Are you going to let me do anything for your party, or was it just lip service to shut me up?"

Ginger patted Saffron's arm with her hand. "What about music? You could put a playlist together for me. You're young and hip."

Saffron snorted. "What I know about music you could write on the back of a postage stamp. But I can look into it."

"I would love that." Ginger was throwing Saffron a bone.

Lizzo's latest track began to play through the café's speakers. Saffron quirked an eyebrow. "I know Lizzo, met her at a party. I could ask her to play live! How awesome would that be?"

Ginger began to laugh, and it soon turned hysterical.

Saffron frowned. "What did I say?"

"Not Hollywood, Saff! I don't want a famous singer. I just want normal music with normal people." Ginger covered her heart with her palm. "For once, I want to be the star attraction, not anyone else."

"Okay, I hear you." Saffron drummed her fingers on the wooden table. "A live band, though? Does that meet your approval?"

Ginger scrunched her forehead before nodding. "Do some research. Run some by me. I don't mind a live band. So long as it's not a 15-piece orchestra flown in from New York. Or Maroon 5."

Saffron's face spelled affronted. "I've got *some* taste."

Chapter 12

"I can't believe the view." Ginger whistled, standing on Saffron's veranda. "And, I can't get enough of the sea air." She spread her arms out, as if embracing her new way of life. "If I were you, I'd never want to live anywhere else."

Saffron uncorked one of the bottles of red Kirsty had delivered. "It's much more relaxing here than my place in London."

Ginger, with a glass in hand, sat in one of the padded outdoor chairs with an *oomph*. "There was a time I'd never live anywhere else than London. Now, I can't imagine going back."

Saffron leaned against the wooden railing, facing her sister, a sense of tranquillity washing over her. "Do you think this is your forever place?"

"My forever place?" Ginger laughed, her eyes clouding over with nostalgia. "I haven't heard that phrase in so long."

"It used to be one of our staple conversations when we'd stay up late, unable to sleep because our parents had thirty of their closest friends over for after-dinner drinks that lasted until dawn." Saffron let out an anguished sigh.

"I still feel like I'm catching up on lost sleep." Ginger yawned, half-covering her mouth. "Do you remember the time

Mum actually swung from the chandelier, pretending to be Tarzan after Dad wouldn't take up the dare?"

"How could I forget? Who would have thought hundreds of crystals smashing to pieces could make such a deafening sound?" Saffron closed her eyes, her heartbeat speeding up. "When I had to film a scene that involved jumping off the side of a burning building, which was all staged, mind you, I froze on the first ten takes. I kept hearing the shattering of glass, followed by Mum's screams."

"How'd you finally jump?"

Saffron opened her eyes and gave Ginger a wistful smile. "I remembered you whispering in my ear that we'd never be like them. Irresponsible. Careless. Never thinking about the consequences. For them, it was all about being the life of the party and getting a laugh, to hell with the carnage." Saffron set her glass down on the railing, her throat constricting. "To this day, I'm still kicking myself for not seeing the truth in the early years. Thinking how cool our parents were for being involved in the West End glitterati scene. All of their friends wanted to be like them. Rich. Fabulous. Adored." She threaded her fingers and batted her eyelashes. "Idolised."

"I remember finding it funny when Dad would bump into things when he was driving. The way he'd say *whoopsie-daisy*, and then break out into his hyena laugh." Ginger sighed, and swiped her glistening brow. "It wasn't until I was much older when I realised that was his drunk laugh."

Saffron cringed, recalling just how often that had been. "It's amazing we survived our childhood with them. It would have been better if they'd kept their theatre jobs and not been fired."

Ginger rested her head against the chair, looking up into the darkness overhead, connecting the dots of light with a finger. "That's why I love it here. All the pressure to be someone I'm not is finally off me."

"I feel that way, as well. I wish I could stay." Saffron gazed at the horizon, not seeing any obstacles, just the open sea as if saying whatever you want, you can have. She knew, though, life wasn't that simple.

Ginger shifted her gaze to her baby sister. "Why can't you?"

"Pearl is pushing me to do the next *Girl Racer* film. If I don't give her an answer soon, she'll send her former MI6 goon with the contract and pen. Or, maybe she'll make me sign with my own blood just to show me who's the boss of my life."

"I never liked Pearl." Ginger's disapproving pursed lips had a stronger effect on Saffron than the words.

"No one likes their agents. They're a pushy breed. That's why we hire them. To do and say the things sane people never dare." There was a time when Saffron unreservedly subscribed to the notion, because that was what every actor told her. But, did that necessarily make it true?

"Do you really need to make another movie you hate? You have enough money for three lifetimes. And, you can't tell me that you've enjoyed one second when making the previous two. You would call me late at night and cry."

"Isn't that what everyone does? Cry about their jobs?" She made a fist, and rubbed her eye like a child, trying to make Ginger laugh and move on to a less troubling topic.

Ginger shook her platinum locks, looking so much like the

older sister who'd kept Saffron in line all those years ago. "To whinge, yes. But sobbing... talk to any life coach and they'd say if you ever reach that point, it's time to quit. There's more to life than a job or, in my case, my marriage." Ginger sat up straighter. "Look at me, I never thought I'd be happy away from Dave, but you know what, I'm in such a better place right now. Just the other night, I participated in karaoke."

"That's great." Saffron sarcastically gave Ginger two thumbs up.

"Don't be flippant. We both know I never would have with Dave around. He stifled me in ways I didn't see until he was out of the picture. I'm free to be me. Part of it is being here in Sandy Cove. Away from my old life that never suited me. I don't care about the latest fashion trends. The hit songs. The hot restaurants." Ginger took another cleansing lungful of sea air. "Another reason for my new-found happiness is making friends here. Real people with real lives. Not what they put on their social media feeds. Meeting Kirsty has been such a blessing for me."

Saffron nodded, afraid to give voice to her thoughts on that front, knowing her sister would pick up on so much more than the words.

Ginger let out a snort of laughter. "I can see it, even if you're looking everywhere but me."

Saffron met her eyes, to prove Ginger wrong, and it took more effort than she wanted to admit to herself. "I'm doing no such thing." She pointed at her eyes and then to Ginger. "Looking right at you."

"I'm looking back at you." Ginger mimicked Saffron's finger-pointing. "Tell me how you feel about Kirsty. Honestly."

"I think she's a great party planner. With her in charge, I don't have to think of a thing, which is good because you hate all of my ideas."

"I don't hate them."

"You don't like them. You've actually called me *Hollywood*. On more than one occasion." The tendons in Saffron's neck tightened.

"It's because you can be sometimes. I know you mean well, and I'm eternally grateful for the reason why. But you don't owe me an apology for missing my wedding. I understood why you had to work. It's how you dealt with Mum and Dad's death."

Saffron looked back to the sea, wanting to sail to the edge to find out what would happen.

Ginger continued, "It's just I'm done doing things to please others. You're so used to the Hollywood way of life you've forgotten about the things we used to dream about, like our forever place. I've found mine. It's time for you to find yours."

Saffron sank into a chair. "What if it's not in my future? I want to stand still, but everyone, not just Pearl, wants me to keep going full speed. I'm getting so many movie offers, and who am I to say no when there are thousands of people who would kill to have my career? My life? The money? The perks?" Saffron curled her arms around herself. "I feel selfish for wanting something different. Pearl's right when she says a lot of people depend on me for their jobs. If I don't sign on for *Girl Racer*, they probably won't make the movie. That means everyone from the director to the caterers won't have a job."

"I don't think it's that black and white. If you say no, they may not make *Girl Racer*, but they'll make a different movie. That's what movie studios do. The entire moviemaking business doesn't sit squarely on your shoulders, Saff." Ginger reached out with a hand, placing it on Saffron's knee.

"Sometimes I feel like it does, though." Saffron massaged her temples.

"I know. You've always taken on the world to prove you can handle anything. You want to be responsible, because you're afraid if you aren't, that means you're like them." Ginger slanted her head to make eye contact. "Tell me, how has that worked out for you? It hasn't made you happy. You're the hottest woman on the planet, but you don't date. It's not like you're hiding your sexuality. What's stopping you from finding your forever someone to live in your forever place?"

"Because neither exists." She ground her teeth.

"Don't talk nonsense."

"Says the woman basing life decisions on a childhood dream." There was a hardness to her voice, because Saffron wanted both. But the choice she'd made when she was so young to go into acting wrecked everything, while giving her all the things people equated with happiness, when most of the time Saffron wanted to smash her perfect life with a sledgehammer.

"Children are more honest to themselves. We knew what we wanted back then. Everything was much simpler."

"Too simple. Because when people grow up into adults, they turn into selfish gobshites." Saffron included herself in that category but ticked the *scared shitless* column for good measure, because wasn't that the real reason she forged on the path of misery.

"Not everyone. Yes, Echo hurt you. She did something foolish, and because of her actions you felt like you did when our parents were raving drunks. Out of control. You hate that feeling, yet you keep making decisions that feed the fear."

Had Saffron said the part about fear aloud? Or was Ginger using her sister connection to dislodge the truth. Curious, Saffron pressed, "Like what?"

"Keeping Pearl. You'll never be in control of your life as long as she's your agent." Ginger sliced a decisive hand in the air.

"You really think I should fire Pearl?" If only it were that easy.

"That would be a step in the right direction."

"What would I do?" Saffron pulled her knees to her chest, wrapping her arms around her legs.

"What do you want to do?"

"I only know acting."

"Luckily, you have the resources to take time to figure out stage two of your life, if you so choose. When we were kids, you wanted to be an artist."

"I am." Saffron snorted defensively.

"In the field our parents found acceptable. Even though they derided your *doodling*"—Ginger made quote marks in the air—"you still sketch whenever you have a free moment."

Saffron blew a raspberry. "That won't pay the bills."

Disappointment and frustration practically drifted off Ginger. "Stop ducking behind your walls. We've already established you don't need the money. What's your real fear if you quit making movies? That you'll slow down enough to realise you want to spend your life with a special someone?

Not your Hollywood girl squad, but a woman who knows the true you?"

"I don't know. I can't see that ever happening." Was that still true? Before Sandy Cove, Saffron thought so. But now?

"I think you can, or you're starting to get glimpses here, and it's scaring the shit out of you." Ginger went to her sister, kneeled down, and placed a hand on each knee. "Come out of your Saffron Oliver fortress. Join the real world."

"It's hard to let the walls down. Not after—"

"Would you advise me to never date again? After Dave?"

"I'd hate for you to spend your life alone."

Ginger slanted her head. "I don't want that for you either."

"How can I truly open my heart?" Saffron needed guidance in this department.

"One teensy tiny step at a time."

"What's the first step?"

"Admitting you like Kirsty."

Saffron snorted and gripped onto the arms of the chair, tapping her fingertips. "Just because you want me to like Kirsty, doesn't mean I actually do." Why was she denying her feelings?

"I want you to see what's right before your eyes. A woman who is about as genuine as you can get. She's nothing like Echo, who is still all over your socials. Why is that?" Ginger's eyes pierced into Saffron.

"You know the reason."

"Pearl," Ginger muttered.

"She's desperate to keep the *Girl Racer* magic going to keep raking in the big bucks."

"As long as Pearl is in your life, you'll never be able to have a normal relationship. You can't look me in the eyes and tell me you don't want to see where things can go with Kirsty."

"What if I get to know Kirsty more and I end up really liking her?" Saffron dropped her eyes, surprised she'd squeezed one of her hands, which was now white and starting to throb from lack of blood flow.

"Isn't that the goal?" Ginger's smile was kind.

"For normal people, yes."

"I have news for you, even Saffron Oliver is simply a woman. You're no different from the rest of us. You just pretend you are."

"My lifestyle isn't built for a happy ever after." She knew this part as fact.

Ginger shook her hands in the air. "Build a life so you can have that. We both know our time on this earth can be fleeting. Grab on to the good bits, because in the end, that's all that matters. Not the next blockbuster. Not the red carpet. Loving someone and being loved back. It doesn't get much better than that."

It sounded nice.

But like their childhood chatter about a forever home, it was only that. A dream that fizzled under the harsh light of reality.

Chapter 13

"One more shell? Five more shells? I never bloody know." Helena stood back and assessed the tasting table display. Bottles of wine clad in knitted mermaid outfits—handmade by Hugh—sitting on a beach of oyster shells and sand. Anna had first made something similar the year the shop opened, and Helena had seen photos. She'd put Hugh to work, and he had made something far more stylish. It made Kirsty smile to see Anna's designs upgraded.

A bit like Kirsty's life since their split.

Kirsty strode over and stood next to her, tilting her head. "It looks absolutely fabulous. As for the shells, you know what my dad always says?"

"You can never have too many?" Helena bumped Kirsty's hip with hers.

"Exactly. It looks perfect." Helena had spent the previous couple of weeks being far more attentive to the shop's festival needs than she ever had before. Kirsty wasn't complaining. She wanted to ask Helena why the sudden drive, but she didn't want to interrupt her flow, either. She'd learned from years of working with her that striking the perfect balance was never an easy task. Helena's interest in the business waxed and waned. Right now, she was the perfect partner. Kirsty did not want to get in the way of that.

The loud beat of a drum made Kirsty open the shop door, securing it with their special wine doorstop. She smiled up at the clear blue sky, as the summer heat hit her airwaves. The festival parade opener was going to be a scorcher. She slipped past a couple of people and peered down the High Street. She could taste the anticipation in the air. She couldn't see the parade yet, but she could hear it. The pavement outside the shop was busy with spectators, but it was nothing compared to the harbour, which would be rammed.

Opposite, Donald's Menswear sat empty, a *For Rent* sign plastered on the window. Strangely, she missed Donald on the pavement. Would the shop be let soon? She hoped so. The other end of the High Street had a few vacant premises, but this end, nearer to the harbour, was otherwise fully occupied. She wanted to keep it that way for their business and for everyone else around them.

Minutes later, the drums were upon them, a troop of ten men in two rows of five, banging hip-level drums. Behind them were members of the Chamber of Commerce, this year dressed as oysters, as they had been for the entirety of Kirsty's life. Two years ago, she'd suggested they try something different. It had been greeted with horror by the whole organisation. The pace of change was slow in this town. As was the pace of the parade, but that suited everyone just fine.

"Show us your thighs, boys!" Helena leaned against the shop doorway, giving the players of Sandy Cove Football Club her best wolf whistle, Hugh in particular.

Kirsty winced as the decibels reached her ears.

The team's red-and-white striped kit was a tight fit, but Hugh carried it off with aplomb. He wore a rainbow headband around his receding hairline, and teased his shorts up a centimetre or two at Helena's command. He dashed onto the pavement to land a smacker on his wife, before jumping back into place.

"Stop objectifying me!" he shouted, giving Kirsty a wink.

"You love it!" Helena replied with a dirty cackle.

Kirsty rolled her eyes. She was glad their son Anton wasn't here. He might have died on the spot.

Next came the Sandy Cove Lawn Bowls Club, with her dad looking splendid in his club whites. He was waving to the crowds like he was a well-worn royal. It always made Kirsty smile.

Fifteen minutes later and the parade had passed, the last two slots being taken up by Catch Oyster Bar, their entire staff dressed as oysters. Originality wasn't a treasured commodity in the town. However, the final pub taking part, The Mariner's Arms, had at least come dressed as three giant crabs. Kirsty hollered loudest for that.

She was just about to walk back into the shop when her mum appeared, sprinting along the pavement as if she was in her 40s, not her 70s. Nobody had told Mum she needed to slow down, so she never had. If she ever did, she might never get restarted again.

"Did you see your dad?" She was hardly out of breath.

Kirsty nodded. "He was doing his Prince Charles wave again."

Helena appeared at Kirsty's side, giving her mum a kiss.

Thankfully, she seemed to accept it. Perhaps Kirsty's words about Helena had sunk in. "Ian looked very statesmanlike today."

Mum grinned. "I'll tell him you said that. He'll love it." She paused. "Are you coming down later? I bumped into Ginger in the Co-op earlier, and she said she was going to the harbour." A loaded pause. "Saffron too." Her mum leaned in a little as she said the final part, raising her eyebrows. Subtlety had never been her strong point.

Kirsty gave her a look. "We'll be there once Anton and his mate relieve us. About five?"

"That's about the time when Ginger said she was planning to go." Her mum paused. "*With Saffron.*"

It was like she thought Kirsty was deaf. "Yes, I get it, Mum. Saffron is going. So is most of the town."

Mum put a hand on her arm. "Yes, but you haven't been spending a lot of time with half the town, have you? Even your dad noticed it at the BBQ, and that's saying something."

"Nothing's going on." Not a lie. They hadn't even kissed. But Kirsty knew, whenever they were in close proximity lately, something had changed.

She couldn't quite put her finger on it.

But she'd like to.

"Stop being coy." Her mum wagged a finger. "I'm just saying when she's around you seem happier. Lighter. More your old self."

"Absolute rubbish." But she knew she was blushing.

Helena nodded. "I agree, Ruth. I think the lady doth protest too much." She put an arm around Kirsty. "But she's young, she's never been in love before. It's all so new."

Kirsty couldn't help but smile. "Shut up, you two." She pointed at her mum. "Don't you have a festival to be at?"

Mum gave her a grin. "I do. I'm meeting Shirley for lunch." She reached up and pinched Kirsty's cheek. "See you later, love refusenik."

Kirsty watched her go, then turned. She walked right into Helena's cheesy grin.

"You can wipe that smirk right off your face, too."

"You love it," Helena replied. "By the way, Anton's done some new illustrations for the website, so he's going to work them up over the next few days."

They walked back into the shop. "Ginger said she could implement our online sales once the party's over, too. Get Anton to whack up the new stuff and the promo pages with locals telling everyone how great we are in the meantime, and then we can get our website into the 21st century, finally."

Helena held up a palm, waiting for a high five. "Sounds good, partner!"

Yep, she was acting really strangely.

* * *

They could hardly make out the harbour by the time they arrived. It was just a din of chatter, a throng of short sleeves, and a sunbeam of collective cheer. Somewhere in there was the market, the cafés, the Crab Star restaurant. Kirsty bristled on sight. She'd never liked crowds. It was part of the reason she'd never done what a lot of her peers did when they left university: move to London. Kirsty loved the capital, but its streets were too packed, and the place was far too impersonal. She loved the simpler life, walks along the beach, the harbour in January when it was just her, a few locals, and Sam who ran the Harbour Oyster Café year-round.

She fought her way through the crowds, to where Sam was serving a queue of people that stretched beyond her eyeline. She gave him a wave when he caught her eye, and he gave her a wide-eyed grin. Next to him, his two brothers were pumping out drinks with machine-like precision, and his uncle John was shucking oysters, making it look easy. When Kirsty had tried it in her youth, she'd nearly sliced into her main artery.

Helena tapped her on the shoulder. "Your parents are over there. And look who's with them." She followed Helena's outstretched arm to where her parents sat at a table in the café garden, glasses of fizz in their hands. Also with them were Ginger and Saffron, the latter wearing a different baseball cap and her regulation shades.

Kirsty's heart did a few star jumps as she walked over to them, her mum standing up and taking her bag and sun hat from two chairs.

"About time! We've had to fend off all-comers for these seats." Mum turned to Helena. "No Hugh?"

Helena shook her head. "He's drinking in the Mariner's Arms with his football mates. Says it's too crowded down here."

"He's got a point." Kirsty sat as her dad poured them both a glass of fizz. She turned to the Oliver sisters. "Have they been behaving?"

"Good as gold," Saffron replied, flashing a slight grin.

It was just a simple movement of Saffron's mouth, but it made every hair on Kirsty's body stand to attention.

Yes, something had definitely changed.

"Did you watch the parade?" Kirsty asked.

Ginger nodded. "Caught it from the start. I loved it, especially the people dressed as oysters."

"I dunno," Saffron said. "My favourites were the crabs right at the end. Showed a bit of originality."

Kirsty's skin tingled. "Mine, too." She stared at Saffron. This was getting more difficult by the day, wasn't it?

Saffron broke their stare. She pushed back her chair and got up, rubbing her hands. "Oysters!" she said. "It's the Oyster Festival, so I'm going to get some for the table." She glanced at Kirsty. "Apart from you, I know you hate them." She pulled on the peak of her cap, glancing around. Nobody was taking the slightest bit of notice of her. Was she missing the attention? Kirsty would love to know.

"Our Kirsty is the opposite of an oyster lover," her dad confirmed.

Kirsty held up a hand. "I might try one this year, actually."
Really, Kirsty? Trying to impress a girl?

Kirsty glanced at her mum, who was giving her the type of knowing smile that told Kirsty she knew exactly what she was doing. She might as well have climbed on top of the table and done a tap dance, while singing "I knew I was right!"

"You hate oysters." Helena gave her a pointed look.

"Tastes change." Kirsty took a gulp of her fizz, steeling her nerves. Would she be able to follow through? She didn't want to think about it. She glanced over at Saffron as she walked to the café. Yep, she still looked good enough to eat.

Saffron arrived back moments later with a huge steel bowl filled with ice, the shellfish sat on top. "I couldn't work out the maths, so I just went for a dozen." She glanced around the table. "Two each, right?" Her gaze landed on Kirsty. "If you only want to eat one, I'll have your second one."

"And they say chivalry is dead," deadpanned Ginger.

The whole table grabbed an oyster in its shell, adding fresh lemon, vinegar, or both.

Kirsty gulped. Now that it was in her hand, she wasn't feeling so brave. She shook the shell left, then right. The oyster wobbled. Nausea swept through her.

"Look at me!" Helena held up her phone.

Kirsty gave her an unsure grin.

Helena took a couple of shots of Kirsty, then a few group shots, making everyone scrunch up together, before grabbing her oyster.

"Ready?" Dad said. "After three, everyone down the hatch." He nodded at Kirsty as he spoke. "One, two, three!"

She didn't think about it. Just eyeballed the oyster, held her breath, and tipped back her head.

The slimy blob slid into her mouth.

She was not going to spit it out.

Kirsty wrinkled her face, chewed once, twice, and swallowed. She took a deep breath. Then another.

She'd done it!

The whole table was looking at her.

She gave them a thumbs up. She wasn't taking a chance on speaking just yet.

"I can't believe it! The effect you have on her, Saffron!" Mum's tone was incredulous.

If Kirsty wasn't trying so hard to control her breathing and not be sick, she might have kicked Mum under the table.

She reached over and gulped the rest of her fizz. No adverse effects. She was amazed.

The rest of the table ate their second oyster, and Saffron her third. Then Saffron jumped up again. "Shall I get more drinks?"

"Just a Coke for me." Ginger checked her watch. "It's still only 5.30."

"I'll have a Sandy Cove Blonde." Kirsty got up, too. "Let me give you a hand."

As if responding to that request, Saffron held out her hand.

Without thought, Kirsty took it. A zap of desire rocketed up her arm. She paused. What the hell was she doing? She knew oysters were an aphrodisiac, but one taste and she was holding Saffron's hand?

"I see those oysters have worked their magic!"

She must not shout at her mother.

Kirsty shivered, then dropped Saffron's hand as quickly as she'd taken it, bundling her away from the table and the spectators.

What was happening? She was acting like she was a teenager. She was 49, for goodness sake.

"Everything okay?" Saffron's cheeks were pink. She wouldn't look Kirsty in the eye.

Kirsty gave her a look. "Let's just get to the bar."

They stood in the queue, Kirsty searching her brain for something to say, but she couldn't think of anything. Not a single, solitary word. All she could think was, "*We held hands!*" Like she was 12.

Saffron turned her head to face a woman standing six feet

away, her phone poised. Saffron held up a hand. "Sorry, no photos today, thanks. I'm just here enjoying the festival, the same as you."

Kirsty stared at her. Then she leaned in. "She wasn't taking a photo of you," she whispered, pointing at the life-size plastic fisherman Saffron was standing next to. Standing on the other side of it was the woman's toddler son and her partner, both giving the woman cheesy grins.

Saffron's cheeks coloured even darker as she turned away. "Can we pretend that never happened?" she whispered to Kirsty.

Kirsty shook her head. "Oh no, I'm logging that." She paused. "Remember when you said I could tell you if you were being a tit?" She quirked an eyebrow. "Stop being a tit."

Chapter 14

A man and woman arrived at the tables outside the Poseidon Inn with an older scruffy dog, the two pups under the table across from them wiggling their behinds in the adorable way puppies do when unable to contain their excitement, but desperately trying to behave. The eldest greeted each excited pup with nose held high, but Saffron spied the scruffy dog's tail whip back and forth with youthful vigour.

All the owners exchanged laughs and smiles, as the man gently guided his senior dog to a table across the way, the puppies hiding out under theirs, rolling on the pebbles, not a care in the world.

"I wonder what it's like to greet each new day and experience with puppy energy." Kirsty opened a bag of salt and vinegar crisps, undoing the seam of the bag to spread it out completely open for Saffron to share.

"I think it's one of the reasons why I want a dog." Saffron crunched into a crisp.

"To live vicariously through one?"

"That and to have all eyes on the adorable pup and not on me."

"That's a tall order for a dog." Kirsty stared past Saffron

at the water behind but ever so slowly dropped her gaze to meet Saffron's.

Saffron wanted to take a gulp of air, but didn't want to be obvious, even if Kirsty's penetrating eyes plucked her heart strings.

As if noticing Saffron needed a lifeline, Kirsty stuck to the dog conversation. "Do you think it would be possible for one to help you maintain your privacy?"

"It might be here." Saffron tapped the top of her baseball hat placed on the table, not her head. "For the most part, everyone has been leaving me alone. Even today, with the extra bodies for the festival, I'm just one of the crowd. Not the one causing people to huddle together to catch a glimpse."

"Is that good or bad? In my life, that would be a tick in the good column. No, make that great. I'm adding great to my imaginary chart." Kirsty made a swoosh in the air. "I hate being the centre of attention. I'm wondering, though, if a movie star would want the same."

"My agent would be freaking out if she knew. She always wants snaps of me on social media." Saffron mimed taking photos. "Me smiling, with my arms around people I don't know, acting like I'm having the time of my life. For her, I have to stay in the front of the public's mind, or what if they forget my existence and don't flock to my next movie on opening weekend? The horror!" Saffron placed her hands on her cheeks and acted out the painting *The Scream*.

"Ginger mentioned you get tense whenever you talk to your agent."

"I think she has that effect on most." Saffron glanced back towards the puppies, one biting the other's ear.

"Nice evasion on that, and since I'm feeling generous, I'll leave it there. Also, I have to admit, I'm curious about my original question, not from Pearl's perspective but from yours. Do you"—Kirsty aimed a crisp at Saffron's chest—"want adulation wherever you go?"

"I see you've changed a keyword from the original." Saffron mirrored the crisp move, wondering why Kirsty was focused on the question. Did she want to be around a movie star to reap the rewards? Not that Kirsty seemed the type. Was there another reason?

"I see you're still evading."

Saffron gazed at the puppies, marvelling over their excitement greeting an English bulldog who sported a Hawaiian shirt and bandana around his neck. "In the beginning, it was exhilarating. Growing up, I never particularly thought I was all that special, but when people started treating me like I was different—"

"Is that your word for beautiful?" Kirsty grinned, not so innocently.

"You like words, don't you?" It was an adorable trait and quite foreign for someone who mostly had words put in her mouth by writers.

"I find them useful when communicating." The grin widened.

"I've always leaned into observing to pick up on things."

Kirsty inhaled deeply. "You really should teach a class for how not to answer simple questions."

"Fine!" Saffron playfully groaned. "Yeah, of course it was flattering to feel beautiful. At first…"

"Then…?" Kirsty waved for Saffron to fill in the gap.

"The thrill of celebrity wears off quickly, or at least, it did with me. I couldn't and still can't fathom why people are so curious to know what groceries I buy at Waitrose."

"If you want to shop at Waitrose while here, you'll have to drive to Winterbury."

"I'm certain I can survive without one." Saffron swilled her drink, feeling the back of her shirt becoming damp from the sweltering night air.

"Are you? I wouldn't want to have your death on my conscience." Kirsty added in a melodramatic voice, "Hollywood star dies of starvation, refusing to step foot into her local Iceland for food."

Saffron tossed a crisp at Kirsty. "So funny. Not."

Kirsty swiped the crisp from the front of her shirt and popped it into her mouth. "Thanks." After swallowing, Kirsty asked, "How are you finding it here? Aside from the subpar food shop choices?"

Saffron smiled and then pointed at her lips. "Firstly, that. There's this sense of peace here. Every morning, I wake to the sound of waves. Not honking cars, or the beeping of a delivery van backing up, or construction. There's always something going on in London."

"Is there a secondly? You did mention earlier you're terrible at maths."

Saffron loved the playfulness in Kirsty's eyes. "I need to be careful around you."

"Why's that?" Her breath had a hitch to it.

"You zoom in on my faults."

"That's not true! It's nice to know you aren't perfect. Besides, being bad at maths isn't a fault. It's a part of you.

And, if you want to know the truth, when you brought the oysters earlier, admitting you weren't great with numbers, you had this adorable blush on your cheeks. It's nice seeing you relaxed. Much different from our first interaction."

"When I acted like a spoiled brat."

"You said it, not me." Kirsty wore an innocent expression, but the way she shifted in her chair suggested she was in full agreement.

"I'm terribly sorry about my first impression."

"It's safe to say, both of us weren't at our best. I'm still embarrassed by the things I said."

Saffron started to rethink the reason for Kirsty shifting in her seat moments earlier. Was she...? No, don't go down that path. "It'll take time not to think everyone wants something from me." Saffron filled one cheek with air, and released it gradually, hoping the action took away the guilt.

"That's got to be hard to live with. Always wondering if someone has a secret mission of some sort."

Saffron leaned on her forearms. "Do you have one? Come on; you can trust me." She offered her best *confide in me* smile.

Kirsty mirrored Saffron by also leaning on her forearms, giving Saffron more than a glimpse. "Why do I have to be the one with the ulterior motive? Are you projecting?"

"Wouldn't you like to know?" Saffron chewed on her bottom lip.

"I positively would." Kirsty nodded enthusiastically.

"That's good, right? Remember, I'm bad at maths. Being in the positive is the right direction."

"Depends on the direction you're aiming for."

Saffron stared into Kirsty's eyes. "Would you like to take

this back to mine? Sit on the deck? Listen to the waves? Contemplate if positive or negative is the correct course?" *Or why my heart skips every third beat when around you?*

"Sounds deep. I'm in."

* * *

"Would you like a glass of wine?" Saffron stood in her kitchen, unable to make eye contact with Kirsty. "Or water? I have sparkling? Bubbles. I like bubbles on my throat. Let's have bubbles."

"I'm making a mental note of that, and I'll include some bubbly in your next delivery." Kirsty's nervous laugh piled onto Saffron's inability to shut off her meltdown valve in the part of her brain that controlled her speech.

So what if there was a woman in her home looking at Saffron like she wanted to get to know her in a biblical way? Were there lesbians in the bible? If so, probably not the right example for the moment. She couldn't imagine happy dyke stories from that time period.

This was real life and Saffron didn't know how to act around normal people. It was possible, this was the absolute worst time to learn this fact about herself. Normal terrified her more than anything she'd faced up until then.

Saffron wheeled about to the fridge, the swirling sensation behind her eyes not stopping with her body.

Kirsty stepped closer. "Let me help."

"I've got it." Saffron placed a hand on the metal door to steady herself.

"Don't take this the wrong way, but you don't, and that's okay. We can do it together."

Needing more support, Saffron threaded her fingers through the handle of the fridge. "It's just sparkling water."

"It is." Kirsty inched closer. "Nothing to be nervous about."

"People drink it every day."

"They do." Kirsty placed her hand over Saffron's, unfurling her fingers.

"What if you don't want it, though? After you find out it's simply water with bubbles. That's the secret to fancy water. Frivolous bubbles. No substance." *Shut up, shut up, shut up!*

Kirsty's laugh was sweet, sexy, and everything in between. "You're putting a lot of pressure on this beverage you won't let out of the fridge."

"It's what I do. Fret about the big picture." *Like how I'll wreck everything in a Saffron-Fucking-Oliver way.*

"I'm seeing that." Kirsty's fingers intertwined with Saffron's. "What if I told you I'm not the type to judge anything by its sparkle factor?"

"I have zero reference point for that." Saffron closed her eyes, sinking into the feeling of having Kirsty standing so close.

"Does that mean you don't believe me?"

"I want to." *Oh God, did I want to.*

"How can I convince you to give me a chance?"

Saffron turned around, her back pressed against the fridge. "I want to," she repeated, unable to find other words.

Their faces were so close together, but the tiniest of space between their lips seemed impossible to breach. Because if Saffron did, it'd only ignite her self-destruct button and Kirsty didn't deserve that.

Yet, a force pulled them closer and closer until their lips met. Softly at first. With all the tenderness, but the nerves bubbled under the surface.

Stop thinking of bubbles!

Kirsty, or was it Saffron, deepened the kiss, Saffron threading her hand into Kirsty's hair, as if needing to hold onto her to know this was real. They were kissing. Not acting, but actually experiencing.

And, it was hot.

Scorching even.

Saffron didn't want it to end, but where would it lead?

Get out of your head, idiot!

Kirsty's tongue dove in deeper, causing Saffron's knees to buckle, but Kirsty held on tightly, pulling Saffron further into the moment. Kirsty's nipples pressed against Saffron, eliciting a surge of warmth down below.

They reached the frantic stage, making it difficult to tell whose limbs became entangled with whose. Saffron's fingers trailed down the side of Kirsty's neck, along the collarbone, and cupped a breast, neither daring to rip their mouths apart.

A gust of wind blasted the house, the garden chairs scraping over the paving stones. Saffron jumped at what sounded like broken glass. "What was that?"

Kirsty cupped Saffron's cheek. "Just the wind." She studied Saffron's eyes. "You okay?"

Saffron nodded, kissing the heel of Kirsty's hand.

Kirsty smiled, panting. "Now, I'm really in need of water."

"Right." Saffron gave Kirsty a peck on the cheek. "This all started because of water. I wanted to be close to the water, so I chose this place. And, tonight, water brought us together."

"Water is amazing that way." Kirsty nudged Saffron to the side and opened the fridge.

Saffron pulled two glasses from the cupboard, placing them on the counter.

Kirsty twisted the cap off the bottle, the fizzy sound echoing off the walls, neither of them speaking, only watching the other with searing expressions.

No lights were on in the kitchen since they both seemed to silently desire the darkness to protect them from their fears. As they raised their glasses in a silent toast, Saffron's phone on the counter-top lit up with a message: *I miss my boo. Our bed is so empty without you.*

Saffron clicked the button to darken the screen, but it was too late.

"It's getting late. I should go." Kirsty set her glass down, never taking a sip.

"No, don't. I can explain." *Could I?* And, why hadn't Saffron disabled notifications from appearing on her home screen when she left the house earlier like she normally did? Because she didn't want to miss one of Kirsty's flirty texts. Not that she could say that now and make it seem believable.

"That's not necessary. Really. The message makes it clear you aren't available."

"It's just something she says. Echo gets lonely at night. It means nothing." If Saffron thought she could get away with it, she'd dance like a court jester with exaggerated hand motions as if saying, *nothing to see here, folks.*

"You know me. I like words as a form of communication. And those words do mean something." Kirsty's nose wrinkled. "I don't understand. You told me your relationship was all for show." Kirsty pressed her palm to her forehead. "That"—she pointed to the phone—"doesn't look like it's for show."

"It's complicated." How could Saffron admit the truth? She wasn't willing on most days to be frank with herself yet. How she'd been conned by Echo into thinking Saffron mattered? When in reality, Echo wasn't capable of love. Image and publicity took precedence.

"I'm not in a place in my life where I want complications." Kirsty stared into Saffron's eyes. "It's just…" She shook her head, her eyes turning glassy. "Good night, Saffron."

Saffron stood frozen in the kitchen, unable to banish the thought that although Kirsty had said good night, what she really meant was goodbye.

Chapter 15

Kirsty was back up the ladder again, trying to fix the festival bunting. It wasn't sitting right. It had been annoying her far more than it should for the past half hour. She was well aware of that. But the more aggravation she could eliminate from her day, the better.

She'd already lived through Sunday dinner yesterday with her parents going on about how wonderful Saffron was, how totally unstarry she was. Kirsty had said nothing, shut down, helped Dad with his crossword and eaten Mum's roast. They may well have been wondering what happened to their sunny, happier daughter who was at the festival the day before. The one who ate the oyster to impress a girl. However, they didn't prod Kirsty further. Perhaps they could tell the wrong question might lead to her biting their heads off.

"Can you go easy on the bunting, Kirst? It didn't do anything to you." Helena walked into the shop, carrying a white box from the bakery.

Kirsty stared out the window, the bunting crushed in her fist.

Helena touched her leg. "Put it back up, get down, put the

ladder away, and come have a tea with me." She held up the box. "I bought iced buns."

That pierced Kirsty's veneer. A glimmer of a smile broke through. "I'm not sure even iced buns can fix this."

"There's no problem iced buns can't fix." Helena made tea and waited for Kirsty to join her at the counter. "So?"

Kirsty took a bite of the iced bun and sighed.

Her friend waited for her to carry on.

"I'm just pissed off that I allowed her in. That's all. She's not available and I should have known that." Kirsty put down her bun. "I *did* know. That's the annoying thing. I'd read the magazines, seen Saffron shift when she spoke about her. What the hell was I thinking even putting myself in that position?" She rapped her forehead with her knuckles. How could she have been so careless? "I thought with age comes wisdom, but I'm a walking, talking example that doesn't apply here."

Helena put a hand on her arm. "Circle back and start talking English, please."

Kirsty took a deep breath. "Saturday was great. You saw that. We had drinks, we ate dinner, and then everyone else left."

"And you stayed for a final drink with Saffron."

"Yes."

"And then ignored my texts all day yesterday asking how it went."

"Not well."

"I'm getting that." Helena paused. "So, tell me."

Kirsty cast her mind back to Saturday night. When she'd been wondering whether or not she'd be going home. To the frisson of walking back to Saffron's house. To being in the kitchen. To finally getting the answer to the question: what was it like to kiss Saffron Oliver?

The answer: beyond magical. When Saffron's lips had met hers, real life had taken on a new, improved quality. It had been so perfect while it lasted. The feel of Saffron's lips on hers. The heat of her tongue. The crackle of possibility.

Until it had been destroyed by the text from Echo Black. Kirsty's stomach rolled just thinking about it.

Fuck Saffron.

Fuck Echo Black.

Fuck both of them.

It didn't matter Saffron was a movie star, did it? All Kirsty's disappointments with women felt exactly the same.

When Anna had told her she'd met someone else, a key part of trusting anybody else with her heart had fallen away. Kirsty had worked so hard to repair the damage over the past few years, but she'd never opened herself up too much. Because deep down, even though she'd never admitted it to Saffron, she agreed with her. People couldn't be trusted.

Saffron had proved that by claiming Echo and her were just a publicity stunt, but Echo's text had told Kirsty a different story. Publicity stunt or not, lines had been crossed. They'd shared a bed. They'd been a thing. Saffron had lied to her. Kirsty didn't need to know much more.

Saffron Oliver might be famous and a big deal, but she couldn't be trusted.

For someone who was just allowing herself to like Saffron, that was a bitter pill to swallow.

Helena clicked her fingers in front of Kirsty's face. "What happened?"

Kirsty sipped her tea before she replied. "We went back to hers, and we ended up kissing."

Helena made a face. "Was she a terrible kisser? I once had a guy who was so enthusiastic when he kissed me, I felt like he'd shredded my lips."

Kirsty shook her head. "No, the opposite." Her body revved at the memory. "She was all the things she should be. Until her ex texted a sweet nothing to her phone. I mean, her ex, her co-star, who the fuck knows? But you don't text someone at gone 11pm if there's nothing going on, do you?"

Helena winced. "Maybe, maybe not. Who knows? It might just be habit."

"Even so, I'm too old for dyke drama. I don't want to be caught in the middle of a break-up that's not quite done."

"But you like her. Maybe you could bend your rules just this once? It *is* Saffron Oliver."

Kirsty frowned. "If this is because you want me to date her for the shop—"

"It's not! I want you to be happy." Helena frowned, pink colouring her cheeks. "You deserve it. Plus, Saffron seems genuine."

Kirsty gave her a resigned nod. "Genuinely unavailable and soon going back to her superstar lifestyle." She threw up her hands and paced to the end of the tasting table. "She's not going to settle here, is she? In sleepy old Sandy Cove?" Acid disappointment fizzed inside her. "It feels like she's just been stringing me along. An amusement while she's here, before she goes back to her real life with her superstar girlfriend. Like I've been her plaything."

"What about after? Did she text or call?"

"Nope. Nothing at all." Kirsty placed both palms on the table and dropped her head. "It's just, I'd started to imagine she might stick around. How it might work. But now…"

Helena walked over and rubbed her back.

Kirsty straightened up, lightheaded for a few seconds until she acclimatised. "Next time I find myself falling for a movie star, slap me, okay? I am not starring in a rom-com. This is real life. In fact, write it down on a piece of paper and hold it up in front of my goddamn face if this ever happens again." Kirsty strode to the counter and wrote on the back of one of the consignment notes Helena had just unpacked: *Life is not a Hollywood rom-com, you stupid fuck*. She handed it to her friend.

Helena held the note between her thumb and index finger, like Kirsty had just weed on it. "But you ate an oyster for her. You haven't done that since school. Not even for Anna."

"More fool me, eh?"

The shop door opening interrupted their chat. When Kirsty looked up, the last person she expected through the door was Saffron, but she was standing right in front of her with Ginger just behind.

Saffron gave her a pained half-smile and hung back, letting Ginger take the lead.

For her part, Ginger gave her sister a brief glance, before smiling at Kirsty. Did she know what had happened? Kirsty could only assume she did. Unless Saffron was so contained she'd told nobody. Kirsty had no idea. She didn't really know Saffron at all.

"Hey, Ginger. I wasn't expecting to see you today." Kirsty's tone was brittle. Not to be messed with.

Ginger gave her a look. "It's the tasting, remember? You arranged for us to go to the Lobster Grill and taste the food they're preparing especially for the party?"

Kirsty closed her eyes. Of course. The Lobster Grill didn't open on a Monday, so this was the only day they could do. Why couldn't today have been a bog-standard Monday where she could stay in the shop and hide?

"I brought Saffron along as her palate has tasted the finest foods in the world, so I figured she might be useful. Also, I thought she might find it impossible to turn down a free lunch as she always says there's no such thing. But I was surprised at the amount of persuasion it took."

Kirsty glanced at Saffron. She wasn't surprised at all.

Kirsty turned to Helena. "It's just for a couple of hours this lunchtime. I didn't think it would be a problem. Sorry I forgot to tell you."

Helena shook her head. "It's not like we're going to be overrun with wine lovers on a Monday lunchtime, is it?"

She was being the perfect business partner again. Just when Kirsty wanted Helena to tell her she couldn't go. But she had to.

Ginger's phone ringing pierced the air, making everyone jump. Ginger took the call into the shop corner.

Which left Saffron standing in front of Kirsty and Helena, who soon departed for the loo.

Saffron moved her mouth one way, then the other. She shifted her weight from one foot to the other, then walked over to the wine shelves to her right, reading one of Kirsty's handwritten notes. "Sunshine Fields Chardonnay is the perfect accompaniment to a summertime meal. Crisp, clean, uncomplicated." She glanced over at Kirsty. "Would you recommend it?"

"I favour crisp, clean, and uncomplicated in my life. Sadly, it's hard to come by. Perhaps you should buy a case so you know what it tastes like." Okay, that wasn't the answer she normally gave to customers. But Saffron Oliver wasn't just any old customer, was she?

She was someone who Kirsty had developed feelings for far too prematurely.

Now, she had buyer's remorse.

Ginger came back just in the nick of time. "So sorry. That was a client I've just taken on, and their website needs urgent attention." She sighed as she looked from Kirsty to Saffron. "I know this isn't the best timing and that you really do need me there, but could you do the tasting for me?"

Irritation slid down Kirsty, landing squarely in her stomach. She'd thought Ginger was her friend. However, she was her party planner, and this was part of her job. Kirsty was going to have to suck it up, wasn't she?

"No problem." Kirsty's words came out flat. It was how she was going to have to play this. All her emotions boxed up and hidden away.

Saffron shrugged, avoiding Kirsty's gaze. "Sure, we can do that."

"Great." Ginger gave Saffron a hug and did the same to Kirsty. "I trust you both implicitly. I'll call you later." With that, she left the shop, apparently oblivious to the tension in the air.

Prickly heat crept up Kirsty's back as she stared at Saffron. Yes, she should be asking her what the hell she was playing at, but she still remembered what it had felt like standing in her arms two days ago. Finally giving in to their attraction for a few brief minutes. She was still gorgeous, still ticked the attraction box for Kirsty. But life wasn't as simple as sexual desire, was it? If it was, she'd slam her up against the shop door right that moment and press her lips to Saffron's.

Longing flooded her once more.

Kirsty closed her eyes.

Damn it.

Helena walked back in, oblivious to Kirsty's thoughts.

Seeing her, Saffron turned and picked up the wine bottle again. "Can you ship me a case of these when you have a chance? I'm keen to know more."

Kirsty turned to Helena. "Can you put that order in for Saffron?" She wasn't going to react to Saffron, despite the heat of her stare.

Helena gulped then nodded. "Sure, sure." She signalled to Saffron. "Can you bring it over so I can get the name right?"

Saffron did as she was told.

Helena patted the counter. "Leave it here, I'll put it back on the shelf."

Saffron took a deep breath, only now looking at Kirsty directly. "We should go. The tasting's booked for midday. You ready?"

Kirsty ground her teeth together. "As I'll ever be."

Chapter 16

They walked to the restaurant, side by side, the awkward silence growing more uncomfortable with each step. Every part of Saffron itched as if she was covered in hives, and it took all her restraint not to scratch all her skin off.

Saffron had experienced perplexing moments before, but this stroll was putting every socially embarrassing situation to shame. Even the time when she was introduced to the director of *Girl Racer* and she stuck her hand out to shake, only to learn after the fact the germophobe never shook anyone's hand. Her hand had hung there for many uncomfortable seconds, the director's eyes locked on hers as if daring to see how long she'd hold out. Turned out for eight seconds, which in hindsight wasn't very long at the moment, though, it seemed like a lifetime.

The walk from the High Street, along the water, to the edge of Sandy Cove on the Branton Bay side eclipsed eight seconds by an eternity. Every damn one of the ticks of the clock seemed to kick Kirsty's annoyance into a higher gear.

A gaggle of tourists in Bermuda shorts and red faces made their way to the beach to catch more rays.

"It wasn't until I walked along a beach in Southern

California that I realised our pebble beaches are shite." Saffron acted out walking barefoot on jagged rocks.

"Luckily for you, your time in Sandy Cove will be short-lived and you can return to your posh lifestyle." Kirsty kept her focus on the promenade, her shoulders squaring for battle.

The first attempt to alleviate the tension had crashed and burned.

"The Kent coastline has more character. It even has castles." Saffron slid her eyes to Kirsty to see if the lamest peace offering in existence had been accepted.

From the clamped lips, it had not, and quite possibly, it made Kirsty disappear further into her protective bubble. Saffron had to control the urge to stab the air around Kirsty to pop the imaginary barrier. But that wouldn't accomplish what Saffron wanted and would probably result in pissing off the woman even more.

If Saffron wanted to apologise for what had transpired after the kiss, she'd actually have to address the ill-timed text. Talking about her personal life wasn't something she enjoyed doing. How could she say, *Hey, Echo Black is your typical obnoxious Hollywood-type whom I unwisely started a relationship with because I thought she actually liked me, but for her it was more about publicity and that hurt?* The icing on the cake was Echo sharing intimate photos of them as a way of fighting off rumours they had separated all in an attempt to keep the frenzy of *Girl Racer* fans alive. Saffron had told Echo, in her Saffron way, that they were done, but Echo wouldn't relent.

The irony wasn't lost on Saffron. If she'd been able to

outright tell Echo they were through, Saffron would have a leg to stand on when explaining everything to Kirsty. Truth was, Saffron hated disappointing people and struggled saying what was really in her heart.

With a smile, she remembered Kirsty saying she found words useful when communicating. The confident Kirsty wouldn't be in this situation. Every time Saffron started to text Kirsty after the kiss, she became paralysed by her inability to let Kirsty take a peek behind the curtain, worried she would see Saffron, quaking like a child.

Saffron had hoped fleeing to Sandy Cove would hammer the point home to Echo. They were through. Apparently, the message hadn't been received. Or Echo ignored it.

The same was true with Pearl. If Saffron could cut the agent's apron strings once and for all, she wouldn't be ducking calls about a movie she didn't want to make with Echo, absolutely making it clear to both that Saffron wanted a clean break.

Children of alcoholics, more often than not, grew up playing peacemaker, never wanting to rock an already seesawing boat in a tempest. Saffron had learned this in therapy and understood the foundation for her need to placate others. Understanding and confronting were polar opposites in her world.

The door of the restaurant came into view, and Saffron legged it to get there first. "After you." She made an exaggerated bow and arm wave, only to be met with a snort.

I guess chivalry isn't appreciated. Saffron crumpled, wanting to sink into the ground.

"Ladies, welcome." The owner pressed his hands together. "Which one of you is the lucky lady?"

Saffron and Kirsty stared blankly at the man.

"Oh, I'm sorry. Are both of you the brides? Such a lovely couple." He put a hand on one of Kirsty's shoulders and gave it a squeeze.

"Oh, no." Kirsty rushed to say, lowering her shoulder to be free of the man. "I'm planning a divorce party for…" She looked to Saffron.

"The person who left you is a fool." He slapped his hands together, but stopped short from spitting on the floor, even if he looked as if he was about to. "An utter fool." The man led them to the table, speaking to Saffron on his right. "Don't you worry. What we've conjured up today will make you feel better. I have no doubt you'll rebound quickly." He winked at Saffron as if hoping to add his name to her *future suitors* list, much to her amazement. Did he have no clue who she was?

Kirsty took a seat next to Saffron, which would have been encouraging, but the way the table was set up, the chairs were right next to each other. Should Saffron take comfort in the fact that Kirsty didn't move one of the chairs to the far side? Was that a sign she didn't hate being in the same space as Saffron? Or was she simply avoiding making a scene?

The owner came out with two plates. "First up, caramelised scallops with cauliflower puree and pancetta. Enjoy."

"They look scrumptious." Saffron unfurled a white linen napkin with a cracking sound, placing it onto her lap.

"I feel like I should tell you something." Kirsty poked the offering with a fork.

"You don't like scallops?"

"I'm not a superfan, but no, that isn't what I want to say." Saffron braced for the worst.

"The other night, I think we can both agree it was a mistake. With the festivities, too much booze, and wanting to… I shouldn't have kissed you."

"Uh—"

"I don't know about you, but I'm not the type to indulge in summer flings. We both know you're only here temporarily, and I'm planning your sister's divorce party, of all things. Us… kissing again, is a bad idea. Absolutely the worst." Kirsty sliced the air with both hands.

"Oh, I couldn't agree more." *Actually, I totally disagree!*

"You're clearly still involved with Echo Black, and I'm not the type to be the other woman. Not that I think whatever we had qualified as that. It's just… yeah, we should cool it. Focus on the party planning and nothing more." Kirsty gestured to the scallops as if they were the only things that mattered in the moment.

"Yes, all this is about Ginger." Saffron noticed Kirsty referred to them in the past tense. The woman moved on quickly, which surely meant it had only been a bit of fun for her.

Kirsty turned to Saffron. "You agree? It was a mistake?"

Saffron nodded, hopefully showcasing a relieved smile when all she wanted to do was crawl back under her duvet and start the day over because this wasn't where she wanted to be. The last thing she had wanted was being told the kiss was a mistake and they should only see each other for party planning business and nothing more.

For Saffron, the kiss had been amazing. The toe-curling kind that she'd heard about but never experienced.

But it wasn't only that. When she was around Kirsty, she felt like herself. Not SAFFRON OLIVER, all lit up in red on a marquee. Allowed to be her dorky, uncool self without fear of being judged. Wasn't that what most people craved deep down? To show their true colours and to be not only accepted but loved for those nutty qualities? That door had just been slammed shut in her face.

Kirsty cleared her throat, still waiting for an answer.

"Yep. I agree." Saffron stared at her plate.

"Our lives are just so different. You're used to women drooling over you, and my life is in this sleepy town with terrible beaches, where I hope to eke out enough wine sales so I can buy frozen salmon and peas at my local Iceland for my version of Friday night dinner. Our worlds couldn't be further apart if we tried." Kirsty spread her arms out wide, one hand barely grazing Saffron's chest, causing her insides to ignite like a stick of dynamite. "Sorry about that." She recoiled in her chair, the chasm between them growing even more.

Saffron tried to blot out how her body still sizzled from the accidental touch. "For the record, I like salmon and peas."

"Have you ever tried it from a shop like Iceland, that has budget in mind, not bells and whistles for the rich? That's the point, Saff, isn't it?"

Saff? Kirsty had called her Saff, but it wasn't meant to bring them closer, only to tear them apart. And, why was the woman so caught up about shopping in Iceland? Would Saffron have to build one of the shops on an actual chunk of ice to get across to Kirsty that she didn't like the so-called Hollywood lifestyle?

Saffron tapped the side of her head, forcing a smile. "Don't worry. We're on the same page."

Kirsty let out a relieved whoosh of air, and her shoulders softened. "I'm so glad. Because this"—she waved to Saffron and then back to her chest, resting her hand on the appetizing swell, causing Saffron to sit on her hands to avoid doing anything foolish—"has been awkward at best. Now that we've cleared the air, we can go back to being what we are: party planner and client."

"Perfect. As the party planner, what do you think of the scallops?"

Kirsty took a dainty bite. "Oh, it's not from Iceland."

"Is that a tick in the right box for you? I know how much you *love* your Iceland." Saffron didn't have to roll her eyes, since her tone made it clear.

"Just as much as you *love* your Waitrose." Kirsty smirked, her red lips pressed together, and Saffron felt a tug of an invisible string pulling her mouth to those lips.

"It's where my assistant does all my shopping, before wrapping everything in gold paper." Saffron snapped her head back, confounded as to why Kirsty couldn't understand Saffron didn't give a fuck about where to shop as long as they did it together. The takeaway point was there was absolutely zero chance between them. Saffron should put it out of her mind right then and there.

"Well, ladies, what do you think of the scallops?"

"Stunning." Saffron stared into Kirsty's eyes.

"Nothing better on the planet." Kirsty held her gaze.

"Magnificent." The man bobbed his head, clearing the half-eaten food. "I'll be right back with the next delectable delight."

Saffron licked her lips.

Kirsty bit down on the left side of her bottom lip.

Saffron tugged on her collar and crossed her legs.

The owner returned. "This will knock your socks off. Grilled lobster with chili and chorizo." He kissed his fingertips. "Fresh and hot."

"She is... I mean, it looks like it is." If the lobster shell had been on the plate, Saffron would have crawled into it. As an alternative she had to settle for her cheeks burning redder than the missing shell.

"Thank you." Kirsty swallowed.

When they were alone, Saffron raised her eyes to those lovely greys, only to be met with a quizzical stare. "Shall we dig in?"

"It is why we're here." Kirsty didn't make a move to sample the lobster.

"Yes, because you're the party planner and I'm the client. Nothing else to see here, folks." Saffron tried to laugh at her own joke but nearly choked. She clenched the water glass with two shaky hands and drank heavily to clear her passageway.

Kirsty slapped Saffron's back. "Are you okay?"

Saffron nodded, still guzzling water, her eyes tearing. After several deep breaths, she recovered, mostly. "These are the moments that are usually cut out of my films."

"The real ones?" Kirsty still had her hand on Saffron's back, rubbing it tenderly.

Saffron stifled the buzzing sensation coursing through her, as Kirsty still massaged her back, worry in her eyes.

"Exactly." Saffron took one final drink of water. "Moviegoers don't want real from me. Only perfection." *Like I have my life figured out, when really, I'm flailing like the rest of the human population.*

"Another reason why we wouldn't work. I revel in imperfection. Maybe it's why I prefer rom-coms, not action flicks. No offence."

"None taken. What's your favourite?"

"*Sleepless in Seattle*." Kirsty spoke the words like she'd tossed down a gauntlet.

"Another problem. I'm a *You've Got Mail* girl."

"I think we'll find, if we continue scratching the surface, we really don't have a lot in common." Kirsty fidgeted with her fork.

"I would like to note, both of our rom-coms star Tom Hanks and Meg Ryan." Saffron punctuated the sentence with an emphatic finger punching the air. "If we agree on absolutely everything, where would the spark come from?"

"Not from water, that's for sure."

"Right. Been there. Done that." Saffron made a check mark in the air. "Just tap water from here on out."

"Will you be able to survive, do you think?"

Saffron clutched her shirt as dramatically as she could. "I don't have a choice."

"You're being so brave." Kirsty placed a hand on Saffron's thigh.

If I were indeed brave, I'd lean over and kiss you to test your we can never be more than party planner/client *resolve.*

Instead, Saffron refused to draw attention to the hand, because she didn't want the contact to end.

A thought struck her. "Did I tell you Michelle, my assistant, shipped my motorbike? Have you ever ridden one?"

Kirsty shook her head.

"Since you taught me to kayak, I'd like to return the favour and take you for a ride." Saffron had to force one image out of her mind. "On my motorbike."

"I thought we just agreed to keep our relationship strictly professional."

"We can still be mates, can't we?" *Please say yes.*

"Mates?"

"Yes. I get that you want nothing more. But, there's nothing like riding a bike. Come on. It'll be fun." Saffron held her breath, waiting.

"I'll think about it."

Saffron could only concentrate on the idea of Kirsty wrapping her arms around Saffron, holding on and not letting go. By the glint in Kirsty's eyes, there might be hope Saffron wasn't alone in this fantasy.

Chapter 17

It turned out Saffron wasn't very good at taking no for an answer. It probably wasn't something she heard often. She hadn't given up, texting Kirsty the previous day after their party planning lunch to arrange a bike ride.

Kirsty was torn. She didn't want to give Saffron the wrong impression. That she was interested. But she was only human.

It wasn't every day that Saffron Oliver from *Girl Racer* offered to take you on a bike ride, was it?

Meet me downstairs in five. I hope you're ready for a thrill. x

It wasn't the first suggestive text Saffron had sent her. Kirsty hoped Monday had gone some way to smoothing things over, that they were on the same page now. Sort of. Friends with a sell-by date of whenever Saffron went back to her normal life. That was how Kirsty was going to view it.

She walked down her stairs and outside, just as the kick of an engine split the air. If she'd been in the shop, she might have tutted. However, Kirsty could do nothing but gawp as Saffron pulled up outside Wine Time. She clicked the motorbike stand onto the ground and swung a leather-clad leg onto the pavement, quickly followed by the other.

Kirsty's throat went dry. This was her ultimate dream fantasy. Every fibre of her being wanted to jump up and down.

Saffron Oliver had come to take her for a ride. In her bike leathers.

Kirsty had officially won the lesbian lottery.

Saffron took off her helmet and shook her hair free.

Kirsty gulped. Her clit sprang to life.

Okay, this was totally unfair.

Saffron got the spare helmet from the bike's sturdy black pannier and handed it to Kirsty. "Ready to go for the ride of your life?" She followed that up with an ironic wink.

This friend thing wasn't going so well, was it? Kirsty shook her head. "Get on the bike, you moron. And by the way, you *really* need to work on your lines." All lies, but making a joke of her feelings was the only way she could handle this. Almost like they were actually friends. Today, she was going to suspend reality and just enjoy the ride. Literally.

"Remember to wrap your arms around me tightly," Saffron instructed. "I followed your advice when we went kayaking, so the same courtesy here, please. I don't want you to fall off, okay?"

Kirsty nodded. She pulled down her helmet and wrapped her arms around Saffron, ignoring the purr of her body.

Then Saffron pulled away, the engine roared, and a whole other dimension opened up.

For the first ten minutes, Kirsty did nothing but hold on, too scared to look left or right. Was Saffron going as fast as it felt? Kirsty had no idea. When she eventually looked up, they were riding through glorious purple lavender fields, no other cars in sight. Kirsty risked a glance left, then right, then wobbled.

She pressed both arms tighter around Saffron. When Saffron pulled up in a lay-by, Kirsty's thighs clenched.

She was straddling leather with Saffron.

It was something she might have dreamed about in another way, too.

Kirsty pushed the thought from her head.

Those were not helpful, friendly feelings.

She stumbled off the bike, dazed. She shook out her wobbly legs, then pulled off her helmet. The scent of lavender filled her nostrils, and she breathed it in, almost forgetting she must look a state. She ruffled her hair, trying to unclench her muscles. But even though she was still getting over her first bike ride, the tension was mixed with a thrill. Kirsty was being a rebel. She was living. That was definitely something her new friend had brought to the table. Since she'd met Saffron, her life wasn't just about work.

New shoots were bursting through.

She liked it. She liked it a lot.

It almost took her back to a time when she had someone to share special moments with.

She missed that.

"Well?" Saffron shook out her blond locks again.

"How come you don't look a sweaty mess like me? Did they teach you that on set, too?"

Saffron grinned. "You look gorgeous. A little sweaty, but in a sexy way." She blushed. "I mean sexy in a friendly way."

Kirsty rolled her eyes, but her heart sang. Saffron thought she was sexy? It wasn't helpful, but it made her morning.

They walked over to the lay-by's solitary bench and sat. Kirsty stretched out her arms and legs and turned her face to the sun. It was hot this morning, just like it had been every morning since Saffron's arrival. She squinted, missing the disguise of her sunglasses. She was completely on show, but Saffron was, too.

"Are you going to tell me what you thought?"

Kirsty glanced right. "It was... scary. Luckily, you're easy to hang on to. But it was definitely something I could get used to."

Saffron quirked an eyebrow. "You're already booking in for another ride?"

"You've got to get me home, so I hope so. I've got a cake tasting with Ginger at lunchtime."

"I wouldn't want to keep my sister waiting." A few moments went by before she spoke again. "You've got a very thoughtful look on your face."

Kirsty gave her a slow smile. "I was just thinking this is nice. To be doing things again that aren't work related. Sharing moments." Why had she started down this road, and how was she going to back up and not make this sound awkward? "It's something I've missed since I split with my ex."

Not like that. Really, Kirsty? You're out on a ride with Saffron Oliver and thinking about Anna?

"I don't know her or what happened exactly, but she was dumb to let you go." Saffron gave her a searching look then turned away. She crossed her legs. She must be baking in those leathers.

Kirsty chewed on her words. "My ex cheated on me. She lied to me. Which is why you lying to me about Echo touched a nerve. I don't appreciate being lied to."

Saffron nodded and turned to face Kirsty. "I get it. I'm

sorry. What went on with us was short-lived, just like my feelings for her. I was stupid to get into it. Which is probably why I lied, because I should have known better. Not an excuse, but that's why." She reached out a hand to Kirsty's arm and drew it back just as quickly. "I'm sorry I touched a nerve. I know how raw they can be."

Kirsty sucked in her bottom lip, her heart beating fast. They were straying back into dangerous territory here, weren't they? She jumped up, brushing down her jeans.

"Shall we get going?" Best to break this up now before it went too far. "I've got a cake tasting to get to."

* * *

"Kirsty, have you tried my new cakes? They're cream cheese frosted, like the ones they did on *The Great British Bake Off* last series. Pimped-up madeleines, as one of my customers called them earlier." Betty grinned from ear to ear as she pointed at the display cabinet. "Can I tempt you? Your mum and dad would love them. Your dad's in here most days buying something."

Was he really? That was news. "No thanks, Betty. We're just in here to order a cake for Ginger's divorce party." They all looked and smelled divine. Kirsty had always said bakery staff must be the most content workers on the planet, inhaling the aroma of cake all day long. The sweetness hung in the air like a warm blanket of love.

Betty frowned. "A divorce party? Is that a thing now? I'm not sure a celebratory cake is what's needed for that, is it?"

"You didn't know my ex-husband," Ginger replied, making Kirsty snort. "Can we try the poppy seed and lemon, salted caramel, and the coffee and walnut, please?" Ginger paused. "And you're invited to the party. Can you make August 17th?"

"Smashing! I do love a party." Betty clapped her hands together. "Take a seat, I'll bring the cakes over. On the house, of course."

"The perfect business arrangement."

"Not the rainbow cake?" Kirsty pointed at the seven-layered cake done in all the colours of the rainbow.

Ginger gave her a look. "We've been through this. You're gay. Saffron is gay. I, unfortunately, am uncontrollably attracted to men."

They walked over to a table at the back of the shop and sat.

"Women aren't any better, believe me."

"So I've heard." Ginger settled in her seat before she spoke. "I know this is none of my business, and you can tell me to shut up, but has something happened with Saffron? She's being evasive, even though she's spent the past ten years of her life telling me she'd love to live near me. Now we live a ten-minute walk apart, and she's hiding. I was wondering if you knew why."

Betty brought over the cakes, along with two teas.

Kirsty waited until she'd gone to speak. "I know she's had a lot of publicity stuff to do with Echo for *Girl Racer*." Even saying her name made Kirsty's brain hurt. "What kind of a name is Echo anyway?" She'd thought that even when she was just Saffron's co-star. However, now she was impacting her life, Echo's name seemed totally ridiculous.

A little like Kirsty developing feelings for a movie star.

"An LA name, sweetheart." Ginger put on her best Californian accent to deliver that line.

Kirsty couldn't help but smile. "Is it real?"

"As real as anything in Hollywood." Ginger sighed. "You know what? I don't know. I don't know Hollywood. I've lived a very different life to Saffron. But I believe what she tells me. She thought things might be different when Echo moved here temporarily. But it turned out, they weren't."

Kirsty nodded. She wanted to know more. But she didn't want to make it look like she was desperate to know all the details.

Even though she was.

Ginger took a bite of the salted caramel cake and tilted her head back, savouring the taste. "This is good." She picked up some stray crumbs with the tip of her finger. "If she could do this as the base layer, and maybe a different flavour for layer two, we might have a winner. I want something funny iced on top. Maybe *Straight Outta Marriage*? Or I have seen people having bride and groom cake-toppers like at a wedding. Only this time, the bride is dumping the groom into a toy version of a bin lorry. That would work, too."

Kirsty was glad she didn't have a mouthful of tea, as she might have spat it out. "How do you think your friends who know both of you are going to take that?"

"If they don't see the funny side, it's their issue. This party is about me and my rebirth, right?"

"Totally."

Ginger put a hand on Kirsty's arm. "Thank you for all your help with it, too. I couldn't have done this without you." She pressed a hand to her chest. "It's funny, isn't it? So much emphasis is put on romantic relationships. But here we are, having only known each other for a few weeks, but we're bonded. Possibly because I'm a wreck and have been drinking your wine and spewing my guts to you." She laughed. "But still, I really do appreciate having you as a friend. It's rare to click with someone like we do." She held up her tea mug. "Here's to many more years of friendship."

Kirsty clinked her mug. "I'll drink to friendship." She was happy to have Ginger in the friend zone, where she belonged. Saffron, on the other hand… Kirsty filled her mouth with cake to stop herself from going down another dead end. "The lemon and poppy seed is great, too. Betty makes a mean cake."

Ginger glanced up at Kirsty. "I noticed you haven't answered my initial question about you and Saffron. Things seemed weird the other day in the shop. Has something happened?"

Kirsty went to speak, then stopped. Should she tell Ginger? If they truly were friends, she would. Her mind raced as she tried to work out what was the right thing to do.

"We kissed." Her mouth made the decision before her mind could catch up.

Ginger's mouth formed an "O." "And?" She sat forward, her forehead creased with concentration.

"And nothing. It was all going great, but then she got a text from Echo. Saying she missed her. And I saw it. So I left."

Ginger threw her head back and let out a sigh. "Fucking Echo."

"Exactly, that's my concern." Kirsty's mind was still filled with images of Saffron caked in leather. But she also knew what Echo looked like in leather, thanks to the movie.

"You know what happened?"

Kirsty shook her head. "No. I know Saffron's going to

disappear. I know I don't want to get in the middle of something that's not done."

"It's done. I promise you."

"If you'd seen this text message, you wouldn't have said so. She told Saffron she missed her in her bed."

Ginger's face clouded over. "She probably does. But that's her issue, not Saff's. She shouldn't have been such an idiot and posted private photos of them on her social media, should she?"

Kirsty froze. Her stomach dropped. "She did that?" How awful for Saffron.

"You didn't see them? Hear about them?"

Kirsty shook her head. "I'm not really a social media person. I'm barely on top of it for the shop."

"You must be the only person alive who didn't see the shots. Echo swore it was a friend who posted them. But it was on her account, and it was conveniently timed when the movie came out. She did it for her career, I have no doubt about that. Sure, she deleted them afterwards, but the damage was done. For someone like Saffron, who has always had trust issues, it was the last thing she needed."

Kirsty sat back. "Wow. I didn't know." She ran through all the conversations she'd had with Saffron so far. She'd never wanted to talk about Echo. Now Kirsty knew why. "But why didn't she just explain things to me? Tell me what happened?"

Ginger sighed. "My sister doesn't open up easily. Even to me. She's also probably still processing it all, as it was only a few months ago. You can ask her for the full details, but she won't want to tell you. She doesn't want to offend anyone. But she needs to remember you can't please everyone all the time.

It's just not possible. And if you try to, you end up pleasing nobody, least of all yourself. Saffron's doing it with her career and her love life at the moment. Quite some feat." She leaned in to Kirsty. "Promise me one thing, though. Don't give up on her. My sister is a wonderful, loyal person. But she's also her own worst enemy."

Kirsty pushed the cake away, suddenly not so hungry anymore. "I'm not going anywhere. This is my home. But the thing is, it's not Saffron's home, is it? Because of that, I'm not sure I'm the person who's going to make Saffron happy, no matter how much you might want me to be."

Ginger shook her head. "I know Saffron wants a change. She's had the next *Girl Racer* script sitting in her house for ages, and she hasn't read it. Maybe now would be a good time for her to take some time out. She's never done that. Slowed down. Cleared her head."

"Shouldn't you be telling her this?"

"I did, the other night. Maybe I need to ring Echo and tell her the same. She's not right for Saffron."

"And I am?" Kirsty's body told her she was, but her mind was shaking its head.

Ginger looked her directly in the eye. "You might not see it now, but I really think you could be."

Chapter 18

At half past nine on Wednesday morning, the sun still hung relatively low in the east, but the pleasant temperature, the cawing of seagulls, and other sounds of summer propelled Saffron to leave her house for her daily walk much earlier than normal.

As she meandered past the beach huts, her mind wandered to Kirsty. What did she do on a beautiful summer morning? Was she in the wine shop already? Seemed early for wine. Well, not for Saffron's parents, who enjoyed what they termed, breakfast wine. Not that Saffron thought of Kirsty as a boozer, but Saffron imagined owning a business more than likely involved loads of tedious and time-consuming tasks, like inventory and spreadsheets.

A shiver put an extra pep into Saffron's step, the harbour coming into view. She loved exploring the stalls of local artists and shop owners, an awe deep within for the creators willingly standing to the side while someone critiqued their work in real time. There was no way Saffron could ever put herself through that. She always showed up for the red-carpet portion of opening night, but slipped out when the movie started.

Given it was still early in the day, the crowd consisted mostly of locals and the owners setting up for the day. Saffron purchased a coffee, buying an insulated stainless steel to-go cup with a blue old-fashioned rowing boat painted on it. Perhaps buying a piece of kitsch was silly, but she couldn't resist having yet another root to the seaside town.

Sipping the piping hot coffee, which combatted the occasional chilly breeze coming off the water, Saffron stepped into a stall with crafty home items. The type of mementos tourists would purchase for their avant-garde family and friends.

Dangling from the ceiling were strings with randomly coloured puffy balls spaced an inch apart, reaching nearly to the floor.

"Are you joining the dark side?"

Saffron whipped around, nearly taking Kirsty out. "Jesus! You startled me."

"I'm sorry." Kirsty laughed, darting her hands up in a *don't shoot* way.

Saffron placed a hand on her chest, in an effort to steady her pounding heart. "Don't be. It's nice to see you. Can't you tell how excited I am?"

Kirsty offered a timid smile, but didn't say the same.

"Er, what did you mean about the dark side?"

"Oh, just a lame joke."

"About *Star Wars*?" Saffron scrunched her brow.

Kirsty held one of the larger sized puffy balls on the string dangling between them. "Wasn't gunning for Darth Vader but referencing a lesbian checking out artwork with 20 or so balls. Seems a bit much."

"Right! Now I get it." Saffron laughed at herself. "I was

thinking of getting some of these for Ginger. Enough to cover a doorway, like those beaded curtains that were popular in the sixties. Or was it the seventies?"

"Why are you asking me? Are you being ageist?" Kirsty challenged, her face frustratingly devoid of emotion.

Was she mad? Teasing? Better to act neutral but close to apologising. "What? No! It was me talking out loud."

"How else do you talk?"

Saffron inspected Kirsty's grey eyes, unable to decipher the tone of the conversation. Christ, the woman could be infuriating, keeping everything bottled up. "Are you giving me a hard time, or have I upset you?"

Kirsty's easy-going smile, with a pinch of snark, put Saffron at ease. "Just teasing. I promise. What have you been up to since we last saw each other?"

Saffron leaned against one of the dangling strings, nearly losing her balance. Kirsty reached out to prevent Saffron from toppling over.

"Thanks." Saffron licked some spilled coffee off the back of her hand. "FYI: these are not a good substitute for a wall."

"Duly noted. It's good to have you around to test these things out."

"Glad my stupidity serves a purpose."

"You made me smile." Kirsty treated Saffron with another killer one.

"Then it was worth it. You have a lovely smile."

Kirsty's eyes dropped to the worn wooden planks under their feet.

"To answer your question, I haven't been up to much. Unless pottering about my house counts as something."

"Is that right? You better watch out. That can lead to slowing down and enjoying life. Before you know it, you'll be strolling the High Street like a local without a care in the world."

"That doesn't sound too bad."

"Maybe it's something you can do for a bit, but it's hard to see Saffron Oliver settling down, not jet setting around the world, filming movies." Kirsty blinked. "You aren't wearing a baseball hat."

"Not needed during the week. It's only on the weekends when the Down From London types invade. Most around these parts have grown used to me and simply say hi and move on with their lives. It's so refreshing." Saffron's massage therapist would be shocked by the looseness of her shoulders and might not feel needed anymore.

"Is it? You don't miss people surreptitiously snapping your photo? Or staring with adoring eyes?" Kirsty batted her lashes.

"I've told you before that type of attention makes me uncomfortable."

Kirsty's expression baffled Saffron, as if Kirsty didn't quite believe that statement.

"Back to Ginger and the balls. What do you think?" Saffron crossed her arms, appraising them.

"In what way?"

"I want to get Ginger a gift for the party, and…" Saffron looked back at the puffy balls on strings. "To be honest, my assistant usually does my gift shopping. From the shocked expression on your face, that's a good thing."

"Buying gifts can be hard." Kirsty studied the dangling balls like they were a masterpiece she didn't understand.

"I bet it's not for you." There was a twinge of tightness in her left shoulder.

"Not true. Every year, I struggle buying my dad something for Christmas. How many silly socks can one man own?" Kirsty panned the contents of the stall. "You know what, just on the other side, I spied something I think would be the perfect gift for Ginger."

"Lead the way." Saffron motioned she was at Kirsty's mercy. If only Kirsty understood the true effect she was having on Saffron, whose heart hadn't settled yet and never seemed to whenever the bedevilling woman was near.

A man in a yellow T-shirt and shorts walked his black lab.

"Hello, Rufus. How are you?" Saffron rubbed behind the dog's ears.

"I swear he looks out for you every day." The man grinned.

"That's quite a compliment coming from such a handsome fellow." Saffron gave the dog one final pet before the two of them took off, Rufus pulling his owner as only a large puppy could.

"My, my, my. You are making friends in town." Kirsty chuckled. "I don't believe I know Rufus and...?"

"I don't actually know the man's name." Saffron hitched a shoulder. "Now, the gift."

"It's over here." Kirsty led them to a jewellery stall. "Here it is." She slid a silver necklace off a hook. "The pendant is a lotus flower."

"It has a pearl dangling from the flower." Saffron tapped it, the gem bobbing back and forth. "It's beautiful."

Kirsty held it aloft, the sun glinting off the silver. "Lotus flowers symbolise rebirth, and that's what Ginger's party is about."

"And the pearl is for Sandy Cove, where she's starting over. It's perfect. I can't thank you enough."

"Happy to help my client."

Saffron's stomach plummeted, but she didn't want the interaction to end so soon. "Can I buy you a coffee? It's the least I can do since you're saving my arse helping me shop. Or do you have to rush off?"

"That'd be lovely. Helena is opening the shop this morning, so I have some time."

"Perfect. What about a pastry? I really owe you. I would have been here all day and still ended up with the balls."

There was a long, uncomfortable pause before Kirsty conceded, "I do have a sweet tooth."

"Fab. I'll pay up here and then get pastries and coffees. Why don't you grab one of the tables, and I can try this new thing I'm learning. I think you'd call it slowing down and spending quality time with a girlfriend." Saffron couldn't believe the word fell from her mouth. "Er, I mean girlfriends like in *Sex in the City*. Not—right. Why don't I stop"—she mimed digging a hole—"and get on coffees and pastries? Even I can't fuck that up."

"Don't sell yourself short." Kirsty's laughter reassuringly wrapped around Saffron. Everything about the woman made Saffron feel better and normal, and when they were apart, she couldn't handle the silence.

Saffron playfully snarled, liking that Kirsty understood her, which only dug the dagger in all the more given Kirsty had been clear that nothing could happen between them. Damn Echo and her mind games.

With the necklace now safely in a box, Saffron marched to the coffee hut. "Joe, I need a refill." Saffron handed him her to-go cup. "Another coffee and…" She checked out the offerings. "I need some pastries, but I don't know which ones. Can you select a dozen to knock my socks off?"

"Leave it to me." He fixed the coffees first before tackling the pastries, selecting ones from the case with tongs, delicately placing them into a pink box. "I wish all my customers were as easy as you."

"Experience has taught me it's best to leave the important matters in life to the experts." Saffron tapped her card and dropped a tenner into the tip jar.

Kirsty had her eyes glued to her phone when Saffron set the box on the table. "What's that?"

"Open it and see." Saffron took a seat in one of the metal chairs with plastic blue slats.

"Let me guess. You panicked and got one of everything."

"Close, but not on the money." Saffron sipped her drink, enjoying the fact Kirsty got that about her.

"Out with it."

"I let Joe select the treats. I just supplied the number."

Kirsty, shaking her head, laughed. "You really are used to having everyone do everything for you."

"Hey now. Joe wished every customer was like me."

"Because you probably bought out half of his stock for the day, and he can close up early." Kirsty picked up the box. "Given the weight, you supplied an outrageous number."

"A dozen."

"I can't eat that much!"

"I'll take what we don't eat over to Ginger's. Are you going to see what's inside?" Saffron scooted to the edge of her chair.

"Probably a million calories."

"I was gunning for a billion. Go on."

Kirsty lifted the lid, her eyes growing large. "Oh, wow. I think you nailed the billion mark."

Saffron leaned over to eye the goodies. "Who doesn't love a fruit tart for breakfast?"

Kirsty placed the tart on a paper plate, giving it and a plastic fork to Saffron. "Me, I like something with a bit more class." She winked at Saffron, putting an iced bun on her plate.

"Yes, dough with icing on top is the pinnacle of class."

"Don't be a hater. Even Paul Hollywood of *The Great British Bake Off* finds the simple delicacies scrumptious with a touch of nostalgia." Kirsty kissed her fingertips with a flourish.

Saffron wiped her brow and ditched the fork, picking up the tart for a bite and moaning in delight. Washing it down with coffee, she said, "You have to eat my tart."

"So early in the day." Kirsty arched an eyebrow.

Saffron, her cheeks burning, held the tart for Kirsty, standing her ground. "You know you want to."

Kirsty met Saffron's gaze. "Just for you." She took it and bit into it.

Saffron widened her eyes. "Well?"

Kirsty swiped crumbs off her chin, handed it back, and mumbled, "You're right. It's to die for."

"Why didn't you have trust?"

"Oh, I do." Kirsty added, "In Joe."

Saffron laughed. "Ouch, but considering you had to select the gift for my sister, I can't really defend myself."

"I think she'll like the necklace." Kirsty licked icing from a finger.

"Are you kidding? She's going to love it." Saffron sighed. "I need to spend more time with Ginger. It's one of the reasons I'm here."

"Do you have another reason?"

"A couple. I needed a break, and I've always liked being near the water." Saffron's gaze wandered to the lazy waves. "I like it here."

"I wouldn't want to live anywhere else."

"Maybe we can spend more time together."

"Of course. When you visit Ginger during breaks in filming, it'd be nice to catch up."

Saffron eyed the lighthouse, wishing it could guide her way to Kirsty's heart, because right now, Saffron seemed to be drifting firmly in friendly waters with no hope of more.

Chapter 19

Kirsty walked along the beachfront to the back deck of Ginger's house, finding its occupant sitting at the table squinting into her phone. Having spent years walking past this house and wondering who lived there, she was more than thrilled she could just walk in now. Especially when the owner didn't see her coming and Kirsty could creep up on her.

She made her final steps light, then sprang forward. "Boo!"

Ginger jumped in the air, her phone leaping from her hand.

Kirsty caught it with her right hand as if it had been choreographed all along.

Ginger moved her sunglasses to sit on top of her platinum blond hair. "You can go off people, you know that?" But her blue eyes told a different story.

"You could never go off me. When it comes to the Oliver sisters, I'm like a lucky charm." At least, she was with one Oliver sister. The other one, who the fuck knew? They were so hot and cold, she'd given up even trying to work Saffron out of late. She'd been very sweet in the market, almost as if none of the previous stuff had gone on. Why couldn't Kirsty meet a woman with no history, no issues to work out? Did they even exist?

She sat beside Ginger, crossing one leg over the other. She returned Ginger's phone, then fished her laptop out of her bag. No more brooding on Saffron and what might happen. She had to live in the present. Ginger's divorce party was in a handful of days. "Ready to go over your drinks order? You're ordering too much, so I've toned it down."

Ginger held up a hand. "You don't know my friends. If there's booze left over, I'll give everyone a goody bag. Leave the order as is, please."

Kirsty raised an eyebrow, but let it go. If that's what Ginger wanted, she could have it. She amended the order. "Next thing. Cake topper. Did you sort that?"

She got a wide grin in return. "Oh yes. Wait till you see it. I've been chuckling since it arrived." She pulled her sunglasses down again, peering up into the blazing hot morning. "I need to get an umbrella for this deck. That's something I never thought I'd say living at the UK seaside." She sat forward. "I wanted to ask you about a suit that turned up this morning. I wondered if you'd ordered it?"

Kirsty frowned. "Not that I recall."

Ginger blew out a breath. "That's what I thought. I've been sitting here wondering if I'm going mad. My parents died too young to get dementia. My grandparents were all dead by the time I was ten. So I've no idea what our family history is when it comes to losing your marbles. Is this the first step? Ordering suits you don't remember?"

"What's it like?"

"Sparkly." Ginger jumped up. "You know what, even though it's not really my style and it's a bit big, I was intrigued. Somebody's put a lot of work into it." She pointed a finger at Kirsty. "Stay there, I'm going to try it on. Help yourself to coffee."

Kirsty did as she was told, pouring herself a cup from Ginger's cafetière. Five minutes later, someone clearing their throat made her look up. She did a double take at the sight in front of her.

"Wow. You look…" Kirsty couldn't quite find the words.

"Like a gameshow host?"

She let out a strangled laugh. "Or perhaps an extra from Studio 54."

Ginger shook her head. "Liberace's love child?" She looked down at the sequined silver trouser suit, tapping its shoulder pads, before stroking its black velvet lapels and pocket trim.

"If you were a pop star, you could get away with it."

"But I'm not. I'm a web developer from Sandy Cove."

A wolf whistle split the air. When Kirsty raised her head, Saffron was running up from the beach. Was she stalking her? It was a small town, but she didn't bump into anyone else as much as she did Saffron.

"It came!" Saffron opened the gate, wiping sand from her jeans. Barking sounded from behind her. She ran back out to Rufus, getting down on her haunches and making a fuss of him. "See you tomorrow, Greg!" She waved them off, then came back in, closing the gate behind her.

"You found out the owner's name, too?" Kirsty asked, impressed.

Saffron nodded. "It seemed rude not to."

Ginger cleared her throat. "What did you just say? This was you?" She swept a hand up and down in front of her.

Her sister nodded. "I know you said you didn't want the

179

Milan treatment, but I asked my LA stylist anyway, seeing as you say no to most things I suggest." Saffron touched one of the sleeves that Ginger had rolled up.

"That's because they're more for you, not for me." She eyed her sister. "In fact, this would look far better on you. Fit you better, too. It's younger, more hip. You could pull it off because you're a movie star. Whereas on me, it looks a little... *Boogie Nights*."

Saffron's shoulders slumped. "I was just trying to surprise you. Do a nice thing. But I can send it back."

Ginger walked over, taking her sister in her arms. She was a few inches shorter, so Saffron put her head on her shoulder.

"It was a nice gesture, but I can buy my own clothes, okay? You should try it on."

Saffron nodded. "I might. Pack it back up and I'll take it home." She untangled herself from Ginger and sat next to Kirsty. "Nice surprise seeing you here."

"Same." Kirsty hadn't meant to be so honest, but she couldn't help it. Saffron brought it out of her. Whatever it was between them, the heat of it was far stronger than the sun.

Saffron's cheeks turned pink as she looked anywhere but at Kirsty. She cleared her throat and glanced over at Ginger. "Anyway, the reason I'm here is because I decided I want to get a cocktail tonight. I thought I'd ask my sister to join me."

Ginger frowned. "Tonight? Hell, no. I've got a mobile beauty lady coming round to pamper me stupid." She pointed. "Ask Kirsty. I'm going to get out of this suit before an agent walks by and signs me up for the remake of *Saturday Night Fever*."

Saffron rolled her eyes. "Very droll." When Ginger was gone, she turned to Kirsty, her sure tone faltering. "What do you think of Ginger's idea? A cocktail with me later?"

Kirsty blew out her cheeks. Was that wise? "It sounds suspiciously like a date, which we agreed we weren't going to go on."

Saffron moved her mouth one way, then the other. "It's not a date. It's an outing. Just two friends having a drink."

"You really believe that?"

"With all my heart." Saffron crossed her own, just so Kirsty understood.

"An outing?"

"Uh-huh. Pick you up at 7.30?"

Kirsty looked her dead in the eye. Saffron would make a terrible poker player. "7.30."

* * *

An impromptu outing. Not a date. *An outing.*

What the fuck did she wear to an outing? Because for all their stop-start so far, Kirsty and Saffron had never actually gone out in the evening just the two of them. No family or friends. Just them. Which made this a very strange non-date.

Should she have said no? Probably. But it was her night off, and she was still in her 40s. She might as well live a little while she could. She'd said something similar to her mum this week and had been clunked over the head with a tea towel. In her mum's world, Kirsty was definitely not old.

Tonight, she was going out with a hot movie star, so she

was going to channel her inner 35-year-old. It wasn't that long ago. She could totally pull it off.

Luckily, she was on top of her laundry, so her perfect outfit was clean. She sent up a silent prayer to a god she didn't believe in. It couldn't hurt to have as many people as possible on her side tonight.

For this non-date.

Very much a non-date.

7pm rolled around sooner than she thought. Kirsty took a breath, recalling the scorched look from Saffron earlier. Had it been scorched? Or had it just been in her imagination? She'd soon find out. She steadied her hand as she applied foundation, mascara, powder, and a little lipstick. She studied herself, then gave a nod. She could pass for late 30s.

Nearly game time.

Kirsty tried waiting on her sofa, but she couldn't sit still. She hoovered her sofa cushions. Dusted the coffee table. Straightened her copies of *Decanter*.

When she checked her watch, it was still only 7.15.

Her phone beeped.

Kirsty's stomach sank. If Saffron was cancelling, she was going to punch something.

It was from Helena, asking her to come down to confirm some website login details.

Kirsty jumped up, checked she had all the essentials in her bag and went downstairs. When she walked in the shop, Helena's eyes widened.

"I don't think I've seen you this dressed to kill since... Well, I can't remember. That's how long it's been."

"It's not too over the top, is it? Too much for a Monday?"

Maybe she should have gone for jeans rather than tapered orange trousers and a figure-hugging shirt? It was just a cocktail on the harbour, after all.

They weren't going *out-out*.

Helena shook her head. "No, it's perfect. It's just, your hair, your make-up, the whole ensemble." She paused. "I love that shirt. The hot pink is fabulous on you. And your shoes."

Kirsty's feet were adorned with freshly shined two-tone brogues.

"I've been waiting for you to wear those again. They're at least three levels up from your slippers."

The blood rushed to Kirsty's cheeks. "Thanks." She wasn't comfortable in the spotlight. Whereas Saffron's job was literally to be in it. But she wasn't going to focus on that now.

"Only, with your shirt showing that much cleavage, she won't be looking at your shoes, trust me."

Kirsty really hoped the make-up was covering the pink of her cheeks.

"You wanted the website details? It's all in the logbook, in the drawer." She pointed under the counter. "I loved the new illustrations Anton sent through. Can't wait to see the new promo pages, too. When Ginger gets the online shop going, we should get some new business." Kirsty beamed. "Thanks for doing this. You've really stepped up of late."

Helena gave her a wink. "Anything to drum up new business. Anton's putting the finishing touches to it this week, pulling all the images I've snapped for the promo pages from my cloud. At least, that's what he told me, so I believe him. I had to check there were no dodgy ones of me or Hugh in there before I gave him access."

Kirsty made a face. "TMI."

The shop door opened and Saffron walked in. Suddenly, all thoughts of Helena and Hugh vanished. Saffron looked every inch the movie star. Her trousers were low-slung, her low-buttoned shirt an invitation, and her open biker boots screamed sex bomb.

This was Kirsty's non-date for the evening.

It was as if she'd been transported to a far-off lesbian dreamscape. She concentrated hard on not letting her jaw hit the floor.

"I saw you through the window." Saffron hesitated. "You ready to go from here?"

Kirsty nodded, her throat suddenly too dry to talk. She turned to Helena, not meeting her wide-eyed stare, wanting to get out of the shop as quick as she could.

Somehow, this moment was way too intimate to be shared, and they hadn't even got out of the shop yet.

She wasn't sure how she was going to cope.

"Have fun!" Helena shouted as they left.

Kirsty guided them out of view down the High Street before she risked a glance at Saffron.

The heat in Saffron's stare made her stop in her tracks. Her eyes raked Kirsty's body.

Kirsty stood stock still, balling her fists so tight she was sure to leave a mark.

"You look amazing," Saffron said. "I feel like I should kiss you on the cheek at least, but it's a non-date."

Kirsty nodded. "Right."

"High five?"

Kirsty gave her a look. "Let's just walk to the bar, shall we?"

Saffron did as she was told.

Kirsty tried to regulate her breathing. It wasn't easy. "By the way, you look incredible, too."

Chapter 20

Saffron continued to sneak glimpses of Kirsty as they walked—no, strolled to the bar. Damn, the woman was the definition of smoking hot and it was going to take a lot of self-control not to keep saying that.

Kirsty cranked her head, looking at Saffron, with a raised brow that meant business.

Uh oh. Think, Saffron. "This is nice, isn't it? Two friends, lackadaisically making their way for a friendly night out."

"I-it is." The words escaped Kirsty hesitantly, as if waiting for the punchline. "Was that your way of saying I'm walking too slowly?"

"Not at all." Saffron bumped her shoulder into Kirsty. "I might be getting the hang of this."

"Of what?"

"Enjoying the moment, not rushing from one place to the next. And, with you, which makes it extra nice." Saffron flinched. Kirsty had been clear. This didn't qualify as a date, so it was paramount not to utter statements like that. Was there a way to suck those words back into her mouth?

Kirsty stopped in her tracks. "Do we need to define what this is again?"

"It most definitely isn't a date." Saffron ground her thumb into her palm but couldn't stop herself from grinning like a fool.

"Your smile says differently." Kirsty also seemed to be losing the *whatever you do, don't grin* battle.

"This is just how I am when I'm totally relaxed. It must be the sea air. It's done more for me than three years of painful massage treatments." Saffron shook her arms out and rolled her neck, the smile still firmly affixed.

"You kind of look like a creepy doll."

"Your digs aren't going to work." Saffron briefly clasped a hand around Kirsty's, but quickly dropped it. "Here we are. Let me get the door. Not because it's a date. It's just the right thing to do." She yanked it open, expecting it to be much heavier than it was, smashing it into her forehead, nearly knocking herself over. "I'm okay. That was totally planned."

"Yeah, right. I never would have guessed an action star would actually be so clumsy." Kirsty chuckled.

"If you could keep that morsel to yourself, I'd greatly appreciate it. I've got a rep to protect." Saffron pressed a finger to her lips, delighting in seeing Kirsty's gaze skim along the finger and landing on the lips. Kirsty visibly swallowing.

Inside the Harbour Bar, Saffron spied a high table with two stools, and placed a hand on the small of Kirsty's back, guiding them, pleasantly surprised Kirsty didn't break the contact. That had to be a good sign, but probably best to keep playing it cool. Or Kirsty would continue to call Saffron out, and she hated hearing how they were only friends.

Saffron pretended to hold an order pad. "What can I get you, Ms?"

Kirsty, though, stared past Saffron as if she'd seen a dead relative spring back to life.

Saffron stood closer. "You okay?"

"It's Anna."

Saffron started to turn her head—

"No, don't." Kirsty held Saffron's chin in place, their eyes locking for a blissful second, before Kirsty's hand dropped like a stone.

Saffron froze before regaining the ability to speak. "*Anna*, Anna? Your ex?"

"Yes." The blood seeped out of Kirsty's thinning lips.

"Do you want to go somewhere else?"

"No, we have a table."

"Are you sure? I can work my Saffron Oliver magic and get a table at any other place." She snapped her fingers.

"I thought you were enjoying your anonymity in Sandy Cove."

"I am, but for you, I would do it." She'd do anything, really, which she absolutely should not say aloud. It was ironic, considering Kirsty liked verbal communication, yet Saffron had to keep her true words in check.

"No, it's fine. As I said before, Anna isn't that far away. The chance of seeing her with a girlfriend is always a risk." Kirsty visibly bolstered her resolve by sitting up straighter and trying to appear relaxed, which only halfway succeeded.

"Do you want me to pour it on? Have her think we're a hot item and make Anna rue the day she broke your heart?"

"Given your track record, or do I need to remind you that you just nearly knocked yourself out with the door, I'm thinking it's best not to put myself at risk. Besides, she's not worth it." Kirsty did a shake of the head, as if resetting a switch. "I'll have an aperol spritz."

"You got it, Captain." Saffron, clicked her boots together and saluted. When her back was turned, she wanted to slap herself across the face. A salute? Why couldn't she stop being so nervous and making an arse of herself?

The woman behind the bar, pulling a pint, raised her brows expectantly.

"Could I have an aperol spritz..." Saffron leaned closer since a group of men charged in, "and a margarita."

The woman with a nose piercing and heavily tattooed left arm nodded.

"Kirsty! Is that you?"

Saffron casually glanced over her shoulder to see Anna and the girlfriend standing at the table.

"Hello, Anna. How are you?" Kirsty's frosty tone could turn a person into a snowwoman in the middle of a heatwave.

"Have you heard the news?" Anna bounced on the balls of her feet, not picking up on Kirsty's stiffening shoulders.

"What?"

Oh God. Was Anna going to announce she was engaged? Saffron wanted to run interference, but her mind went blank. Using her hair to protect being spotted, Saffron shamelessly eavesdropped.

"Saffron Oliver has been spotted all over town," Anna squealed like a fourteen-year-old girl.

"Is that right?" There was a hint of a knowing smile on Kirsty's lips.

"All the lesbians in town must be swooning. I mean, she's the hottest dyke walking this earth. I was hoping to spy her tonight"—Anna glanced around—"but sadly, my wish hasn't come true."

Kirsty shifted on her stool, glancing down at her lap.

The bartender finished both drinks, and Saffron paid.

"Here you go, darling." Saffron set the aperol spritz in front of Kirsty.

Anna's and her girlfriend's jaws dropped.

"Hi, I'm Saffron." She put her hand out to the girlfriend first, who shook it, but didn't supply a name. No matter.

Anna, slightly recovered, gushed, "I can't believe this is happening. Can someone pinch me?" She held her arm out and Saffron wanted to give it a painful twist.

Instead, she laughed as if that was the funniest thing she'd ever heard, but it wasn't by far and not the first time she'd heard that exact line.

"What are you doing in Sandy Cove?" Anna still held her arm out as if Saffron should pinch her.

Stop tempting me, bitch.

"I heard it was beautiful here." Saffron stared intently at Kirsty. "And, I'm happy to report, I haven't encountered anything more stunning."

Kirsty's face could rival the ripest of strawberries.

"I bet you can't wait to get back to the city, though. I mean"—Anna looked to her right and left—"this place doesn't have a lot to offer the likes of you."

"Oh, I'm not sure I agree. I've found it to be just what I need." Again, her eyes were glued to Kirsty's.

Anna's girlfriend whispered something. Anna seemed to argue against whatever was said, but then let out an angry rush of air.

Painting on a fake smile, Anna said, "We're meeting Jane's parents for dinner, so we can't stay."

"That's too bad." Saffron blew out a disappointed breath in a *maybe next time* way.

The two left and Saffron took a seat, reaching for her margarita, doing her best to focus on the lack of ice and not melt from Kirsty's glare.

Kirsty snorted to snag Saffron's attention and for added measure, she crossed her arms. "I thought I said not to play it up."

"Who says I was?" Saffron sipped her drink, licking some salt off her lip.

"Are you kidding?" Her eyes bulged. "You laid it on pretty thick."

Saffron placed a not-so-innocent hand on her chest. "Are you calling me a bad actor?" She released a fake titter. "Besides, I don't think Anna noticed a thing. She doesn't seem the sharpest. You deserve so much better than a woman who had to be reminded they had plans."

"She was never much of a family person."

Saffron cocked her head. "That strikes me as odd, since you're close with your parents."

"It may have been an issue." Kirsty adjusted her shirt sleeve.

"I'm serious, though. You deserve better." Saffron leaned over the table, her head ever so close to Kirsty.

For a split second, it seemed that Kirsty might brush her lips to Saffron's, but pulled back instead.

"This is hard, isn't it? Staying in the friend zone?" Saffron didn't budge, but the hope burning inside churned into unease in the pit of her stomach.

"Maybe we should call it a night to be safe. I mean, we've both been clear. Nothing can happen between us."

"Yes. You've been *adamant* about that." Saffron gestured she was only calling a spade a spade.

"Oh, nice guilt trip. If I remember correctly, you also said it wouldn't be a good idea since our lifestyles are so different."

Saffron slouched, but wasn't ready to give up the fight. Not one that mattered this much to her. "You know what they say, opposites attract."

"Been there. Done that." Kirsty hooked a thumb over her shoulder, indicating Anna who was long gone.

"We can't let the booze go to waste." Saffron gestured to both of their full glasses. "Tell you what, we can talk about Ginger's party. Keep it strictly professional."

"Can you keep the compliments to yourself?"

Saffron rested her head on bent elbow, letting out a frustrated breath. "What woman hates to hear how amazing she is?"

Kirsty made a circle in the air with two fingers. "Bullseye! That's exactly what I'm talking about. You can't keep doing that."

"What?"

"Being charming. It's driving me insane. This isn't a date. Kindly refrain from saying things you would say on a date." Given Kirsty was admonishing, her tone didn't come across like she meant it.

"You have a lot of rules for friends." Saffron crossed her arms to tamp down the desire to grin. Kirsty was doing her best to stop whatever was happening between the two, but

Saffron guessed from the desire building in those sexy greys, Kirsty wasn't being all that honest about staying friends.

"Do you agree to the terms?"

"Can you refresh my memory?" Saffron tapped her temple.

"Here's the gist. The moment you start being charming, I'm outta here."

"I will do my absolute best to be nothing but a beast." Saffron offered the smile that made movie audiences swoon, according to numerous sources.

Kirsty licked her lips.

Saffron continued her smouldering look.

Kirsty cleared her throat.

Saffron boosted her left eyebrow to the perfect angle. It'd taken years in front of the mirror to master it and to make it look effortless. And, Saffron believed deploying it right then would be make or break.

"Fuck." Kirsty blew out a breath.

"Yes." Hopefulness whooshed through Saffron.

"This isn't going to work, is it?"

"What do you mean? I'm having a grand time." Oddly, even with all the back and forth, Saffron didn't want to be anywhere else.

Kirsty started to speak, her lips forming the word no, but she stopped, sighing. "Shall we go back to yours?"

"I thought you'd never ask." Saffron let out a victorious whoop.

"You really can't control yourself, can you? Everything about you exudes charm."

"Not sure about that. Most think I'm stuck up, because

I hide behind a bitchy veneer. With you, I don't want to be anyone else but the real me."

Kirsty's chest hitched. "Are you okay with ditching the drinks now?"

"I don't see anything but you." Since the moment Saffron first laid eyes on Kirsty.

Chapter 21

They swerved a gaggle of teenagers on the way back, both Kirsty and Saffron keeping their heads down and feet moving lest the group spy who Saffron was. Now was not the time to stop and pose for selfies. Not when the air around them was thick with unsaid words and feelings.

Kirsty still wasn't sure how that sentence had dropped from her lips, but it had. Her heart jumping ahead of her mind. "*Shall we go back to yours?*" Daring. Kirsty had taken control and rolled the dice. From here on in, it was unchartered territory.

That thought made her heart skip a beat.

Saffron glanced Kirsty's way as the Beachcomber came into view.

Beside them, the sea shimmered under the burnt orange sunset. But all Kirsty could see were the flash of Saffron's eyes, a strip of white when she smiled. Even in dim light, her smile had wattage.

Saffron took Kirsty's hand as they climbed the stairs to her veranda and front door. Still no words had been spoken.

Every muscle Kirsty possessed contracted at the thought of what might happen next. Had they been building up to this moment since the day they met? Perhaps.

Saffron managed her front door far better than the one in the bar, pulling Kirsty through with no ceremony. She walked straight through to the open-plan living space with purpose, snapping on the lights.

Kirsty blinked, glancing around. There had been changes since she was last here. A new painting. A fresh rug. Some flowers in a vase. Stylish patterned cushions. It even smelled more lived-in, like Saffron had settled.

"Have you been shopping? It feels different in here. More like someone actually lives here full-time."

Saffron turned, draping all nearly six feet of her against her kitchen island.

Damn, she was sexy.

She nodded. "What you said got through. I've never put down roots, so why not start with a vase or a local painting of the harbour? Even though I might not stay in this house, whatever I buy can come with me. So, I did a little shopping. Made the place feel a little more like me. Turns out, I have an eye."

"Good for you. I know that's not your normal."

"None of this is." Saffron's stare was loaded. "Do you want a drink?"

"Sure."

"Wine, beer?"

Kirsty shrugged. "Surprise me."

She walked over to the island. Somehow, the lounge was too far from Saffron. The bar had been too public and had too much of Anna. The walk home had been too concrete and crowded. Now it was just the two of them, she wanted it to be softer, closer. She hoped that's what Saffron wanted, too.

Unless she'd read this wrong.

She really hoped she hadn't read it wrong.

Saffron busied herself in the fridge, getting drinks. The pad Kirsty had seen before was on the island. The one Saffron carried everywhere with her. The one she guarded with her life.

Kirsty couldn't help it. She lifted the cover. When she saw the intricate work there, she couldn't stop herself looking closer.

"These are incredible. Did you do all these?"

Saffron cast her gaze to the floor, then returned it to Kirsty. She nodded.

Kirsty flicked through some more. "You're not just some hobbyist. These are so richly drawn and beautiful. Have you worked these up into paintings, too?"

"Some of them." She gave Kirsty a glass of sparkling wine before shutting the pad. "It's just some stuff I've been working on." She glanced up into Kirsty's eyes, her sapphire gaze reaching in and gathering Kirsty close. "A lot of the reason I started sketching again is you."

Kirsty put a finger to her chest. "Me?" Electricity crackled in the air.

Saffron nodded. "You told me to be who I wanted to be. To slow down. You and Ginger both." She gave a wry grin. "So, I did. I finally remembered who I am and who I *really* want to be. When I got into acting, I thought that would make my parents proud. It didn't." She shook her head. "Then, after they died, I stopped caring about anything else. All my old passions. The things that truly make me tick. I threw myself into my work and put my art aside. I even put my sister aside, which I'm not proud of."

Kirsty reached out and took Saffron's hand. A bolt of desire flashed through her. Her breath hitched in her chest.

Had Saffron felt it, too?

"You were young."

"Still." Saffron's chest heaved. She put down her wine.

Kirsty followed suit.

Saffron stepped closer to her. "But now I live here, I've reconnected with Ginger. Nothing has made me happier in ages. Spending time with my sister, having time for my art. But what's been the icing on the cake is meeting you. Because you care about everything you should. You always have. Your family. Your friends. Your passions. I love those handwritten notes you put on your wine: it shows who you are."

Kirsty's heartbeat roared in her ears as the weight of Saffron's intense stare pressed into her. "I love my job, that's all."

"Most people don't. Most people settle. You didn't."

"You know who you are, too." Kirsty gripped the island with her right hand. "You're Saffron Oliver, movie star supreme."

Saffron smiled. "Also Saffron Oliver, stupidest woman alive when I'm around you. You might have awakened my soul and told me to be true to myself, but you also make me walk into doors. Did you ever wonder why I did that?"

Kirsty shook her head. "Because you're clumsy?"

"Only when I'm around you. Because what you think matters." She lifted Kirsty's left hand and gently kissed her knuckles. The effect was the same as if she'd just pressed her tongue to Kirsty's core. Thunder rolled down Kirsty. She gripped the kitchen island like her life depended on it.

"You matter, Kirsty McBride. You matter far more than I've been prepared to admit until now. Yes, I've fallen for the town, but in doing so, I could easily fall for you, too."

Saffron moved forward, closing the gap between them.

Kirsty tried to take a steadying breath. It didn't work. She didn't want it to. When Saffron Oliver was this close to her, she wanted to feel *everything*.

Only, it wasn't the movie star she was about to kiss. This was Saffron Oliver, the real deal.

Saffron reached out and cupped Kirsty's cheek with her palm.

An arrow of lust rooted Kirsty to the spot. If she'd had doubts before, they were all gone now. Her body leaned forward at the same time Saffron's mouth edged closer to her.

"You think we can do this without any interruptions this time?" Saffron's voice was so quiet it was almost a whisper.

As Saffron's warm breath caressed her lips, there wasn't a single atom of Kirsty that didn't swoon. "I really hope so."

At last, Saffron pressed her lips to Kirsty's. It was worth the wait.

This time was different. They both knew where this was going. They were both on the same page. Saffron couldn't have been clearer.

She could fall for Kirsty.

As that thought almost made her fall forward, Kirsty airbrushed it from her mind and focused on the here and now.

On Saffron-Fucking-Oliver kissing her into next week.

No cameras needed to roll for this. This was the movie star working without a script, her lips whispering sweet nothings right into Kirsty's soul.

Kirsty gripped Saffron's waist, pulling her closer. She turned so the kitchen counter pressed into her back as Saffron advanced, one hand on Kirsty's bum, the other skating up and down her side.

Kirsty closed her eyes and let herself be swept away from all the stresses in her life. From all her doubts. They'd all disappeared, with one sweep of Saffron's lips.

She wanted Saffron, and the feeling was mutual. Her heart burst as that thought soaked through to her bones.

Saffron reached down and cupped her breast.

Something fluttered in Kirsty's chest. The counter-top was still pressing into her. Reluctantly, she pulled her lips away.

"Saff?"

Exquisite blue eyes focused on her.

"You never did show me your bedroom. Now would be a good time."

Saffron took a deep breath, then gave her a nod. She gripped Kirsty's hand. When they arrived, the biggest bed Kirsty had ever seen took up half the room.

She blinked. "That's a big bed."

Saffron ramped up her heated stare. "I've got big plans."

Kirsty gulped. Had she ever been this turned on by anyone? She couldn't recall.

She was about to see Saffron Oliver naked. Kirsty stilled as Saffron's arms encircled her. This was where the age gap was going to be most apparent, wasn't it? Seventeen years wasn't something you could hide.

Saffron must have noticed the hitch in her breath. Her brow furrowed. "What's wrong?"

Her voice was so tender, Kirsty almost melted. She shook

her head. "Nothing. This is perfect. You're perfect." She wasn't lying. Saffron's skin was unblemished, not a wrinkle in sight. "It's just, I'm 49. And you're not."

But Saffron just pulled her closer. "You're beautiful, and that's all that matters to me. Scratch that, you're exquisite. I want to know you and *everything* about you." Her tone was no-nonsense. She left Kirsty believing every single word.

Saffron stripped Kirsty of her top and bra with consummate ease, marvelling at her breasts before turning Kirsty around and holding her.

Kirsty was transfixed as Saffron's hands caressed her from behind, Saffron's mouth nuzzling her neck, her soul being coaxed by Saffron's words.

"I don't want you to be shy around me. You're spectacular. In fact, spectacular takes on a new meaning when I'm with you."

Saffron's hands went south, just like Kirsty's blood supply, all pumping down her body. When Saffron undid Kirsty's trousers, she wondered if her legs would hold. When Saffron's hand slipped into her pants and then lower still, she whispered again in Kirsty's ear.

"*Spectacular.*"

Kirsty was so wet.

They tumbled to the bed, Saffron ridding Kirsty of the rest of her clothes, along with her own. She kissed her way up her body, before rolling on top of her, making Kirsty groan.

"You feel absolutely incredible."

Saffron kissed her neck in response. "So do you," she rasped before crushing Kirsty's mouth with her own.

Kirsty's vision went into romance mode, all fuzzy around the edges. She hadn't expected this when she woke up that morning. To spend the evening with Saffron. To bump into Anna. To be propelled back here. To be naked in Saffron's bed.

Anna was another life, one Kirsty was well and truly done with. Now, right here in this bed, it might not only be Ginger rewriting her future. However, Kirsty wasn't thinking long-term. There was no point. Right now, her future lasted till tomorrow morning. She was ready to jump in with both feet.

Saffron was already in with both hands. One on her breast. The other travelling south.

Kirsty breathed in pure desire as Saffron's hand swept through her centre.

"Fuck," she said.

Saffron kissed Kirsty's lips before her fingers went back to what they were doing.

"Like this?" Saffron started slow, slipping in, then out.

Kirsty gasped. She was falling fast. "Yes," was all she could manage. Her focus was elsewhere.

"And this?" Saffron's hands were all over and inside her, until Kirsty couldn't even recall who she'd been before this all began.

All the pillars of her life crumbled to dust, reduced to just this moment. The most important. The one she and Saffron were sharing.

They began their own rhythm.

Saffron pressing, sliding, kissing.

Kirsty arching, thrusting, longing.

The fire was lit, then the flames began to lick their way up through Kirsty as she writhed on Saffron's sheets, pulling one corner of the fabric into her balled fist.

Saffron was giving her all she had.

Kirsty's eyelids flickered open.

Their gazes locked.

Saffron changed her rhythm, making Kirsty gasp.

She could feel it building, feel every muscle she had tightening to Saffron's touch. Some moments later, the beautiful cacophony her body was playing reached an ultimate crescendo. Kirsty let herself fall into Saffron's safe embrace, coming undone with some style as all the emotion and the pent-up desire of the past few weeks flooded out.

Saffron held her tight, then kissed all the way down her body, breathing hard. When that hot breath landed next to Kirsty's pussy, Kirsty purred. Before she had time to process, Saffron took her into her mouth and devoured her.

Kirsty could do nothing but come again, then again. Fireworks burst in her heart. Every cell of her body lit up with pleasure.

Saffron stopped only when Kirsty put a hand on her head.

When Saffron looked up, her grin was pure bliss.

Kirsty could hardly process anything, let alone speak.

Once again, Saffron kissed her way up her body, then settled on top of her, pressing a thigh between Kirsty's legs.

Kirsty shuddered once more. "I could seriously get used to you." She drank in the beautiful view.

"That's what I was hoping." Saffron kissed her lips again. "I'll tell you one thing."

"What's that?"

"We make terrible friends. But excellent lovers."

"No argument here." Kirsty leaned in for another lingering, slow kiss. Her head spun. It was going to be one long, delicious night.

Chapter 22

The sound of the waves gently tugged Saffron from a peaceful slumber to nearly awake, where she knew it was early morning, but still wasn't jazzed to open her eyes to greet the day.

Especially not after last night, which had been mindblowingly fantabulous, leaving Saffron brimming with hope and desire to be the person she so much wanted to be. Not the person her minders wanted, but her true self. If she could bottle this emotion, she would. Not to share, but to lean on when *Saffron Oliver, Superstar* needed to remember life could be bloody amazing, not the slog she'd been living through for what seemed like forever.

Because as good as she felt right here and now, she worried—no feared—it wouldn't last. How could she make a relationship with Kirsty in Sandy Cove work? Kirsty wasn't the issue. Neither was the town. It was the movie career. This summer was the longest she stayed put in one place when not filming.

What could she offer Kirsty? A day here. A weekend there. Always rushed and never long enough. How long until Kirsty demanded more? Or until Saffron wanted to give it up?

An arm wrapped around Saffron, stilling her mind, and yanking her back into the moment.

"Good morning," Kirsty's voice was laced with sleepiness, which was another fabulous reminder of the previous night.

"Your first thing in the morning voice is pretty damn sexy." Saffron rolled onto her side, propping her head up on bent elbow.

"Right back at you." Kirsty also rolled over to face Saffron. "Is this actually happening?"

"I feel like you're trying to trick me into saying something I shouldn't. What do you mean by *this*?" Saffron ran a finger down the side of Kirsty's face, admiring her striking cheekbones many in Hollywood would pay top-dollar for.

"I'm waking up with you, who is literally Britain's lesbian icon. No. The world's. How many women have wanted this to happen to them? There's no way this can be real, right? I'm dreaming. The past several weeks have all been one long and delightful hallucination and I'm about to crash back to reality."

All the doubts sloshing through Saffron's mind fizzled while staring into those stunning grey eyes, right behind the adorable button nose. "Would it be okay if it were real?"

Kirsty bolted upright, looking every bit as confused by her action as the situation.

Saffron laughed, and pulled the startled woman on top of her. "You're not going to get away that easily. Now that we've actually moved past the terrible friend zone, I'm not going to pretend last night didn't happen. Or this."

Saffron kissed Kirsty on the tip of her nose, and then peppered her lips and face with soft and delicate smooches.

"Every morning should be like this. I haven't felt so alive and happy in—come to think of it, I'm not sure I've ever experienced euphoria like this."

Kirsty gazed down at Saffron. "Even if it is a dream, I'm determined not to get out of this bed."

Saffron flipped Kirsty onto her back and climbed on top of the woman, playfully holding her arms above her head. "I've always wondered what it would be like to have a sex slave."

"Have you now? It seems like a really bad time to break the news to me that you're some type of sex monster."

"Why's that?" Saffron's gaze travelled down those toned arms, past Kirsty's perfect face, and landed on the hollow of her throat before she leaned down to kiss it.

"I'm not sure I'll fight you off. Even if that's what you need to get turned on." Kirsty jerked a hip into Saffron.

"You. That's what I need. Kirsty McBride and no one else."

"You make it sound like it's so easy." There was a tremor in her voice.

"Can't lie. It feels really easy at the moment." Saffron kissed her again. And again. "I'll never get my fill of you. Never."

"Now there's a cheesy line."

"Mock me all you want, but I am being completely honest with you." Saffron crossed her heart.

"Really?" Kirsty squinted one eye, measuring up Saffron.

Saffron nodded. "I can't lie until I have at least one cup of coffee."

"Would it be wrong for me to take advantage of that?" Kirsty cupped Saffron's bum.

"By all means, have your way with me."

"Is it true that you have a script in the house you haven't read?"

Saffron's eyes narrowed. "You tricked me with arse play."

"Now there's something I've never been accused of before. Still waiting for an answer." Kirsty tugged on her own earlobe.

Crestfallen, Saffron grunted and asked, "That's what you want to talk about right now?"

"It's been bouncing around in my head since Ginger told me."

"Ginger has a big mouth." Saffron crinkled her brow.

"Not the point." Kirsty placed a finger on Saffron's lips. "Hear me out, will you?"

Saffron nodded, still not liking the turn of events.

"One of the reasons I was adamant about this not happening was I couldn't shake the idea that it'd only be for a fleeting second and then you'd have to leave." Kirsty inhaled deeply. "Why haven't you read the script?"

"It's the last thing I want to do." *I'd rather eat my own toenail clippings.*

"Read it or do it?"

"Both." Saffron rolled off Kirsty, and collapsed onto the bed with a thud.

"Can you extrapolate on that?"

Saffron laughed, sinking her head into the pillow. "Do you always talk so fancy when in bed with a woman?"

"Not going to work. You're not going to distract me with that killer smile of yours and incredible body." Kirsty lifted up the sheet, swallowed, then let it fall back into place. "Use your words, big or small. Talk to me."

"It's nothing, really. I'm just feeling burnt out. I've been

acting since I was fifteen. All of my adult life. I need a break."
Saffron let her eyes close and took a deep breath.

"Why'd you get into acting in the first place?"

"I thought it'd make my parents happy. They always talked a big game about how important it was to be a star in one's own life." Saffron waved a hand in the air, indicating her name in lights. "They meant for them, though. When I actually became a bigger deal than my parents—let's just say they changed their tune and fast."

"That must have hurt." Kirsty's comforting tone gave Saffron the impetus to continue, not shutdown.

"It did, but I'm not sure I understood why I felt such a gaping hole inside. By the time I figured it out, they'd already died in the car crash. I was doing my thing. Ginger was doing her thing. And..."

"What?"

"I'm thirty-two and I'm learning that acting wasn't ever my dream. Aside from making me loads of money, enough to live off of for the rest of my life, I actually hate it. All the people in my life outside of Sandy Cove just want something from me. They don't know me and have no desire to change that, as long as I smile pretty for the cameras. So, yeah, I don't want to read the script that's been sitting on my kitchen counter since the day I arrived here."

"Can't you quit?" Kirsty lay a soothing hand on Saffron's chest.

"And do what? Even though I have money, I can't not work. I'd go mad. I'm an actor. I just need to accept that and—"

"No. I don't believe it's as simple as that. You're a creative, but there are other outlets."

Saffron pinched her eyes shut.

"Don't shut off. Listen to me." Kirsty cupped both of Saffron's cheeks. "Maybe you need to take a sabbatical. Open up a gallery here. You said last night you have an eye for art. I wholeheartedly agree. Your drawings are brilliant. Switching it up might just be the solution to your problem. And, I happen to know a shop right across from me is up for rent."

"An art gallery!" Saffron winced from her own shriek. "Having an eye for tossing some cushions on a sofa and being able to doodle on scrap paper doesn't qualify me to open a gallery." She took a deep breath. "I appreciate what you're trying to do, but I'm well aware I need to stay in my own lane. The acting one."

"That's the safe way. Come on. You're Saffron Oliver. You've jumped out of planes!" Kirsty bounced up and down on the mattress.

"In movies, which I hate to break it to you, are all make believe. Besides, my stunt double does all the crazy shizzle."

"Just walking onto a movie set takes nerve. Don't sell yourself short in the confidence category." Kirsty gave a *level with me* expression. "What are you really afraid of?"

"The same thing as every other sucker walking on this planet. Falling flat on my face." Saffron slapped one hand hard into her other, the sound stinging her ears. "Mostly trust, though."

"In general…?" Kirsty waved for Saffron to fill in the blank.

"In my abilities. In me. In you. In every part of my life."

Kirsty's expression softened and she took Saffron's hand, threading their fingers together. "You can trust me."

Saffron swept some hairs out of Kirsty's eyes. "I do believe that."

They kissed. A long and lingering lip lock, neither of them making a move to end it.

Right when Saffron started to explore Kirsty's supple skin with her mouth, a buzzing sound ripped them apart. Saffron stared at her phone, wanting to take a hammer to it.

"You don't have to look at it."

"Wouldn't that be nice." Saffron still had her eyes on the device that kept her tethered to the life she wanted to leave in her past to focus on the present. "But Ginger said she might pop by this morning and it'd be rude to ignore my sister." She swept it into her hand, groaning when the text appeared on her home screen. Saffron bolted off the bed, pacing to the large window overlooking the sea, then flipped around and strode to the other side of the room.

"I know what that signifies." Kirsty pointed to Saffron. "It's from your agent."

"Bingo!" Saffron ground a fist into her palm.

"This only reinforces my belief you need a break from making movies. One text sends you over a cliff." Kirsty sat up in bed, tugging the covers to keep her hidden. "What does she want?"

"A meeting in London." Saffron raked a hand through her hair. "Apparently I can't miss it. Something about there being a clause in my contract with Pearl."

"When?"

"Tomorrow afternoon, but I think I need to go today to meet with my lawyer about this clause I've never heard of." Saffron spun around, heading back towards the water, away from Kirsty's disappointment.

"But the party's only a few days away."

"I know." Saffron made her way back to Kirsty and sat on the edge of the bed. "I'll only be gone one night. Two at the most. I won't miss Ginger's party. Not after pulling a no-show for her wedding."

"Why's this meeting so important?"

"It's about the *Girl Racer* franchise." Saffron gestured la-di-da.

"Will Echo Black be there?"

"Yes. Not only is she my co-star, but one of the producers." Kirsty started to get out of bed.

"Please, don't." Saffron reached for Kirsty.

Kirsty stopped, but her stiffening body didn't put Saffron at ease. The exact opposite, really.

"It's not like I want to see Echo. Between us, I can't stand her any more than you."

"Then don't go," Kirsty pleaded.

"I don't have a choice." Saffron smothered her face with her hands.

"There's always a choice."

"Not when it comes to Pearl and *Girl Racer*. There are millions of dollars at stake. Not just my pay, but for the studio. They'll do everything to wreck my career if I don't cave and sign on for the next one." Saffron wanted to rest her head on Kirsty's shoulder in the hope of making everything go away, so Saffron could live the life she wanted.

"Let them." Kirsty gripped each of Saffron's shoulders and spoke with confidence. "We were just talking about you starting over. Finding work that makes you happy."

"It's something to talk about, but doing it, that's entirely another matter." Saffron leaned into Kirsty. "Trust me. I'll make it back in time for the party. I'm not going to let down my sister or you. Please, believe in me."

Because Saffron needed one of them to.

Chapter 23

The light coming through her window woke Kirsty earlier than she wanted. When she opened her eyes, Saffron wasn't beside her. She'd only experienced sleeping together once, but she hoped it would happen again. Yesterday's plans had been cruelly cut short when Saffron was summoned by her agent.

Kirsty ground her teeth. Saffron had told her the meeting wasn't optional, but it did nothing to quell Kirsty's nerves. She'd slept with Saffron, and then Saffron had driven to London for a meeting with her agent and Echo Black. As beginnings went, it was as far from Hollywood as Kirsty could imagine.

She put her feet on the ground and padded over to her window, drawing back the curtains. The light marched in. It was another gorgeous day in a summer that hadn't stopped shining for the past two months. Up until yesterday, Kirsty had thought the weather knew something she didn't. That the spring in its step mirrored her own.

Now though, she wasn't so sure. She walked to the kitchen and flicked on the kettle. Saffron had said all the right things, reassuring Kirsty it was just business. Kirsty wanted to believe Saffron, but her heart had been down similar paths before.

It knew the previous outcome and the odds of it working out. Her heart was in self-preservation mode.

Kirsty understood about having work meetings you'd rather not have. She'd fired suppliers who messed her around. Held serious talks with Helena when she'd tried to steer the wine side of their business. Since then, their business relationship had been far better. In fact, since the Oliver sisters arrived in town, Helena had been a total rock.

Saffron was a big deal. She had to go to meetings. It was just her meetings were with Pearl, who certainly didn't have her best interests at heart. Also with her ex, Echo Black.

How could Kirsty compete with Echo-Sodding-Black? No matter what she'd done, she and Saffron were unfinished business.

She made herself a tea, then grabbed two crumpets. She peered closely. There was a bit of green mould on one. She cut it off. Enough butter and jam, and you'd never know. She put them in the toaster and pressed down. She bet Echo never ate crumpets. Too many carbs. Although Saffron did.

Saffron wasn't at all who Kirsty had imagined she'd be. She was a lost soul, just coming to terms with her life. Kirsty had wandered into it, and they had a connection. Saffron felt it, too. She'd told her, and she'd showed her. All night long.

A wave of lust rolled through Kirsty.

She grabbed the toasted crumpets and put far too much butter on them, watching it seep through the holes and onto the plate. So what if she put on a few pounds? She might need it to wallow if Saffron went to London and stayed there.

All it was going to take was one word from her agent,

one veiled threat, and the promise of their new relationship could fly out the window.

Kirsty walked through to the lounge and took a bite of her crumpet.

She was right.

They tasted delicious.

* * *

Two hours later, Kirsty stared up at their shop sign. They still needed to get that repainted. She added it to her mental to-do list and pushed open the shop door. Helena was already there, dealing with a delivery. She waved to get her partner's attention.

"You okay here if I go for a walk?"

Helena nodded. "So long as you bring me back a treat."

Kirsty strode out wondering how she coped before Helena. Anna had never been fully invested in the business, so it was good to have someone who was.

She needed air this morning to clear her head. Within ten minutes, she was on the start of Fisherman's Way, a disused railway line that was now a trail all the way to Winterbury, their nearest big city. At eight miles, she wasn't planning to walk it all. But walking the local coastline, she ran the risk of bumping into someone she knew. When she walked this trail, she was pretty much guaranteed solitude.

The fields around her were straw-coloured from so much sunshine, the mud underfoot dry and cracked. Kirsty put on one of her favourite podcasts and fixed her headphones.

"*Welcome to this week's Lesbian Life podcast with Jade & Candy! This week, we've got all the latest happenings in the sapphic world, including an interview with Saffron Oliver and her co-star, Echo Black! Who doesn't love those two?"*

Kirsty picked up her pace, a frown settling on her face.

Candy made a noise in her ear like she'd just eaten something delicious. *"Oh yeah, I can't wait! Having listened already, it's a fabulous interview. The two of them just look so fantastic together both on-screen and off."*

"They sure do, Candy," Jade agreed. *"The latest Girl Racer has got all our pulses racing. They were both very coy about whether or not they were together in real life. What did you glean from the interview?"*

"I think there's still something going on. There was just something in their voices, you know?"

Kirsty's stomach gurgled. Her blood twisted. Acid rose up her windpipe. She rolled her shoulders and took in the countryside view.

"Or perhaps that's just wishful thinking on my part and the whole of the lesbian world," Jade added. *"Let's face it, the pair of them have got incredible chemistry on-screen. If it's the same off it, it would make my lesbian heart skip a beat."*

Kirsty pulled her phone out of her back pocket and snapped off the podcast.

She wasn't going to listen to the interview.

If she did that, Echo Black would start to walk around her head, and that was the last thing she needed. She was already a striking movie star, just like Saffron. Perfect for her, just like Jade and Candy had said. Kirsty's mind didn't need any coaxing.

She stared hard at her phone, then clicked off the podcast app altogether.

She was not going to listen.

Even though she really wanted to.

Kirsty carried on walking, the path ahead clear. She could work out her excess energy here and nobody would know.

Saffron had made sure she had energy to burn. Heat and anger slammed through Kirsty's system at the thought of Saffron. *Damn her.*

Kirsty saw a nearby tree stump and kicked it.

The pain whizzed from her toe right up through her body and to her brain.

Fuck. That *really* hurt. Saffron was already causing her pain. The last thing she needed was to add a dollop of her own on top.

Kirsty liked to think she knew Saffron. Saffron had told her she and Echo were over. She'd also told her not to believe whatever she read in the press. Kirsty guessed podcasts went under that umbrella, too.

But it was hard. *So very hard.*

The path took a steep incline. To her right, large cows lazed on the earth. To her left, hay bales were rolled up in neat rows.

Kirsty climbed the dry path, enjoying the effort. Doing something this physical took her away from where her mind wanted to go. She breathed in the fresh air. Stopped, closed her eyes and bathed in the silence. For a few brief moments, Saffron was put on mute. Now, all Kirsty could see was sunshine, daisies and blue sky. She remembered why she loved it here. The ability to be in the middle of nowhere in no time at all. Away from people.

It was what Saffron had told her she wanted, too.

But did she really? Her flat was in London. Half her life was in LA.

Kirsty shook her head, filled her lungs again and let out a piercing scream. The blood that had previously been tangled in her veins began to pump.

She screamed again.

A grin split her face.

This was what she needed. To shout and scream. It was a cheap therapy, but it worked wonders.

"Kirsty?"

Kirsty turned, then did a double take. Walking towards her was her dad. Dressed in hiking gear with those Nordic poles that were proving so popular with pensioners. However, this was the first Kirsty knew of her dad using them.

"What are you doing here?"

"Same as you, getting some air on this gorgeous day. If I want to eat cakes and pastries, your mother insists on it." He patted his belly, then gave her a hug. "Did you hear that screaming? I was looking around, but I couldn't see where it was coming from." He regarded his daughter. "It wasn't you, was it?"

Kirsty shook her head. "I didn't hear anything."

Her dad frowned. "Whatever it was, it sounded wounded."

Kirsty was not going to fess up. Even though Dad was spot-on.

"You walking back?"

Kirsty checked her watch. She'd already been gone nearly half an hour.

"I'll buy you a coffee and a cake, my treat," he added.

That sealed the deal. Kirsty fell into step beside him as they clumped down the hill.

"Everything okay? You seem preoccupied." Dad glanced her way. "Nothing to do with a certain movie star, is it?"

He always had been able to read her like a book. "Might be. Could be." Kirsty shook her head. "Is." A sigh. "It's just, she's gone back to London to talk to her agent about her next film. She doesn't want to do it, but she doesn't know if she might have to."

"Doesn't she have a say? It's her life, after all."

"Apparently, it's not that easy. Plus, she's going to be in the same room as her co-star. Who she had a thing with." Kirsty's chest tightened again.

"Everyone's got a past." Dad gave her a look. "You've seen Anna since you split up."

"But I haven't been contemplating working with her again. That would be a nightmare."

"She might have gone to London to get out of it. I imagine that might take a few meetings."

Kirsty kicked a stone with her foot. "I know."

He put a hand on her arm and they stopped walking. "You know what they say. If you love someone, set them free. If it's meant to be, she'll come back."

Kirsty bit her lip, then nodded.

"You're just going to have to trust her on this. And if it doesn't work out, it wasn't meant to be." He took her hand and squeezed. "Come on. I'll get you two cakes with your coffee. You look like you need it."

Chapter 24

Saffron dashed from her flat after a rushed shower; her run to clear her mind had taken longer than she intended. Her London lunchtime attire, which would be absolutely out of place at the Poseidon Inn, but was necessary for the poshest restaurant in Soho, felt like a betrayal to who Saffron wanted to be.

Stepping out of the black cab, she checked her reflection in the glass, adjusting a wisp of hair before entering.

Pearl, with phone in hand, stalked the inside like a shark trying to pick up the scent of blood. "Don't you look good enough to eat."

Saffron offered her a tight-lipped smile, not trusting herself to speak.

"Echo's running late, so let's start in the bar." Pearl gave a shrug that she probably hoped implied rolling with the punches, when Saffron suspected Echo was the one person who intimidated the agent.

Saffron wasn't surprised at all Echo was running late. The woman was entirely convinced the sun revolved around her and no one could survive without her commanding presence.

The hostess led them to a quiet table in the bar, the place

buzzing, but the scene reeked of overly made up people, all of their movements seeming to be directed by an invisible hand. A deadening sensation congealed inside Saffron.

After ordering a bottle of chilled white wine, Pearl, her eyes widening with anticipation, turned to Saffron. "So, how's Sandy Cove? Going mad from boredom?"

"Not yet, no."

"Well, that's a blessing, I suppose." Her face didn't register a flicker of happiness, but calculation to twist things in her Pearl way. "We don't have time to put you into some type of treatment to fix your mental state from taking months off."

Saffron couldn't comprehend how any of that made sense to anyone. More proof agents weren't human.

"At least tell me you've had your fun and are ready to come back to work." Pearl tapped her fingertips together.

Saffron ducked answering by nodding thank you to the woman who poured her drink.

Pearl's bob of the head was much more dismissive, instead of grateful. "Here's to your next great venture with Echo."

Saffron sipped the wine, the trail of ice-cold liquid going down her throat leaving her numb.

Pearl's gaze dug into Saffron. "Well?"

"Well, what?"

"Are you ready to get back to work?"

"Not really. I'm thinking I need another month—"

Pearl stuck a hand in the air, gold bangles clinking on her wrist. "Not possible. Do you think everyone involved in the project can wait for you to work out whatever angst you're having? Millennials have no idea how the real world works. I've got news for you, dear. This sabbatical, or whatever you want to call it, is over. I'll send someone to your Sandy Cove place and pack up your belongings. I've let you have your fun. It's over. Got me?"

"I wasn't aware you controlled all the aspects of my life, not just my career."

"It's all rolled into one. It's best for you to accept that to avoid whatever this summer has been." Her look of exaggerated disgust nearly caused Saffron to burst into laughter.

Once, the two of them had been to a curry place in Brick Lane, and a man sitting near them started to have a seizure. Everyone in the restaurant leapt into action, including Saffron who pulled the table and chairs away from the poor man. Pearl, though, grunted in disgust and continued eating naan.

Why did that memory flood Saffron at that moment?

Because Kirsty was right. Saffron needed to call time on her movie career.

"I'm starting to understand how all of this works with you in the picture." How had it taken Saffron this long to see Pearl for who she really was? A greedy, vindictive, controlling arsehole.

Pearl softened her facial features, a heroic feat given the recent Botox injections Saffron knew the woman was addicted to. "I know you're struggling with motivation right now. I'll hire you the best people. The perkiest and liveliest to get you up in the morning and ready for this new and exciting adventure. This will be the best instalment of the *Girl Racer* franchise and I'm willing to bet, there'll be five more after this."

Saffron gulped her wine, needing the numbing sensation to return before she exploded and tossed the liquid in Pearl's face.

Pearl reached for her hand, and gave it a pat. "We've been through worse together. Like when your parents died. I was there for you every day. I'm still here for you every day. We'll navigate these troubled waters. Tell me what you need and—" she blew on her fingers, "And poof. I'll make everything better."

It was lines like the navigate one that had made Saffron feel better after her parents' deaths. Making her feel like she wasn't all alone and maybe Pearl actually did care. But the passing years proved beyond a doubt, Pearl only cared about what made her richer and more powerful.

Saffron slanted her head and crossed her arms. "Funny, because from my viewpoint, I have been telling you what I need—time away, and yet you're insisting I stay your hostage."

"Hostage!" Pearl scoffed. "I've done more for you than any of my other clients."

"I make way more than all of your other clients combined."

"Exactly! Which is why we have to nip this in the bud. Get you back in the saddle." Pearl, much to Saffron's horror, pretended to ride a horse, hollering, "Yee-haw!"

How had Saffron ever accepted the gauche woman? Had Pearl always been this Pearl-y or had Saffron's success gone to the agent's head? Either way, Saffron was horrified she'd kept Pearl in her life this long.

"Good afternoon, so sorry I'm late, babe."

Saffron braced at hearing Echo's voice, momentarily pressing her eyes shut, not wanting to have to confront Pearl and Echo in one go. Saffron wished Kirsty was there, giving *a you can do it* smile.

Before Saffron reopened her eyes, she prayed that the present circumstances were a bad dream and she'd wake in her bedroom in Sandy Cove. The sound of waves rolling in. Seagulls cawing. Children squealing in delight. And, she was tucked safely in her bed in Kirsty's warm embrace.

Instead, the sound of glasses clinking and obnoxiously fake laughter invaded her ears and the sight of raven hair falling in waves around Echo's shoulders, a faint constellation of freckles dusting her cheeks, and penetrating black eyes brought Saffron back to reality and she wanted to kick, punch, and scream.

Instead she said, "Glad you could make it on time, *babe*."

Echo kissed Saffron's cheek, ignoring the comment. "I swear you get lovelier every time I see you. But—" she glanced to Pearl and back to Saffron—"Why are you hiding at this table in the corner? This won't do. Not at all." She whirled about and an employee practically materialised from thin air. "We're ready for our table."

Pearl made a gasping sound, her hand clutching her throat. Echo spun in her heels. "Are you dying?"

While Echo had a hand on Pearl's shoulder, there was no hiding what her tone implied: *You'd better be dying because you're annoying the fuck out of me and sucking all the attention from me.*

Oh Christ. Both of these women were embarrassingly terrible. Saffron's insides went cold with the knowledge she'd let them into her life.

Pearl sputtered, letting lose a string of sounds that bore no resemblance to the English language all the while pointing at whatever was on her phone.

Echo met Saffron's eye, silently asking, *Can you believe this act?*

In the beginning, one of the things Echo and Saffron had bonded over was their annoyance with Pearl. How ridiculously pushy and over-the-top Saffron's agent could be. But when Saffron started to dig beneath Echo's surface only to discover what the woman was truly like, there wasn't much to be desired on that front. Echo was a petty person in pretty packaging used to being fawned over and her star had risen so high, she no longer had to disguise her controlling, bitchy nature.

Like showing up to lunch late to make a stunning entrance. Everything about Echo was staged. She was exactly like Saffron's parents.

Wait. Saffron shook her head. What just happened? When the thought Echo was like her parents slammed through the walls around Saffron's heart, she let out a yelp.

Echo focused on Saffron, wrapping an arm about her. "Are you okay, babe?"

Saffron tried to free herself from Echo's grasp, but ended up being pulled closer, Echo placing Saffron's head to her breast, stroking her hair with a tenderness Saffron knew the woman didn't possess.

"I'm sorry, but I have to go." Pearl hopped off her seat. "One of my client's wrapped his Porsche around a palm tree in Beverly Hills and the story is about to break on TMZ. I have no doubt you two can work out the particulars."

With that, Pearl fled the restaurant, and Echo slid into the empty bar stool, dismissing the poor server with a flick of the wrist. Reaching over, she held Saffron's hand. "Tell me what's troubling you, doll."

"Why does everyone keep asking me to open up my heart only to ignore the words that come out? It's like I don't exist."

"You haven't told me a thing. You haven't answered one of my calls or texts." Echo painted on an Oscar-worthy worried and caring expression.

And Saffron noted her hand was still enveloped in the viper's caress, which undoubtedly to the casual observer would appear to be affectionate. In the poor lighting, no one would notice Echo was crushing the hand she held to keep Saffron where she wanted it. At her mercy.

"Please release my hand," Saffron said through gritted teeth.

Echo leaned forward. "What, baby? It's loud in here."

At least that much was true. It was loud in the bar, but Saffron took note of the surroundings with fresh eyes. Everyone had their attention and phones on the *Girl Racer* stars as if enjoying a live performance. Exactly what Echo wanted.

"Oh my God, I can't believe I fell for this!" Saffron whipped her hand from Echo's clutches and leaned back in the chair, folding her arms over her chest. "This was all a set up. Showing up late so Pearl could lay the groundwork, playing the bitch ordering me back to work and then you swooping in to save me while simultaneously Pearl hears about a client in dire straits." Anger crashed through Saffron. "Every damn part of this evening was scripted to get us alone so we look like a couple for the whole world to see. The question is, why?" Saffron tapped a finger on her chin. "Knowing you, this is all about building a buzz for the next *Girl Racer*. That's why you demanded I do the podcast interviews. Did you plant all the questions that implied we're a couple and reveal to the hosts behind the scenes that we are indeed an item, but we're trying to keep it on the down low?" Saffron's gaze swept the bar. "Is everyone here extras or paps you tipped off?"

Echo inclined her head just right for some of her hair to swish into place, and she batted those long, sensuous eyelashes. "I don't know what you're talking about." In a much quieter voice, she added, "Do we need to get you *mental* help?" The word mental had been mouthed.

"I think so because that's the only explanation as to why I ever found you attractive."

"Should we take this somewhere more private?"

"You can by all means. I'm going back to Sandy Cove without you and whatever this is."

"You can't," Echo snapped, losing her famous composure.

"Oh, I can and will. Yesterday, I bought the clause in my contract ruse. But I forwarded my contracts to my solicitor and surprise surprise, the clause Pearl mentioned in her text doesn't exist. It never did. I didn't have to come here after all." She'd been such a fool for far too long.

"And, yet, here you sit, still." Echo waved dramatically, her gotcha smile firmly in place.

"To tell you that I'm done. No more *Girl Racer* films." Saffron slapped her palms together. "Never again."

"If you back out of one of the most successful action-movie franchises, you'll never get another acting deal. Not even a dog food commercial."

"Can I get that in writing?" Saffron tapped the table, wanting Echo to fulfil the wish right then and there.

"I'm not following." Echo cockily folded her arms over her chest, like a parent dealing with a petulant child.

Saffron splayed her hands on the table. "Let me see if I can get through to you. I don't want to be an actor. I don't think I ever wanted to be one. I'm done. D. O. N. E."

Echo shook her head, implying she now knew the game Saffron was playing. "If you want more money, we can talk. Just tell me what you want."

Saffron threw her hands in the air and leaned over the table, speaking in a hushed, but livid whisper. "Jesus Christ! I have been. Will you listen to me for once in your fucking life? I'm quitting the business. I will never act again. Not on stage. Not in movies. Not in local theatres. I can't stand it. I can't stand the people involved. I can't stand Pearl. And, I unquestionably can't stand you."

"Will you keep your voice down? You're making a scene. That's what happens when you grow up with drunks as parents." Echo tapered her eyes, grinding her teeth.

"You can be such a fucking bitch."

"Is this about the woman in Sandy Cove? The one you took for a ride on your motorbike. I've seen photos of you two all over social media. This is my fave—" Echo whipped out her phone, clicking on a photo of Saffron and Kirsty at the Harbour Bar, both leaning over the table, looking like they were about to kiss. Saffron hadn't seen the photo, but she'd trade her millions to go back in time and stay in Sandy Cove.

"This is about me wanting to live my own life."

"Please. You won't be able to survive without Pearl and I guiding you every step of the way." Echo walked two fingers on the table. "You've always needed someone like me by your side or you'd fall apart."

"If you say one more word to me, I'll stand on top of this

table and tell the world the truth. I can't stand you, Echo-Fucking-Black. We are not a couple. We were and it was one of the worst periods in my life. Now, I just want to be free of you."

Echo started to speak, but Saffron stabbed the air with a finger. "Not one word."

Echo shut her mouth, her eyes filling with hatred.

"There's probably a hundred actors who would love to fill my shoes. Hire one of them for your precious series. I'm going home to Sandy Cove."

Chapter 25

Helena had insisted Kirsty take her dad up on his offer of dinner that night. Kirsty didn't have much appetite, but she also didn't have the energy to say no. This wasn't game over yet. Saffron had just gone to London for a meeting. Like her dad said, if she was hers in the first place, she'd come back.

Kirsty had forgotten this part of getting together with someone. The part where you constantly second-guessed yourself and felt like you were going mad. She hadn't missed it one bit. And yet, on the other side of this madness and uncertainty lay the pot of gold. What was that old saying? No lotus without mud? Right now, Kirsty was covered head to toe.

At least her mum had acquiesced to the fact it was summer: tonight they were eating outside. She was whipping up a speciality paella. Mum bought the paella spice mix every year when she and Dad spent the first two months of the year in their timeshare apartment in southern Spain. Kirsty had offered to help in the kitchen, but had been shooed out by her mother. Now she was relaxing in the lounge with her dad. He'd made a jug of sangria to complete the authentic Spanish experience, which made Kirsty smile. At least they hadn't produced a straw donkey and started performing the Macarena yet. Perhaps after dessert?

She sipped her drink and coughed. Her eyebrows shot up her head. "How much wine did you put in this, Dad?"

He glanced over the top of his paper. "What the recipe said, plus a glug for luck." He gave her a grin. "Remember when I taught you to make cocktails? A glug for luck is the secret home ingredient."

"I remember." She paused. "You're doing your crossword late."

"I was out walking, wasn't I?" He put his paper down. "Are you feeling any better? Any communication from you-know-who?"

Kirsty ground her teeth together. "Not yet." She said it like it meant nothing, but it didn't. Saffron had texted her once since she left, saying 'Sweet dreams' last night, but she hadn't received it until this morning. Since then, nothing. After a steady stream of messages the whole time she'd been in Sandy Cove, Kirsty wasn't sure what it meant. She was going with the *just busy* excuse. She wasn't focusing on what Saffron might be busy doing.

She took another glug of her sangria. This time, the strength pleased her.

"Here's one you might know. Fourteen down. Singer and performer, son of musicians Loudon and Kate. Five letters."

"Rufus," Kirsty replied.

Dad looked down, then cracked a smile. "It fits! I knew I had a daughter for a reason!" He gave her a wink and filled it in.

Even saying the word caused Kirsty's heart to deflate.

She recalled the morning on Ginger's deck with the silver suit. Meeting Saffron in the harbour market. Both times, Saffron had been on her knees playing with Rufus the dog. Would she be back to do that anytime soon?

Kirsty glanced up at the TV, which was on mute. It was on a channel she didn't recognise. Her parents were normally on the first five stations, not known to stray off the well-trodden path. She picked up the remote and was just about to turn over, when an image of Saffron and Echo flashed up on the screen.

If Kirsty's heart had deflated at the thought of Rufus, it shrivelled up into a kernel and almost stopped beating at that. She located the mute button and stabbed it.

"The two were dining at Haze, very much on show for all the waiting paparazzi," said the channel announcer.

Kirsty's heart rallied as the camera zoomed in on Saffron. She was so incredibly beautiful. Also, incredibly styled in a black tux and crisp white shirt that Kirsty had seen her wearing before in photos online. But where was Pearl? Where was the meeting room? If Kirsty didn't know better, this looked very much like a date.

Was her date with Echo going to end with the same dessert Saffron had given Kirsty?

Kirsty put her drink down, her hands automatically going to her face to cover her eyes. Her heart, recovered from its temporary slump, was now booming in her chest for all the wrong reasons.

Every muscle in Kirsty's body tightened. Her hairs stood on end. She struggled to control her breathing.

Saffron was in a posh restaurant with her ex, and the way

Echo was gripping Saffron's arm and staring at her left little space to jump to anything but the obvious conclusion. Echo's grip was possessive.

Saffron was letting her do it.

Perhaps Saffron had missed her doing it.

Had Kirsty been played by a movie star? Had all Saffron's words meant nothing? Had she been acting all along?

Please say it wasn't true.

However, the announcer was oblivious to her internal strife. As was her dad, still frowning at his crossword.

"We all know that Girl Racer 2 has broken all box office records for a female-led action movie, especially one with two out lesbian leads. Could it be that the on-off couple are back on in real life, too? If that's the case, it's going to make the shooting of Girl Racer 3, due to start next month according to my sources, even hotter than the last. It's also going to tip fans of the franchise over the edge! We'll bring you all the latest news on the film and the romance as we get it. Now, back to the rest of our Hollywood round-up."

Kirsty jumped up from the sofa, then switched off the TV.

Her dad looked up. "You okay? That was a very sudden movement."

"I have to go." She couldn't get through a dinner with her parents without cracking and she didn't want them to see she'd failed again. It was becoming more and more apparent by the minute that she had. Why did she keep failing at romance? What was wrong with her? She had the perfect role models with the perfect marriage, but she couldn't emulate it, no matter how hard she tried. All Kirsty wanted was normal. It turned out, that was the hardest thing to find.

How could she have been so stupid to think Saffron would choose her over Echo Black? Even those words skating across her mind made her shake her head and let out a despairing snort.

She was Kirsty from Sandy Cove. Not Echo from LA. She'd never stood a chance.

"Go? But we're having paella. It's your favourite."

"I know. It's just, something's come up. I'll tell you more another time."

He stared at her, then nodded. If there was one thing she'd always been grateful for, it was her dad always knew when to stay silent. It was a talent her mum had never cultivated. She leaned down and kissed his cheek.

"Can you tell Mum?" She would never take Kirsty fleeing without an explanation.

He nodded. "I'll take care of it. Go do what you have to do."

She squeezed his hand and walked out of the house.

Once in the fresh air, she almost crumpled. She'd kept it together in the house because she'd had to. But now, replaying that image of Echo holding onto Saffron's arm and staring at her with her movie-star smile, she paused. She had a sensation like the soft tissue in her chest and throat had hardened, making it difficult to breathe. Kirsty stopped walking and leaned over, a hand to her heart. The pain was so visceral, it was pulsing. She never wanted to feel it again.

She hobbled along her parents' road, running parallel with the beachfront and the High Street. She cut down an alleyway with some graffiti of a heart exploding and stopped to soak it in. The wall was a graphic representation of what was happening inside her body. She'd walked past it a million times before, and yet it'd never hit home like tonight. It was as if Saffron had reached in and scrunched Kirsty's heart into a ball, then ripped it out and thrown it away.

Like it was disposable.

Like it meant nothing.

Tears welled up inside. Kirsty shook herself. She had to get back to her flat before she fell apart. She wasn't doing it in an alleyway. Not when everyone in town knew who she was. Somehow, though, even with the shop mere minutes away, it seemed to take forever.

When she finally passed Wine Time's window, Helena was grabbing a bottle from the display. Her face broke into a smile when she saw her business partner.

Before Kirsty could stop her, Helena had yanked open the shop door and was beside her. "Can you believe it? We've sold out of that new Chilean Cabernet you ordered. Going like gangbusters. So much so, I had to steal one from the display for an order someone just called in." She paused. "Why do you look like you've swallowed a bee?"

Kirsty slumped against the doorway, but said nothing.

"You haven't swallowed a bee, have you?"

Kirsty let out a strangled yelp as she shook her head. "No, but I have swallowed a whole bunch of lies."

Helena's face spelled alarm. She grabbed Kirsty's arm and dragged her inside. She scooted around the counter and snapped her laptop shut. Then she pulled out a chair at the end of the tasting table and put Kirsty on it. She put the bottle of wine down, too. "What's happened?"

As Kirsty filled her in, Helena's eyes widened.

"You're sure it's not just a set-up? Just something for the cameras?"

Kirsty shook her head. "She told me it was a meeting with her agent and Echo. Then I find out through some crappy TV channel it's just her and Echo, looking very cosy." She threw up her hands, swallowing down the tears that were threatening. She pulled a tissue from the box on the table and blew her nose.

"If this was you, what would you think? Saffron can have me or Echo Black." Kirsty jumped up and paced the shop. "What have I been doing these past few weeks? Apart from deluding myself." She shook her head, then stopped pacing. She swivelled on her right foot and marched to the counter, scrabbling in the top drawer until she pulled a piece of paper out.

Then Kirsty turned to face Helena, waving the note in the air. "Remember this? *Life is not a Hollywood rom-com, you stupid fuck.* How damn prophetic was I? It's more like a slasher movie right now." Kirsty scrunched up the note and flung it behind the counter. Then she sat again, shaking her head.

"Oh fuck! I'm doing her sister's divorce party. Saffron said she was coming back for it. Maybe that was a lie, too." Kirsty put her head in her hands, her insides collapsing, her voice scratchy. "I can't go to that now. I can't possibly face her and everybody else." For some reason, Anna's face flashed through her mind, full of fake pity for her.

Kirsty brushed it aside. She didn't need her romantic failures lined up in her mind right now.

"You bloody well can." Helena reached over and put a hand on Kirsty's arm. "Listen to me. You're doing that party.

You live here. This is your manor. If Saffron has played you, you hold your head up high. You did nothing wrong. If she's chosen Echo Black over you, that's her loss. You're worth five movie stars all stacked on top of each other." Helena's face was bright red as she stabbed the air above her head. "I tell you what, if she wants a fight, she can have one. Sandy Cove is on your side, not hers. If she comes in here, I'll punch her lights out."

Kirsty blurted out a cry-laugh at that.

Then Helena wrapped her arms around her.

Kirsty let her as her tears fell.

Chapter 26

Saffron parked her car, but didn't get out, all ten digits white-knuckling the steering wheel. Her publicist had been calling non-stop, wanting to know what to say about the Echo Black rumours? Were they back together or not?

"It's okay, Saff, if it's just for show, but I need to know the truth so I can spin it the right way to maximise your image," Andrea had said, after Saffron had shouted for the umpteenth time she never wanted to hear Echo's name again.

No. None of this was okay. Not by a long shot.

Pearl didn't get it.

Nor did Andrea.

Echo had been her cagey self on the socials, posting old photos of them together, with hopeful messages like: *will be back together soon.*

How would anyone believe Saffron had been played like an unsophisticated rube? She was known for portraying the bad-ass motorbike chick, brimming with confidence and intelligence. Saffron always smoked the bad guys. Always!

When Saffron had watched the clip zinging through the ether on every platform all over the world, she knew she was in deep shit with Kirsty. Saffron wanted to text Kirsty not to believe everything she saw or heard, but couldn't find the words necessary to convey the message.

Ultimately, she decided it'd have to be done in person and there was no time like the present. Too many priceless hours had slipped past since the date setup. All because Saffron was terrified of losing everything that was outside of her control. She hated the swirling sensation, as if her life and happiness were being flushed away. All because of Echo Black!

Had Kirsty seen the footage or photos? She wasn't exactly the type to watch rubbish on the telly, but someone in her circle had probably been exposed to the lie on social media at the very least. Sandy Cove protected its own, and Kirsty fell into that category, not Saffron.

But she couldn't go to Kirsty in her London clothes. They weren't part of Saffron's new life, but weighed her down like a ship's anchor. It seemed an insult to the Sandy Cove way of life. Which was real and pure. On the flipside, everything about her life in London and LA was utter filth. How had Saffron not realised until this summer how much she hated her life at every level?

It was imperative to express this to Kirsty, but would she believe Saffron? Their last time together, they'd talked about the importance of trust. Since then, Saffron had been seen looking cosy with Echo. How many women would take Saffron's word that nothing had happened? It had all resulted from a huge lapse in judgment on her part. Her pushy agent and manipulating *Girl Racer* co-star had staged the meeting just to get the hopes up of the fans the love affair had been rekindled in the nick of time for filming. Before Saffron had made her escape from Haze, the prospect of her getting back with Echo was already trending on Twitter.

Another confirmation that Pearl and Echo had planned everything, proving how neither would stop their machinations to squeeze every last drop of blood out of Saffron.

Even though Saffron hadn't reacted the way they probably desired, it still played out perfectly for mass consumption. The *are they/aren't they* debate was publicity gold for the next movie. People loved to choose a side and to argue why they were right, even if it had zero impact on their life. Actually, that component seemed to add to the fun, because no matter the result, it didn't alter someone's life.

Aside from Saffron's happiness.

No one seemed to care about that, including Saffron. Until she came to Sandy Cove and met Kirsty. Then things started clicking in her head and the conclusion was Saffron hated her old life and wanted to start over before it was too late to let the real Saffron flourish.

"Better get your arse out of the car, then." Saffron's hands still gripped the steering wheel.

Prying her fingers off, she got out of the car, and entered the beach house, her mind flitting to the times Kirsty had been there. Kirsty exploring the main area, commenting the place lacked personality. The kiss in front of the fridge.

In the bedroom, Saffron stood at the foot of the bed, remembering how bloody fantastic it'd been to wake up with Kirsty.

Was it too much to ask the universe to have protected Kirsty from hearing a thing about what had transpired between her and Echo? Yes, because in today's world, there were no such things as privacy for the likes of Saffron Oliver.

I can't go to her!

Not yet at least.

Saffron needed to clear her mind and the best way to do that was to hop on her motorbike. Hurriedly, she changed into her gear, and within minutes, she zoomed away, feeling the heaviness lift.

Hunched down, she reached the open roads, taking the turns at speed, making her lean low to the ground, feeling the thrill of having a powerful machine between her legs, and knowing there was no room for a mistake. But the control excited her, along with the vrooming sound when she revved the bike.

With her mind on autopilot, it didn't sink in until the fragrance of lavender tickled her nostrils. She'd taken the exact route with Kirsty, not even a week ago. Slowing down, she pulled over to sit on the bench where she and Kirsty had spoken about Anna. The woman who'd lied and cheated on Kirsty.

Would Kirsty think Saffron was no better?

It was true, Saffron hadn't been entirely honest, but it wasn't because she was purposefully lying to Kirsty, but to herself. It was hard to confess she'd fallen for Echo, who was nothing more than a con artist, and Saffron had felt foolish for needing to feel loved so she'd ignored all the signs that in hindsight flashed overhead like a neon sign.

It started off small. Echo sharing too much about their private life. Details that Saffron wanted to be just between them. Even Echo's jealous streak, when Saffron talked to someone too long at a party. At first, that seemed kind of sexy.

Echo wanted her that much. Soon enough it'd morphed into Saffron never being able to see or confide in friends, out of fear of igniting Echo's temper. And, it wasn't even like Echo had ever loved Saffron. No, she liked how the connection played to movie audiences. All she was to Echo was Saffron Oliver, a commodity to be guarded at all cost.

Soon enough, Saffron was hostage to Echo and her control, afraid to walk away because she didn't want to be all alone. Just the thought of that used to send her into a frenzied panic, especially late at night, when the darkness seemed to swallow her whole.

Saffron's phone rang.

"What?" she snapped at her publicist.

"I need to know everything about Wine Time."

"The shop in Sandy Cove? How do you know about it?" Saffron swiped hair out of her eyes.

"Because your photo is all over their website, claiming it's the only place to buy wine in your adopted town."

Saffron saw black. Then streaming sunlight. More black. It took several ticks of her heart to figure out she was blinking excessively and unable to speak or comprehend what she'd just heard.

No.

This wasn't happening again.

Being played to boost someone else's business.

Please, God. No.

"Saff—is there something going on with the wine shop? Have you invested in it? What's your connection?"

"I don't have a connection!" Saffron slammed her fist into her own thigh, ignoring the spasm of pain.

"The photos are of you in the shop. Are you sure?" Andrea asked, her strained voice not trying to upset Saffron further.

Yes, she had a connection, but how to explain she'd fallen for Kirsty, who only cared about one thing. The Saffron Oliver name and photos to sell booze.

How had Saffron been such a fucking idiot to think Kirsty wanted the movie star for anything else? Her parents had never put her first. Pearl had repeatedly used her. Echo had kept her under lock and key all for publicity. Why would Kirsty be any different? When would Saffron learn she couldn't trust anyone?

* * *

Unbridled rage hummed through Saffron, when the motorbike's tyres screeched to a stop outside of Wine Time. She leapt off the bike and ripped her helmet off by the time she reached the shop door.

"What's the meaning of this?" Saffron, with her helmet tucked under her left arm, held up her phone with her right hand. "All this time, you've been lying to me!"

Kirsty, who'd been unpacking bottles from a box, took a step back, giving Saffron the once over. "What are you raving about?"

"This!" Saffron shook her phone.

"Who do you think you are? Barging in my shop, ranting like a lunatic." Kirsty planted her feet, readying for battle.

"Who do you think you are? This entire time, you planned on using me. I give you credit for all your showboating, claiming we couldn't be more than client and party planner, when all the while you wanted nothing more than to get close to me." She snarled and then hurled the words, "All to get an endorsement starring moi."

"M-moi?" Kirsty stuttered.

"Yes, me." Saffron stupidly thumped her phone into the centre of her own chest, hitting bone.

"Why would my website have you on it?" Kirsty knitted her eyebrows.

"Exactly! Why would it, Kirsty?" Saffron stepped towards the woman, the rage continuing to boil. "Why?"

"Can I see whatever you're talking about?" Kirsty bared her palm.

"It's your website. How do you not know what's on it?"

"Can you please just show me your fucking phone?" Kirsty shook her hand.

Saffron slapped it into place. "By all means. Keep this façade going. Maybe you should be the actor, not me."

Kirsty shot her a venomous glare before giving the phone the time of day. "What the fuck?"

"You really are good." Saffron applauded, managing not to drop her helmet.

"Just stop, okay." Tears brimmed in her eyes. "I haven't seen it since Helena did the rejig. I had no part in this." Kirsty held the phone by a corner, as if not wanting the lies to contaminate her.

"Yeah, right. After everything between us. I thought I actually meant something to you. Like you believed in me and my ability to quit my career. To be a real person, not a commodity." Saffron willed herself not to break in front of Kirsty. When she got home she could let the tears flow.

"Oh, get off your high horse. You're only trying to shift the blame onto me because within 48 hours of us shagging, you rekindled your relationship with Echo-Fucking-Black for all the world to see. I've been dumped before, but never on such a grand scale. Bravo, Hollywood. Bravo!" Kirsty clapped her hands like she was congratulating the queen herself.

"I've done no such thing." Saffron took a shallow breath, feeling faint.

"What *thing* are you talking about?" Kirsty made sarcastic quote marks in the air.

"Rekindling things with Echo. That lunch was all a setup."

"You led me to believe it was a business meeting. One you were legally required to attend. From what I saw, it didn't look business-y. Not with the posh setting and romantic flickering candlelight. I'm surprised Adele wasn't serenading you two as you held hands, staring lovingly into the other's eyes." Kirsty pressed her palms together, batting her eyelashes.

"At least with Echo, I know what I'm getting. You've been lying to me since day one." Kirsty held a finger up in the air, but Saffron continued to steamroll. "The worst part, I actually believed you. I believed what we had was real. I've been such a fool!"

"Why would Pearl set you up on a date? Why should I believe a word you say?" Kirsty's expression turned to stone.

"Can't you see? It's the perfect stunt to drum up publicity for the next *Girl Racer*."

"It definitely worked! Even in this small town, all the tongues are wagging."

"On more levels than you know." Wetness formed in the corner of her eyes.

Kirsty placed a hand on her hip. "And, what's that supposed to mean?"

"Here are the facts. You and the shop will be famous. The paparazzi are already camped outside and they'll hound you for days, if not weeks. Wine Time will become one of the must-stops for the UK Dyke Tour. For me, the whole experience has drilled into my head that I can't trust anyone. Not one soul."

"That's rich coming from the woman who said she wanted to quit the business, but her next movie will begin filming in a month. So, when will you be leaving to be with Echo every single day and night?" Kirsty wrapped her arms around herself, fixing Saffron with a death stare.

"You're just like everyone else!" Saffron slammed her helmet into her thigh.

"Meaning?"

"No one listens to me. I don't want to be in the next film. Or any film, but whenever I say that, the words don't compute." Saffron tapped a finger to the side of her head. "People, even you, just want to hear the words that fit their own script."

Kirsty sucked in a deep breath. "You know what, I don't have time for dyke drama. As you can see, I'm very busy." She waved to all the boxes that needed unpacking.

"I'm glad using my name has brought the prosperity you so much desired. It must have been such a hardship spending time with me, when you clearly didn't respect me as a human being."

"I didn't respect you?" Kirsty clutched the front of her shirt. "I can't trust you!"

"Neither can I!"

"I was right all along. This. Us. It wasn't ever going to

work. Just go back to being a movie star. Jump back into bed with Echo. Leave me to cobble back the pieces of my dignity."

Saffron gaped at the woman, swooshing her away like a pesky insect. "I can't believe all of this has been a lie. All of it."

Chapter 27

When the shop door slammed and Saffron was gone, along with the paparazzi, Kirsty was left all alone. She stood for a full few moments listening to the whoosh of her heart, and the familiar noises of the shop. The hum of the fridges. The creak of the polished floorboards under her weight. It took a few more moments to notice she was shaking.

She stared at her hand. The bottle of wine she held almost fell from her grasp, but she managed to put it down.

What the hell had just happened? None of it seemed real. She'd told Helena to join Hugh at the pub as the shop was quiet. Kirsty had decided to unpack a couple of boxes to take her mind off the whole Saffron debacle. She'd just about managed to convince herself there was a sliver of hope that Saffron wasn't cheating. However, then Saffron had come in and said all those things.

Kirsty walked over to the counter and almost crumbled to the floor. She and Saffron were done. That's all she knew. The hope and anticipation of the past few weeks were done. No more flirting. No more thrills circling her body.

She clutched the counter harder as a wave of doom crashed through her, almost taking her breath away. She grabbed her phone and pulled up the website. Anton's new graphics looked great, but that was by the by. She clicked on the promo pages and the first one that came up was plastered with photos of Saffron. There she was, holding up wine in the shop. Standing smiling at her parents' barbecue. Grinning beside Kirsty after she'd eaten her first oyster in years. Kirsty shook her head. No wonder Saffron was mad.

What the hell had Helena done? After everything they'd built, everything they'd done to get the shop on an even keel. All the trust they'd rebuilt over the past two years. Had Kirsty been unclear in her instructions about Saffron? She didn't think so. But now it was too late.

The plummet of doom was now met with an uprising of anger.

How dare Helena do this to her. *To them.*

And how dare Saffron think Kirsty could do that to her.

It turned out Saffron had been right all along: trust nobody.

Kirsty locked up half an hour early. Outside, a light blinded her. She held up her hand to her face. What the hell was that? More paparazzi? If Kirsty and Saffron were done, this would be her last experience of it.

Anger propelled Kirsty down the High Street at record speed to The Mariner's Arms. She crashed through the door, eyes flitting wildly. Kirsty took in the shine of the beer taps, the smile of the bartender, the crackle of laughter in the air.

But she only had eyes for Helena. She spotted her sitting near the end of the bar, tilting her head back, laughing at something Hugh said. Such a perfect couple.

They had what Kirsty would never have.

Helena had seen to that.

Kirsty thundered over to their table and stood beside it.

Hugh clocked her first, standing up to greet her. "Kirsty! Didn't expect to see you here tonight."

Helena jumped to her feet, a worried expression on her face. "You look like you need a drink. Hugh, go get her a wine."

Kirsty held up a hand to stop him. "I won't be drinking with you, tonight or any night." Her words curdled on her tongue. She still couldn't believe she was having to say this to Helena. "How could you do what you did? To me? To us? Maybe my mum was right all along."

Kirsty's raised voice made a few people nearby turn their heads.

Helena frowned, holding up a palm to Kirsty. "Slow down, what's happened? Why are you shouting at me?"

"Like you don't fucking know." Venom rattled through her. "I just want to know why? You can't bear me to be happy, is that it? All that guff about thumping Saffron if she came in the shop. I should punch you instead."

"Please, Kirsty." Hugh stepped between them. "No punching Helena."

That blew the lid off Kirsty's anger.

"This is between us, Hugh."

He stepped back as Kirsty edged forward.

"Although, you should know what a Judas your wife is. Betrayal doesn't even cover it." She stared at Helena so she got the point. "Using Saffron's name to promote the shop after everything I said, everything that's happened."

"I didn't!" Helena's voice scratched the air. "I would never do that to you!"

The pub hushed as Kirsty and Helena's voices scaled the octaves.

A collective intake of breath waited for the next verbal blow.

"Nice try, but you already did. Snapping covert shots, using personal ones of us. Even from the day I ate an oyster. I didn't think you'd stoop so low." Every word sounded like a slap. "Saffron and I have split up, so if that was your aim, job done." Kirsty pointed a finger as if it was loaded. "Just know that as soon as the bank opens tomorrow, I'll be asking about a loan to buy you out of the business. I can't work with partners I don't trust. You fall into that category." Kirsty shook her head, her anger still fizzing through her like a firework.

Helena was shaking her head, her eyes wide. "I didn't do whatever it is you're saying. There must be some mistake."

"You're not wrong there. My mistake was trusting you. I've been defending you, singing your praises to anyone who'll listen. Fuck you, Helena." She hoped her gaze burned her friend. Scrap that, *ex-friend*.

Kirsty turned and walked out of the pub, passing a few locals with open mouths.

She didn't look back.

Chapter 28

Kirsty dragged her kayak up the stony beach, the lone person on this part of the beach at 8am. It was heavier after her ride, but she didn't mind. She hadn't been able to sleep, so she'd decided to commune with nature. Kayaking had been the perfect remedy for that. The smell of the sea in her lungs, the supreme tranquillity calming.

Her wetsuit clung to her body. Kirsty shivered. She needed to get into dry clothes. She abandoned the kayak at the top of the beach, then sprinted across the path and up to their hut. Within 30 minutes, she was hosed down and changed. She sat on the porch in her favourite shorts and T-shirt, coffee in hand, staring out at the beautiful vista, the lighthouse regal as always.

Greg and Rufus walked past and gave her a wave. It took everything Kirsty had to wave back and *not* take it out on them. To everyone else, she probably looked like she had the world at her feet. To some extent, she did. She had her health, her family, her hut, a fresh mug of coffee. However, everything else she counted on—her business and her love life—had broken in two yesterday. Just like that: snap.

Her insides wobbled anew.

She sat up straighter and took a deep breath of the ocean. Not even that soothed her. She'd allow herself some time to wallow, but after that, she had to get a grip.

She was Kirsty McBride.

She'd dealt with worse.

A divorce.

Her business in peril.

She'd risen from the ashes before and she could do it again.

She dropped her head. Only, losing Saffron was going to take some getting used to. Even the thought left her winded.

Kirsty picked up her phone and clicked on Saffron's Instagram account. It was full of images of her and Echo, and she'd been glued to it all night. Why had she never looked before? It told her everything she needed to know. She'd been blind, she saw that now. Blind and stupid. In both love and in friendship.

She took another deep breath, staring out to the flat sea beyond, the sun just starting to bathe its surface.

When it came to Helena, she was still in shock on a completely different level. Kirsty expected lovers to fuck her over, that wasn't new. But friends? It was almost too much to bear.

Helena had sent her a barrage of texts last night. Kirsty hadn't read them. What more was there to say? The damage was done, and Helena was the architect.

When Kirsty lifted her head and glanced down the coastal path, her stomach rolled. Anger uncoiled in her gut.

Talk of the devil. Helena was walking her way. She had some front, Kirsty would give her that.

Helena approached the beach hut slowly. She was carrying something in her hands. It was only when she got closer Kirsty saw what it was.

"What do you want?" She wasn't going to be bought that easily. "You can't just turn up here with an iced bun round and think that'll make everything okay."

Helena nodded. "I know. I owe you a huge apology. The biggest one in the whole wide world. I just thought if you were eating an iced bun, I'd have time to speak." She walked slowly up the short grassy incline, then stepped onto the white wooden porch. Helena put the bun round on the table next to Kirsty's coffee.

Kirsty's stomach growled. *Traitor.* She wasn't going to eat it. She was going to stay strong.

"I don't see there's anything you can say that's going to change what's happened." Kirsty stiffened. She hated conflict, and the last 24 hours had been a clusterfuck of it. "I came here for some peace. I don't appreciate you disturbing it."

But when Helena's face fell, Kirsty gave in a little. Perhaps Helena had an explanation? Kirsty sighed. "Just say what you've got to say, then go."

Helena gave her a firm nod. "Okay." She pulled back her shoulders. "I completely get I'm in the wrong and I fucked up here. So let me put that out there right now. What happened is not okay and it's my fault."

Kirsty nodded. "You got that right."

Helena took a deep breath before she continued. "However, they're not the promo pages I've had Anton working on for the past few weeks. Yes, I was going to do a page using some photos of Saffron that I'd snapped, saying she loves our wines, using her celebrity. I was hoping you'd say yes when you saw it was tastefully done, just to drum up a bit more business. I really couldn't see why you didn't want to. Saffron was a gift dropped in our lap." She held up a hand to stop Kirsty from speaking.

"And yes, I know that was wrong. After a while, I got that. I mocked up the page after the Oyster Festival, but I told Anton to ditch it. I created the ones that are there now with quotes from people all around the town instead, just like we agreed. It was the right thing to do. Particularly after you got to know her, and you got to like her." She put a hand to her chest. "I really liked her, too. Until she broke your heart."

Helena shook her head. "Anyway, the new promo pages celebrate our wines and Sandy Cove wine lovers. But Anton put up the Saffron page by mistake, too. The photos were still in the promo pages folder, which is my fault. He's corrected it now and it's already live. When I got home last night, I made sure he worked on it until it was fixed."

Helena stared at her anxiously.

Kirsty held her gaze. Her anger was still red hot in her throat. "I specifically asked you not to do this. I *trusted* you. Mistake or not, that still stands."

Helena dropped her head. "I know. I've learned a lesson, believe me. Especially if it costs me my business." She raised her head. "You *can* still trust me, even though it might take a while to rebuild. I get it." She stabbed her chest with her finger. "But I'm begging you, Kirsty. Please don't go to the bank. Don't break up the business. I love working with you, and yes, this was a massive misstep. Anton is so sorry, too. He's said he'll work at the shop for free for as long as it takes to make up for it. But just to make it clear, this is *my* fault, not his. I'm not shifting the blame."

She cleared her throat. "What's more, I *hate* the thought I've contributed in some way to you and Saffron breaking up. Especially after it had only just begun." Helena got down on one knee and clutched Kirsty's balled fist. "I *really* hate it. With every atom of my being. You of all people deserve happiness."

Kirsty's stomach rolled again. But this time, the anger was flushed away. They'd known each other since school. There was no malice behind Helena's actions. Could she forgive her for a simple but costly mistake? She still wasn't sure.

"I love you, Kirsty. I wouldn't do anything intentionally to hurt you." Helena's eyes were watery. "Anton and I have just come from Saffron's place. We went round and explained, so she knows you had nothing to do with it."

Now Kirsty welled up. "Did she believe you? Or did she think I was responsible?"

Helena shook her head. "She believed us. And by the way, she looked just as much a wreck as you do. Red eyes. She'd been crying. She was unpacking boxes, too. Looked like she'd brought stuff back from London. If she needs to be reassured it really was me, I can go round again every day till she believes me."

Kirsty shook her head, unfurling her fists. "What's the point? She didn't trust me, and I didn't trust her. If that's the case so early in our yet-to-get-off-the-ground relationship, I'd say it's doomed." She pulled her hands from Helena. "Plus, as soon as she got the chance, she ran back to her superstar."

"You might think that today, but maybe tomorrow may be different. She didn't look like she was heading back to

Echo Black any time soon." Helena stood up with a groan, then eyed the other chair. "Can I sit down? Am I at least semi-forgiven?"

Kirsty leaned back in her chair, before letting out a frustrated breath. "You might want to make yourself a coffee if we're going to have an iced bun together."

A half-smile split Helena's face. She stepped towards Kirsty.

Kirsty held up a hand.

Helena stopped in her tracks.

"I'm still mad at you. You still have a lot of making up to do. But one break-up is as much as I can take in 24 hours." Kirsty pointed at Helena. "You're on probation, okay?"

"Probation is as good as I can hope for." She stepped inside the beach hut, before coming straight back. "Shall I make a fresh pot?"

Kirsty gave her a nod. More coffee was definitely needed.

Chapter 29

Ginger swung the door open, took one look at her baby sister, and then opened her arms wide. "Come here."

Saffron unable to lift her own arms to return the hug, fell stiffly into Ginger's embrace.

"I'm guessing this is girl trouble. Nothing in the world wrecks a person more than a broken heart." Ginger held on tight.

"I should have known better than to get involved with anyone," Saffron mumbled into Ginger's shoulder.

Ginger wrapped an arm around Saffron's shoulder, guiding them to the back door. "Let's chat in the garden. Go on. I'll get the wine."

Saffron sat in the chair closest to the door, not caring the view of the sea was blocked by the dark green clematis climbing a trellis, the white flowers long gone for the season. The sound of people merrily chatting as they strolled on the promenade and the whiff of grilled fish irritated Saffron. How dare people go about their happy lives while hers had been smashed to pieces by Echo Black, Pearl, and Helena. Not to mention, Saffron had started to believe she found her forever home, along with her forever person.

That'd gone up in smoke almost as swiftly as the flame had sparked between them.

Movement outside of the garden caught her eye, and she lowered the brim of the baseball hat where she could hardly see. The paparazzi had been relentless since the Echo stunt.

"Kirsty gave me this bottle of white and I think it's the perfect chilled wine for whatever this is." Ginger circled a finger in the air.

"You don't drink white," Saffron snapped, regretting immediately biting Ginger's head off simply because she'd dare mention Kirsty's name.

"This is part of my rebirth. Kirsty's been showing me how a lot of what I believed about myself was based on Dave's likes and dislikes. And, as it turns out, I dig white wine."

Saffron refused to accept the glass, still unable to set aside her bitterness.

"I don't think I've ever seen you like this." Ginger forced it into the clenched hand.

Saffron took a deep breath.

Ginger grabbed a chair, placing it in front of her sister. "Start at the beginning."

"Why? The only part that matters is the end."

"Not true, because what led to this moment is the part that can be fixed." Ginger sipped the wine, crossing her legs.

"Not every problem has a solution. It's not like I inserted the wrong number into a Sudoku puzzle."

"You're terrible at maths, so I can't picture you trying one." Ginger's face crumpled with disbelief.

"I find them oddly calming when flying." Saffron picked at a thread on her shirt cuff.

"Stop stalling. What happened between you and Kirsty?"

"I never said anything about Kirsty." Saffron's nostrils flared.

"Not with words, but your puffy eyes, pouty expression, stuffy nose, and refusing a glass of Kirsty's wine are screaming heartbreak." Ginger slanted her head. "If you don't stop stalling, I'll ring Kirsty and have her explain."

"Go ahead and please enquire why she's convinced I'm shagging Echo Black. The one person on this planet I wouldn't be caught dead with, let alone fuck." Saffron dug her fingernails into her own palm.

"The video wasn't great." Ginger pinched the bridge of her nose.

Saffron's eyes narrowed. "You watched it?"

"It's safe to assume everyone in your life saw it. I have to hand it to Echo, she knows how to go viral. Too bad she hasn't caught the clap or syphilis. I think the latter could kill her."

"It wouldn't kill her. She would have just given it to me. The woman is great at walking away after blowing everything to smithereens." Saffron made a kaboom sound.

"Let's circle back to Kirsty."

Saffron ground her teeth.

"Okay, since you refuse to speak, which I'm willing to bet is one of the sources of trouble with Kirsty, I'm going to take a stab at it. Kirsty won't listen to you about Echo and how much you despise her. I can see her point—"

"How?" Saffron roared.

"Because there are countless photos of you two together looking beautiful and happy together. Even before the other night. How many red carpets have you graced together? Award shows? Nights out?"

Saffron rested her head on the back of the chair, gazing into the violet sky as night slowly descended. "That's all for show. Everything about that part of my life is for others, not me."

Ginger squeezed Saffron's arm. "I know that, but not everyone understands that. You're so secretive, which keeps everyone away from you, and I understand that's your goal. However, if you want a chance to let Kirsty in, you can't bury the parts of your life you don't want on display for the public."

"I don't know how to do that." Saffron wiped away a tear.

"I've found talking helps when communicating."

Saffron levelled her gaze on her sister, the wetness making it difficult to see clearly. "That's not what I meant."

"Explain it to me, please."

"How can I trust her? Or anyone? Helena explained about the website, but still, it happened. What's to stop something like that occurring in the future? It'll always be in the back of my mind." Saffron flicked a hand in the air, before letting it fall into her lap.

Ginger perked up in her seat. "What happened with what website? Remember, you have to fill in the gaps and not assume everyone knows all the important details."

"The website isn't the actual issue. It all comes back to the same thing. Someone sharing photos that weren't meant to be shared. Echo is the master, but Helena comes in second."

"How does Helena factor in?" Ginger squinted one eye, as if trying to slot everything into place, but failing.

"She's been taking photos of me, and building a promo page on the shop's website, because why not." Saffron flicked a helpless hand in the air. "I don't deserve privacy or respect from anyone. Maybe I should become a hermit."

"No hermitting," Ginger scolded.

"That's not a word."

"Doesn't matter." Ginger reached for her phone and spoke in an exasperated voice, "Just tell me what website you're talking about."

"Wine Time, but that particular page is down."

Ginger acted out throttling Saffron. "Words. I need them to know what the bloody hell is going on."

"Helena had Anton, her son, created a promo page for the shop that exploited my name saying Saffron Oliver gets all her wine from it. An endorsement I never gave permission for, not to mention the photos Helena had furtively snapped. The night I went to London, Anton *accidentally* made it live." Saffron made quote marks.

"Do you think Anton and Helena are lying?"

"No." Saffron tugged her shirtsleeves past her wrists, the night air growing chilly.

"Do you believe Kirsty had a role in it?"

"No."

"Then what's really bugging you?"

"Both things happened on the exact same night. Echo and the website. And both Kirsty and I believed the absolute worst about the other. Doesn't that say something?"

"Two things: bad luck and lack of communication." Ginger displayed two fingers in the air.

Saffron shook her head. "No. It's not that simple. Every time I trust someone, I get burned."

"If I'm following the story, Kirsty didn't betray you."

"She didn't believe me, either. I told her that lunch with Echo was a setup, but…" Saffron hitched a shoulder.

"Can you try seeing it from her side?"

"Are you implying I'm not trustworthy?" Saffron's blood turned to molten lava and she forced her sleeves up her forearms.

"Not at all. I think a lot of women would be jealous of Echo Black. Not only is she insanely beautiful, successful, and rich, she's confident as hell. That combination would be difficult for many to banish from their thoughts."

"She's not that confident. She constantly needs praise and to be admired."

"You know that, but the rest of the world doesn't." Ginger sighed. "Just because you understand what's in your heart, doesn't mean anyone else does, no matter how close they are to you."

"Do you think I'm shagging Echo?"

"Not a fair premise. You've opened up to me about her. And, I've known you since the day you took your first breath." Ginger leaned forward in her chair. "If you want Kirsty to believe you and Echo are over, have a heart to heart with her. Let her in completely."

"It's not just Echo. I don't want to go back to London. I don't want to act anymore. I need a fresh start. On every front. I'm exhausted and if I don't make changes now, I don't know how I'll survive."

"Are you serious? About giving it all up?" For the first time during the conversation, there was hopefulness in Ginger's expression.

Saffron nodded.

"You have no idea how happy that makes me. You've been miserable for so long."

"I really have." Saffron sniffed. "Why did it take me so long to see what was right in front of me?"

"It's hard to pinpoint the source of misery when you don't allow yourself time to stop and think. You've been going full speed for half of your life. Running further and further away from the shadow of Mum and Dad. Maybe it's time to stop running. Start confronting your demons. I've been so worried I'd lose you forever and only be left with the shell of my beautiful baby sister."

Saffron wiped her eyes with a sleeve. "Why didn't you tell me?"

"Sometimes you have to come to these realisations on your own and besides, would you have listened?" Ginger's slanted head said no.

"I guess we'll never know."

"Nice try, Saff. You're the most stubborn person I know and you have to figure out things on your own. I'm just glad you no longer take appliances apart to see how they work. I can't start my day without a coffee and toasted tea cake."

"Where's your tool kit?" Saffron started to rise from her chair.

"You're such a pain in the arse. Sit down. Tell me what your plan is." Ginger eagerly tapped her fingers together.

"I like the beach house. I'm going to put an offer on it. One that can't be turned down."

Ginger squealed. "I like what I'm hearing so far. Go on."

"Maybe I'll adopt a dog. Take long walks every morning and night."

Ginger nodded her head enthusiastically. "Still good. Keep going."

"I've thought about buying one of the beach huts. Spend the day sketching or painting."

"Excellent. Creating art has always soothed your soul."

Saffron leaned back in her seat, taking a sip of the wine. "What should I name my dog?"

"Wait." Ginger bolted upright. "Is that the end of your plans?"

"What else is there?"

"Kirsty." She made a *duh* face.

"She doesn't trust me." Saffron pulled her own *don't be daft* face.

"It has to be earned."

"What's the point, now?"

"Don't you dare do this to me!" Ginger waggled a finger threateningly at Saffron.

"Do what?"

"Give up on happiness because it scares you. I'm having my divorce party tomorrow—"

"Exactly!"

"No. Don't try that shit with me. I married the wrong person. It took me this long to figure that out, but it doesn't mean there isn't the right person for me. Or for you."

"I'm not sure I believe that." Saffron hunched her shoulders, sinking her head between them.

"Is that right? Then why are you wallowing in self-pity? If you didn't believe in love, you wouldn't be hurting this much."

"Oh please—"

"You and Kirsty make sense. You're an old soul. She's young at heart. When I see you two together, it's clear as day that you guys belong together. Don't give up on happiness because it got hard. I have news for you. The most worthwhile things in life take a lot of work. Every single day. The way I see it, you need to convince Kirsty how much you love her. Or you'll never forgive yourself or be at peace."

Chapter 30

"This pinata is bloody heavy." Helena's gaze was on Hugh, as he lugged the ring-shaped papier mâché pinata from one side of the venue to the other.

"It needs to be. It's a divorce party. There's going to be a whole lot of anger to work through." Kirsty checked her phone, then put it in her back pocket. She'd had no urgent messages in the past hour, which was a miracle.

"Everything okay?" Helena's cheeks were flushed after wheeling in some of the party wine.

"Absolutely." Kirsty raised a clenched fist. "Fired up and raring to go."

Helena set down the trolley and put an arm around Kirsty's shoulder. "You should be very proud of yourself. Doing a divorce party in these circumstances is beyond brilliant."

Kirsty snorted. "Understatement of the year."

"Exactly. But you haven't let it derail you. You've been professional to the last." Helena swept her hand around the venue. "This place looks amazing, and that's all down to you."

Kirsty had to admit, the venue looked stunning. The bare bones were great, being that the building was on a jetty with the open sea as its outlook, picture windows framing the vista all the way around. However, Kirsty had strung the place with fairy lights, and the small tables set up to make the most of the view were festooned with seasonal cosmos flowers. The tables also had laminated photos of Ginger with friends and family, showing she didn't need a partner to be happy. It was a sentiment Kirsty could get behind.

"It looks okay, doesn't it?"

"It looks stunning! I particularly like the bitchy cupcakes." They wandered over to the table that held them. "Whoever came up with the slogans stuck in the top was genius. Was that you?"

Kirsty nodded. "I ordered them online, but I'm still worried what Betty is going to say when she sees them. She bakes delicious cupcakes, and then I stick signs in them that say 'Fuck You!', 'Good Riddance!' and 'Solo is My Jam!'"

Now it was Helena's turn to snort. "She'll get over it." She paused. "I also want you to know, you've been incredible the way you've dealt with the whole website hiccup, too. You've been the bigger person, and I appreciate that."

Kirsty nudged her friend with her elbow. "I couldn't deal with my whole world falling apart at once. I needed some stability." Plus, Helena had been a huge help the past two days since everything kicked off. Kirsty hadn't heard from Saffron, which spoke volumes. She assumed she was turning up later for Ginger's party, but who knew? The lure of Echo Black and the movie world might have whisked her away. Kirsty had removed Instagram from her phone so she couldn't fixate. She had to get back to thinking about her new business venture and making tonight the best she could make it. If Saffron turned up, she would be polite but distant. She wouldn't crumble to dust in front of her.

Even though the thought of Saffron made Kirsty pine. She pressed her feet to the floor and focused on the sea out the window. It was calm, with no waves. Kirsty needed to emulate that body of water tonight. Not the wave-inducing kind.

"Where do you want these balloons strung up, love?"

Her dad's shouting broke her thoughts. A swell of love made her heart expand as Kirsty looked over to her parents, who were both busy blowing up purple and pink balloons, then fastening them together. When finished, the balloon banner was going to spell 'Happily Divorced!', and hang on the far side of the space for everyone to see.

"Right above the cake table." Kirsty pointed towards the ceiling where she was standing. "The hooks are already there." All that bunting hanging in the shop meant she was a pro.

Her dad gave her a thumbs up.

Mum put down a finished balloon and walked over, chuckling at the cake topper that had the bride throwing the groom into a toy bin lorry. "We never had this in my day, but I know a few friends who would have loved to have had one." Her mum put a hand on her hip, and glanced up at Kirsty. "Would you have wanted to do one after you and Anna divorced?"

Kirsty shook her head. "I don't think so. I was too upset. But a party to draw a line when the dust had settled would have been nice. I think Ginger's very brave doing this, making a statement."

Her mum rubbed her hands together. "It's the Butlers in the Buff I'm looking forward to. When are the naked waiters getting here?"

Kirsty laughed. "You'll notice them when they arrive. Look for the naked arses and the aprons that barely cover much at all."

* * *

Three hours later and it was all systems go. The main food, to be served in bowls throughout the night, was seafood based and so would be cooked right before it was eaten.

Kirsty stood at the end of the chef's main pass, the staff a blur of activity around her. The oysters sat to her left in a vat of ice, the prawns beside them. She recalled the food tasting with Saffron. When things had just started to thaw after their first Echo Black interruption. Kirsty should have called it off there and then, shouldn't she? Hindsight was a mighty impressive thing.

She pushed open the door to the main space, loving the buttery afternoon light that flooded the space. They'd moved the cakes to the chiller cabinet to avoid them melting to gloop. The deck out front was going to be in full use tonight, so Helena and Hugh were decorating it with bunting and balloons. Kirsty was happily trading on their guilt to make them work and it was panning out well. To her right, the live band had arrived and were setting up on stage. In the far corner, the photobooth was being assembled.

Kirsty turned her attention to the cocktail bar and Mia, their head bartender for the night. How old was she? 25? Almost half Kirsty's age. She hoped working a divorce party wouldn't scar her too much.

"So you're good on our Divorce Sour cocktail?" This was Ginger's creation, emailed to Kirsty at 3am the night of her and Saffron's meltdown. Just two days ago. It felt like two years. Kirsty had opened the email wondering if Ginger was playing go-between for her sister, but no. Instead, she'd received a badly spelled email listing the cocktail's ingredients, also telling Kirsty that Dave could 'go fuck himself'.

"Got it." Mia put her hand on top of a bottle of Bombay Sapphire gin. "Gin, bitters, egg white, sugar syrup and lime juice. I just boiled down some sugar syrup so we've got plenty of it." She pointed to the basket of limes behind the bar. "Plus, Luke is arriving soon, and he's got big muscles. I'm going to make him use them on these limes."

"Excellent." Kirsty paused. "Have you tried it?"

Mia nodded. "Made a couple last night. They were pretty good. The punters should be happy."

A tap on Kirsty's shoulder made her jump. She turned, clutching her chest, to find Ginger behind her. "You scared the shit out of me!" Kirsty gave her a hug.

"My apologies," Ginger replied. "How's the Divorce Sour coming along?"

"Full of bitter regret, just the way you wanted it." Mia gave Ginger a grin.

"Cool." She paused. "Do you mind if I steer Kirsty away for a few minutes?"

It was a rhetorical question. Ginger took Kirsty by the elbow and out onto the deck, past Helena and Hugh, right to the edge.

"Another step and I'd be in the sea."

"Don't do that. Not until the party's over."

Kirsty gave her a smile, staring across the water. The ocean never failed to calm her. She'd been kayaking again this morning. It had proved a lifeline in her stormy emotional seas.

"What are you doing here, anyway?" Kirsty wagged a finger. "You should be getting your glad rags on and gearing up." She pulled her phone from her shorts' pocket. "It's nearly 4.30."

Ginger gave her a dismissive wave. "I'm not high maintenance. Half an hour will do me. I just wanted to say thank you, before the party kicks off, for all your hard work. I know it hasn't been easy, given the circumstances."

Regret slid down Kirsty, but she ignored it. Today was about Ginger and her new life. She wasn't about to steal the limelight. "Whatever's happened with your sister is nothing to do with the party. I'm still here for you 100 per cent."

Ginger stroked her arm. "I know, and I appreciate that." She paused. "But I also wanted to let you know that you shouldn't give up on Saffron. Nothing happened with her and Echo. I really think tonight could be the start of another story, too. You and my sister."

Kirsty shook her head. "I can't think about that right now. I have to focus on my job. Plus, she thought the worst of me. I'm not sure that's a great basis to start from."

Ginger gave a slow smile as she looked out to sea, before turning her gaze to Kirsty.

"You and my sister are very alike, you know that? You're both looking for love, but you're both scared shitless. Plus, you're both damaged from the past. But isn't everyone?" She turned and pointed at the venue. "Look at me. Some people might see this as me celebrating a failure. That's one way to look at it. Maybe I thought like that at one point. But today, thanks to your help, I see this as the start of a new future. Plus, a reason to drink fabulous cocktails and eat delicious cake. We need more of that in the world."

"Saffron and you are a bit like the sea." Ginger waved her hand again. "Calm on the surface, but raging emotions underneath. Those emotions could be explosive in a good way, not a divisive way. I believe you've both experienced the worst side this week."

Kirsty dipped her head. A cannonball of emotion rolled through her, steamrollering her heart. "You could say that."

Ginger shook her head. "I can't believe I'm saying this on the day of my divorce party, but I am, so you'd better listen." She paused to check she had Kirsty's attention.

She did.

"You're both scared, but somebody needs to make the move. You could be happy. I think deep down, you both know that. Grasp happiness while it's on offer. I still intend to when it next presents itself to me. I've just got divorced, but I'm still advocating for love. If I can do it, so can you."

Love? Kirsty's heart clambered to its feet. She went to speak, but her throat was dry. Eventually, she spluttered: "Love? Has Saffron been talking about love?" Kirsty's heart glowed like never before.

Ginger reached out and squeezed her hand. "What do you think has been going on with the two of you?" She smiled. "Think about it. Do the party tonight, but when everything's done, don't run off. Talk to Saffron. You might just find what you've been looking for."

Chapter 31

The band started to play "I Will Survive" and everyone hit the dance floor with Ginger in the middle, her arms raised as she continued bumping and grinding with all willing partygoers, singing along like her life depended on it. Even Ian danced with Betty, Kirsty's father showcasing bumbling dad moves, but Saffron liked how he didn't seem to give a damn.

Everyone was pleasantly buzzed and having a ball.

Well, everyone but Saffron, who'd been putting on a brave face and making small talk with the guests. Odds were no one suspected Saffron would rather be swimming naked in a pool of piranhas.

The only person who Saffron hadn't spoken to was Kirsty, the one Saff wanted to speak to most of all, but was terrified to the core. Apparently, Kirsty wasn't in the mood for chit-chat either, because whenever Saffron was on one side of the party, Kirsty was on the exact opposite with her back turned. One time, they were almost in the same airspace, until Kirsty dashed off on some party mission.

Surely, that meant Kirsty had made up her mind, and Saffron should steel her heart to forever being alone. The sole good news was she'd talked to a shelter about a rescue dog and would be meeting her the following day. Saffron had been bouncing around possible names, but the one that hung over her head like a cartoon bubble was Kirsty.

Kirsty.

"Yes?"

Saffron spun around. "Um... did I say that aloud?"

"You did." Kirsty wet her lips.

"Are you sure?" Saffron took a step back.

"Are you calling me a liar?"

"Not intentionally, no." A sheen of sweat dampened the back of her shirt.

"Does that mean your subconscious thinks I'm a liar?"

"This isn't going well for me, is it?"

"Are you implying it's going well for me?" Kirsty's facial muscles lost some of their rigidity and her eyes glistened with interest.

"You're feisty today." Saffron put a hand up. "No, I wasn't hinting at anything by that. I'm just doing a terrible job of communicating tonight. I wish I could blame the Divorce Sours, but I haven't had one."

"I recommend correcting that immediately."

"Are you saying I have a broken heart?" Saffron playfully crossed her arms.

"I wouldn't dream of inferring anything when it comes to you. It's become apparent, I don't know you all that well."

Saffron swallowed, unsure how to come back from that, because it was reminiscent to what Ginger had said the other night.

"How's Echo?"

Saffron heaved a frustrated sigh. "I have no idea."

"Please. According to her socials you two plan to have a week away before filming starts for the next *Girl Racer*." The only way to define the tone was ice-cold.

Saffron slit her eyes to the point she could only see gold. Gold? Not red? She widened them enough to see the massive gold-ring pinata. "It's a shame Ginger only took one whack."

Kirsty glanced over her shoulder. "Unfortunate timing with the arrival of the Butlers in the Buff."

Saffron snorted. "It's hard to compete with nearly naked men."

"I never saw the appeal." Kirsty's gaze found one of the butlers, his black apron barely covering the goods aside from his exposed arse.

Ruth's friend seemed to intentionally drop something on the ground, that rolled behind the gentleman, who felt compelled to turn around and retrieve it, ensuring he gave Shirley a jolly good show.

Shirley and her gaggle of women cackled with joy, and Saffron shook her head, laughing.

The band started "It's Raining Men" resulting in Ginger shrieking.

Kirsty returned a thumbs up from Ginger, before saying to Saffron, "Good job with the music, even though you've been a tit the last few days. I shouldn't be surprised since you look like a pop star in that suit you ordered for Ginger."

Saffron looked down at the sequined silver trouser suit, tugging awkwardly on one of the black velvet lapels, but she looked back to the ring. "You know the saying: waste not, want not?"

"Is that why you wore the suit?"

"What? No. I was referring to the pinata. The party's breaking up, aside from the diehard dancers. Shall we give it a go?" Saffron pointed to it.

"I've never hit one."

"A pinata or a wedding ring?" Saffron jacked up one eyebrow.

"Both."

"There's a first for everything. Like when I went kayaking with you."

Kirsty started to smile, but it froze on her lips. "I'm not good at hitting things."

"It's easy. Just pretend you're striking my head with a bat." Saffron handed Kirsty the weapon. "Whose idea was the rainbow-coloured stick?"

"Mine. Every time I suggested something rainbow, Ginger shot me down, thinking I was on some not-so-hidden lesbian agenda. But I wanted to keep the party theme as light-hearted as possible. It's not an end, but a beginning."

"Is there a pot of gold at the end of the rainbow?"

"For Ginger." Kirsty clutched the stick with both hands, looking unsure of what to do. "I think I'm supposed to be blindfolded."

"Right." Saffron took up the scarf from the nearby table. "Turn around."

"How can I trust you won't strangle me or anything?"

"Says the woman holding a whacking stick."

"I'm harmless. The weapon in question is rainbow coloured. That should put you at ease."

"This is silk, not piano wire." Saffron held it in both hands, like an offering to a Greek goddess. "You can trust me."

"Can I?" Kirsty's penetrating grey eyes locked onto her target.

"Yes. Look—can you lower the stick, rainbow or not? You wielding it like you're about to smash my skull in, is intimidating as hell and this is hard enough." Saffron slouched her shoulders to appear less intimidating.

Kirsty let it drop to her side.

"I know I mishandled the website snafu—"

"How could you believe I was involved?" Kirsty tapped the stick against her chest.

"It was my worst-case scenario coming to fruition, or so I thought. Having someone use my name for their own profit. I didn't stop to think. I only reacted. I'm sorry." Saffron splayed a hand over her chest. "Really, *really* sorry."

"Are you going to blindfold me or not?" Kirsty used the stick to point to the scarf.

"Does that mean you accept my apology?"

"I'm considering it." Kirsty wheeled about. "I want to whack this ring."

"Is that right?" Saffron tied the cloth around Kirsty's eyes. "Do you have a thing against rings?"

"Not necessarily, but it's here and I think better when in motion." She pranced on her feet like a prize fighter. "I'm ready."

Saffron laughed and placed a hand on each of Kirsty's shoulders. "I'm going to spin you three times, and then you can take a swing."

"Why do you have to spin me?"

"It's the rule."

"Why do Americans like this?"

"Got me." Saffron twirled Kirsty once, keeping her hands firmly on her. "Ready for another?"

"Yes."

After the third rotation, Saffron steadied Kirsty. "On the count of three, do your best. One... two... two and a half... three!"

Kirsty took a swing, barely hitting the pinata, shuffling on her feet as if she was about to fall.

Saffron reached out to steady her, but Kirsty, still blindfolded, was already winding up for another whack, with Saffron as the target. "Whoa! Don't shoot, cowgirl. You're aiming at my head."

Kirsty slapped the weapon into her palm, making a thwacking sound. "And, you think that's an accident?"

Saffron laughed. "I'm an optimist that way."

"You hurt me." Kirsty whacked her palm with a much louder slapping sound.

"I'm truly sorry." Saffron tried to swallow the lump in her throat, but it took a couple of attempts.

"That night was also my worst-case scenario coming to life. I've been taken for granted and cheated on."

"It breaks my heart that you thought me capable of hopping from your bed into Echo's." Saffron massaged her heart.

"Try being me. I remember her text saying her bed was lonely without you." Another thwack of the stick into her palm.

"Okay, I see your point and I want to clear this up right now. I didn't sleep with her that night."

"You didn't?" Kirsty asked in a tiny voice.

"No."

"The video made you two look like love birds."

"I'm aware. Echo is a pro when it comes to presentation." Saffron had to suppress her anger at Echo and focus on what truly mattered. "You probably don't know what to believe, but you said you need to move to think better. I'm going to reposition you to hit the ring. Not me. Okay? You promise not to hit me?" Saffron held her palms up in spite of Kirsty not being able to see.

Kirsty nodded.

Saffron helped her get into the proper stance. "Hit as hard as you can. Get the anger out. Like I said, pretend it's my head. Don't keep it bottled in."

Kirsty whacked the fuck out of the ring. Then again. And again.

Wrapped sweets dribbled out from a tear.

Saffron whistled. "You really like smashing my skull in."

Kirsty nudged the blindfold up. "I pictured Echo."

"That's a relief." Her laughter came out shaky, like she'd been terrified Kirsty really did want to bash Saffron's skull in.

"Why don't you give it a go?" Kirsty's shoulders seemed much lighter.

"Can I picture Echo?"

"If that's who you want to hit." Kirsty prepped Saffron, and spun her around. "One more for good measure."

Saffron chuckled. "This really is a bizarre party tradition."

"Okay, pard-ner," Kirsty's over-the-top American West impression brought a smile to Saffron's face. "Do your best."

Saffron's wild stab made contact, followed by the trickle of more sweets. "Did you check out my social media accounts?"

"I did." Kirsty kept her voice neutral.

"Did mine say anything about this week away with Echo?"

"You don't know?" Kirsty sounded dubious.

"My team handles all that. I've never tweeted in my life. I don't see the point." Saffron swung again. "So, am I going on holiday with Echo-Fucking-Black?"

"Not according to your socials, no."

"At least my team is listening to me."

"Out of curiosity, what did you tell them about Echo?"

Saffron planted her feet and gave the stick a shake, prepping for a wallop. "Let's see if you can guess from this." She released hell.

Kirsty whooped.

Saffron hoisted the blindfold off, zeroing in on the broken ring on the ground. "Just in case you need more of an explanation, I can't stand Echo. If I never see her again, it'd be too soon."

"Won't that be hard when you start the movie?"

"I'm not doing the movie."

"You're not?" Kirsty's eyes widened.

"Nope."

"Why?"

"Besides the fact that I don't want to go to prison because I may bash her brains in if I'm in the same room with her?"

Kirsty started to speak, but stopped, letting Saffron continue.

"I don't want to make movies anymore."

"Not at all?"

"My solicitor is crafting a suit to get me out of Pearl's clutches. I've put in an offer to buy the beach house. Tomorrow I have an appointment to see a dog I want to adopt."

"Wait." Kirsty put her arms out as if trying to stop herself from spinning. "You're not going back to London?"

Saffron shook her head.

"Or LA?"

Another shake of the head. "I'm putting both places on the market. I realised I hate both places. Sandy Cove makes me happy. Being near Ginger. And the sea." Saffron pointed the rainbow stick at Kirsty. "But there's no ifs, ands, or buts, it's you who makes me the happiest."

"But... we were tested and we both failed."

Saffron bobbed her head, taking that onboard. "It's true. The question is: will we learn from it or will we fail every other test?"

"I don't know, Saff. The fact that we're having this conversation the night of your sister's divorce party speaks volumes, doesn't it?"

"It does."

"Then why are you smiling like that?"

"Because you're still talking to me and we're getting our feelings out." Saffron used her hands to demonstrate unburdening herself. "That also has to mean something. I know a simple apology won't wipe away my mistake. But— I want to show you something." Saffron dashed for her bag and pulled out a sketch. "I want to paint this for you."

"It's my shop." Kirsty squinted one eye at Saffron.

"Yes."

"It's incredible."

"And, here's one of the beach house."

Kirsty took the paper from Saffron. "Oh, wow. Look at the detail." She brought the paper closer. "Is that me?"

"In the garden, yes. I never would have finished either of these sketches before coming to Sandy Cove. I'd start one, but would get busy, losing steam. Sometimes, I'd misplace the scrap of paper. I want to slow down. I want to learn to appreciate the small things in life. I want to always stroll on the promenade. Most of all, I don't want to be miserable anymore."

"Were you?"

"Yes. You helped me see just how trapped I'd let myself become."

"I fear I've made things even worse, though." Kirsty tucked her elbows into her sides.

"Yes, but I've been doing a lot of thinking lately. I've decided all of it was necessary. Okay, maybe not necessary... sorry, Ginger has been encouraging me to communicate more to avoid trouble, but..."

"Go on..." Kirsty prodded.

"Are you busy next week?"

"Like every day next week?" A cloud of confusion overtook her face.

Saffron balled up a fist, her nails digging into her palm. "Geez, you're aren't making this easy, are you?"

"What?" Kirsty's eyes sparkled.

"Me asking you out on a date. I've never done it before."

"And here I thought we were turning a new page." Kirsty mimed this.

"We are!"

"I'm supposed to believe you've never asked a girl out on a date?" Kirsty tapped a foot, shaking her head.

"I really haven't. I started acting when I was a teenager. This kind of thing wasn't allowed."

"Dating?"

"Being normal. Everything was staged. For the public."

"Will you miss it? Even a tiny bit." Kirsty held two fingers in the air, barely apart.

"Living in a fishbowl? No."

"You say that now."

"Shall we bet? One year from now, I bet I don't miss it at all." Saffron stuck her hand out.

"What do I get if I win?"

"What do you want?"

"I'm not sure you can give me what I want."

"Movie star." Saffron waved a hand in front of her face. "Try me."

"You know you're proving me right well ahead of the deadline?" Kirsty smirked.

Saffron snorted impatiently. "Still waiting for your answer. What do you want to wager? Because I'm all in on restarting my life away from the spotlight to be with you."

The band started to play the Abba song "Take a Chance on Me."

Kirsty looked at the stage and then back to Saffron. "Did you plan that?"

"What?" Saffron didn't have to feign innocence.

"You were in charge of music. But how did you get them to sing that song right now?"

Saffron bobbed her head as realisation washed over her. "I think fate gets the credit and I'm still waiting to hear what you want from me. Tell me how hard I have to work to convince you I'm in this for the long haul."

Kirsty pulled Saffron close. "I want this."

They kissed.

"Christ! That took you two forever," Ginger shouted.

There was clapping and hooting.

Neither of them stopped kissing.

Chapter 32

"Can I walk you home?" Saffron tossed some party hats into a bin, wiping away glitter from her shirt.

Kirsty emptied her arms of *Single AF* bunting. "Is this another new thing for you?"

"Cleaning up?"

"Walking a girl home."

"Yes. Usually my driver takes a woman home, after he pays her, of course."

"You're incorrigible."

Saffron cupped her ear. "I haven't heard a yes or no if you're ready to go."

"Let me say goodnight to the staff, first. Don't wander off."

Saffron made a show of planting her feet. "Not moving an inch."

"Maybe being a living statue is in your future."

"Hurry up, this is exhausting." Saffron shooed Kirsty away, wanting to leave the party so they could be alone.

Ginger sidled up, bumping her shoulder into Saffron. "Check you out. About to get lucky."

Saffron twisted her hair to get it off her back. "Stop. Don't curse this."

"I'm the curse? I'm the one whose been playing peacemaker."

"You talked to Kirsty?" Saffron craned her neck to see into Ginger's face, unsure if she should be irritated or grateful for her sister's meddling.

"Yep. You can thank me later, but do me a favour?" Ginger gripped Saffron's arm.

"Can't wait to hear this one." Saffron waved for Ginger to get it out, bracing for a very Ginger-like demand. Given they'd just wrapped up Ginger's divorce party, Saffron wasn't sure if she should do whatever was asked.

"Don't mess up again. She's worth a million Echo Blacks."

Saffron sought out Kirsty, who was hugging her mum goodnight. "You can't put a price on her."

Ginger melted. "Why are you wasting that line on me? Go. She's waiting."

Saffron gave her sister a one-armed hug, and rushed to meet Kirsty halfway. "Ready?"

"Kirsty! Wait." Out of breath, Helena slipped something into Kirsty's pocket and said, "Read it in the morning."

"Are you sure?" Kirsty's eyes clouded over.

"Yep. You have better things to do. Now, skedaddle!" Helena gestured for the two of them to get going.

Saffron gave Kirsty a questioning look, but she simply shrugged, and asked, "Water or the short way?"

"Come again? Do you need water for the walk?" Saffron glanced about for a bottle.

"How do you want to get to mine?" Kirsty looked at Saffron like she was adorably clueless.

"Oh, right. The short way."

"I was hoping you'd say that. I'm knackered." She let out a breath.

"Shall I get a car?" Saffron got out her phone.

"I'm sure I can last the five minutes."

"Let's roll, then." She pocketed her phone and crooked her arm for Kirsty.

"It's moments like this when I remember how bloody tall you are."

"Do you want me to bend my knees or walk on them?"

Kirsty swatted Saffron's arm, both of them giggling.

After they started out, Saffron turned her head to Kirsty. "When I finish your painting, will you hang it up in the shop? If you like it, that is?"

"Why wouldn't I like it?"

"I might be a rubbish painter."

"I seriously doubt you could fail at anything. But why do you want me to hang it up?" Kirsty's voice tightened with confusion.

"Because I flipped out over the website. It's like a peace offering."

They turned left onto Kirsty's street, her shop not too far off in the distance.

"That's sweet of you, but not necessary."

"I think it is." Saffron rubbed the back of her neck.

"Seriously. An apology was more than adequate."

"Damn. You may not like what's coming next, then."

Kirsty stopped in front of her shop, looking slightly unsteady on her feet. "What?"

"Look up." Saffron pointed to the sign overhead.

"Why?"

"I see we're back to not trusting." With a nudge, Saffron tipped Kirsty's head up.

"My sign has been painted." Kirsty blinked. "You paid someone to paint my sign?"

"No. Anton and I painted it. Along with the front of your shop."

"You painted my shop and sign? Why?" Kirsty had her eyes on Saffron.

"You said it needed a makeover." Saffron's shoulders fell. "You did say that, didn't you? I'm not losing my mind."

"Yes, but how? When?"

"While you were setting up the party. I knew you'd have your hands full. Helena told me you wanted burgundy. It is the right colour, I hope?"

"It is." Kirsty ran a tentative finger over the wood trim as if it was still wet and then slowly looked back up to the sign. "That's why you were running late tonight. I'd assumed you didn't want to see me."

"That's never the case, even when you're mad at me."

"I don't know what to say."

"No words are necessary."

"Stop right there. I think we've learned communication is indeed needed." Kirsty edged closer.

"I love words. I say them all the time." Saffron shuffled forward.

"You know what's better?" Kirsty's breath tickled Saffron's ear.

"What?" Saffron whispered.

"This." Kirsty pulled Saffron in for a kiss.

Saffron walked them back, pressing Kirsty against the

glass of the shop. "I never thought we'd do this again." She cupped Kirsty's face in her hands. "I thought I'd fucked up beyond belief."

"I believed the same—that you'd never speak to me again." Kirsty placed a hand over Saffron's heart. "The thought nearly killed me."

"It's funny. I've been paid so much money to say other people's words, but when it came to that night…" Her throat thickened and it was hard to get out the rest. "I couldn't find the ones I needed to tell you how I felt."

"Try saying them now." The softness in Kirsty's eyes emboldened Saffron.

"I'm scared." Saffron pressed her forehead to Kirsty's. "It's so much easier building walls than letting someone in."

"Speaking of that." Kirsty rolled the back of her head on the glass to the left and right. "Do you think we should take this inside? Someone might snap a photo of us?"

"Can I send it to Echo with *fuck off* written in your lipstick on it?"

"How did I miss this anger?" Kirsty's smile had bite.

"I'm used to shutting off around others." Saffron ran a hand in front of her face, like a curtain falling, her expression turning perfectly bland.

"Can you not do that? It's disturbing."

Saffron moved closer to Kirsty as if compelled. "I don't think I can resist you anymore. You have no idea how much energy it's taken all this time. To fight this feeling. To stop myself from getting close to you in every way."

"Stop fighting it," Kirsty pleaded.

"You have to as well."

Kirsty inhaled a deep breath, her chest hitching.

Saffron clasped Kirsty's cheeks with both hands, their mouths finding the other, Saffron's heart flitting about as if taking a victory lap. At first, their lips were pressed together, but Saffron lost control and deepened the kiss, her arms wrapping around Kirsty.

Kirsty briefly yanked away, to fish for her keys in her bag, resuming their kiss, simultaneously attempting to put the key into the lock for the door leading to her flat.

Saffron placed her hand on Kirsty's. "Let me help."

The door clicked open.

Still kissing, they crossed the threshold.

"Why did we waste so much time?" Saffron asked in between kisses.

"We're idiots?" Kirsty raked a hand through Saffron's hair.

"Don't hold back." Saffron planted her lips hard onto Kirsty's. "You have the softest lips. I can't stop kissing you."

"Does that mean you don't want a glass of wine?"

"You. Want you."

"I see words are still difficult for you."

"Take me upstairs or we can shag here. Dealer's choice." Saffron growled saying she wouldn't be able to hold back much longer.

"I've never had sex in the hallway." Kirsty, not breaking free from Saffron, swivelled her head back and forth, inspecting the space. "It's pretty cramped."

"Is that a surprise to you?"

"I've never considered using it for anything else before.

It's inadequate for what I want to do to you." Kirsty reached for Saffron's hand. "Upstairs, then." Her pupils tripled in size, lust burning.

Saffron froze, her vision going dark, and a buzzing sound in her ears.

Kirsty tugged harder, but Saffron couldn't move.

"Are you okay?" Kirsty snapped her fingers in Saffron's face.

"I—" Saffron reached for her throat.

"We can stop. For the night." Kirsty's gaze brimmed with compassion. "A lot has happened."

Saffron's heart thudded in her throat, her tongue stilled.

Kirsty gently shook Saffron. "You still with me?"

Saffron glanced over her shoulder as if Kirsty was speaking to someone else, but slowly turned her head to face those lovely grey eyes. Her heart poked holes in all the dark thoughts bubbling in her head. *She can't love you for who you are. She's using you. She'll hurt you.*

Saffron made her decision, and kissed Kirsty hard. "Bedroom. Now."

Kirsty led Saffron upstairs and once in the room she shoved Saffron against a wall. Both of their hands slipping under shirts, savouring the touches of the other's skin. Kirsty fisted Saffron's blond tresses, bringing forth a throaty moan.

Saffron gazed at Kirsty as if not believing this was happening. But there wasn't time to contemplate. She'd wasted too many precious seconds locked inside her head. Action. Her focus had to be on action. She needed to keep chipping away at her walls and let Kirsty in.

Kirsty nodded as if reading Saffron's mind.

Their bodies pressed together once again, both of them hungry for the other's flesh and lips.

Kirsty pulled the neck of Saffron's shirt, to give her tongue the freedom to roam the exquisite collarbone.

Saffron shifted her weight, her knees nearly buckling.

Kirsty lifted Saffron's shirt off, tossing it over her shoulder. Kirsty cupped Saffron's right breast, running a thumb over the peaked nipple battling the restraint.

Saffron reached around, and undid her bra for Kirsty. Together they slid the straps down Saffron's arms, letting the bra fall to the floor, revealing creamy skin, perky breasts with pink nipples, and a spattering of freckles.

Kirsty traced some of the spots, forming a star. "It's like you were born to be famous."

Saffron looked down. "Or cursed."

"Oh, no. Not with this body." Kirsty licked her lips. "How did I get so fucking lucky?"

"I could say the same thing."

"Are you sweet talking me because I have you half naked?" Kirsty boosted a teasing eyebrow, pinching one of Saffron's nipples between two fingers.

"Keep that up, and I'll be begging soon." Saffron let out a whoosh of air, excitement building.

"I wouldn't be opposed." Kirsty pulled Saffron from the wall, and walked them backwards, easing Saffron onto her bed, and climbing on top. Straddling Saffron, Kirsty gazed at the breasts on display. "So fucking lucky."

Saffron nibbled on her lower lip.

Kirsty lowered, her tongue stroking the hollow of Saffron's throat, eliciting a *fuck me* moan.

Kirsty licked a path to the left breast, sucking the nipple into her mouth, hardening it, allowing her to softly bite down on the nub. She alternated between sucking and biting, increasing the pressure incrementally with her teeth.

"Oh, yes," Saffron moaned.

Kirsty didn't let up.

A shiver worked its way through Saffron, her hips rocking upwards. Kirsty rubbed hers into Saffron, the women moving as one, Saffron clawing Kirsty's back, not wanting their connection to break, but there was one problem.

"This needs to come off!" Saffron ripped Kirsty's shirt over her head. "I need to feel your skin against mine."

Kirsty stared down into Saffron's eyes. "Better?"

"Halfway."

Kirsty laughed. "Patience, darling."

Saffron jerked her hip into Kirsty with palpable need.

"So bossy." Kirsty winked and leaned down, taking the neglected nipple into her mouth, staying long enough to make it hard, but not wanting to tip Saffron into desperation.

Kirsty began her journey down, her mouth meandering from one freckle to the next as if following them like sailors seeking a port.

The trail left Saffron aflame with desire, her fingers digging into Kirsty's shoulders and back, all the while her mouth and tongue continued the trek.

Every nerve ending in Saffron's body lit up and she sank her body deeper into the mattress, unable to control her writhing, a growl escaping.

"You sound a bit hoarse. Do you need a glass of wine? I can pop downstairs." Kirsty gripped the top of Saffron's trousers.

"Don't you dare leave me like this," Saffron demanded.

"Like what?" Kirsty undid the top button, but made a show of not continuing without more instruction.

"I need you, not..." Saffron's mind went blank.

"Come on, use your words. What do you need?" Kirsty lowered Saffron's trousers.

"You seem to know." Saffron gave Kirsty a suggestive look.

Kirsty stopped, with the trousers only halfway down.

"This is so unfair." Saffron took a deep breath.

"From my viewpoint, it's so fucking amazing. You're underneath me, begging. You are begging, aren't you?"

"It seems I have to."

Kirsty ran her tongue up Saffron's inside right thigh, stopping on the scarlet knickers. "Poor you. Such torture."

"Please." Saffron swallowed, her body aching with desire. "Don't stop."

Kirsty removed the trousers. "See how easy that was?"

"Aren't you forgetting something?" Saffron eyed her knickers.

"I'm rather enjoying seeing them on you." Kirsty lowered the top enough to permit her teeth to rake pubic hair. "However, it'd be such a disappointment not to be able to taste you."

"I agree. P-please do that," she stuttered.

"Well, since you asked so nicely." Kirsty slipped one finger under the silk, seeking the slippery surface of Saffron's outer lips. Going up. And then down. Again and again, until her finger was wet. Then she carefully eased it out and sampled the goods, never breaking eye contact with Saffron.

Saffron's chest hitched. "You're killing me."

"Can't lie. I'm loving seeing how much you want me in your eyes."

Unable to speak, Saffron couldn't rip her eyes off Kirsty, as she motioned for Saffron to lift up. Before Saffron could comprehend how quickly Kirsty removed the last barrier, her head lowered closer and closer to Saffron's throbbing pussy.

Saffron closed her eyes.

Kirsty's tongue delicately licked Saffron's clit. Flicking it once, before moving on to explore. Saffron's hand sought something overhead to hold onto, but she had to grip the corner of the pillow, her legs parting further, to give Kirsty complete and total access.

Kirsty's tongue dipped into Saffron with uncertainty, as if needing to bolster the nerve to dive inside.

"Please." Saffron fisted the pillow.

Kirsty did, her tongue going in deep.

"You feel so amazing." Saffron's hips writhed.

Kirsty removed her tongue from inside, and focused on Saffron's clit, lapping it slowly and sensually.

Saffron twisted and turned her upper body, doing her best to keep her centre available, as Kirsty eased a finger inside. A shudder working through Saffron.

Kirsty seemed to read Saffron's need and added another finger, going in deep.

"You're amazing. So f-fucking amazing," Saffron stammered, having such a hard time focusing on anything other than the explosion that was building. "Don't stop. Please... don't."

Kirsty somehow seemed to plunge deeper with each thrust, her mouth not letting up.

Saffron latched onto each side of Kirsty's head.

Kirsty didn't let up, circling the exact spot, which was a minor miracle, because Saffron couldn't keep her body still.

"More." Saffron's back arched.

Kirsty added another finger, her tongue kicking it up a notch.

"Oh, fuck me!"

Kirsty plunged in deeper.

Saffron's upper body bucked up off the bed.

Kirsty curled her fingers upwards, lighting Saffron up. The first wave of ecstasy spilled over the crest, firing every nerve ending in her entire body.

But Kirsty had no intention of letting it stop there, because she dove in again, her fingers easily triggering Saffron for the second round, the orgasm morphing into a second force of nature.

Then another.

Saffron writhed, as the orgasm continued.

After another full-body jerk, she collapsed back onto the bed.

Kirsty rested her chin on Saffron's leg. "See how communication pays off."

"I can't see a thing right now. Just light. Lots of light." Saffron flicked her fingers indicating fireworks.

Kirsty laughed. "I'll take that as a win."

Saffron reached for Kirsty, pulling her up to hold onto. "Most definitely."

"Are you sure you don't want a glass of wine now? You sound parched." There was smugness in her tone.

Saffron tightened her squeeze. "I don't want to let go of you. Stay."

Chapter 33

Kirsty blinked herself awake, but something wasn't normal. Her head was buried against something strong and warm. She pulled back. It was only then she smiled.

The warm thing was Saffron. Kirsty had a movie star in her bed. Correction, *ex-movie star*.

At least, for now.

Kirsty moved back to where she'd woken up and snaked an arm around Saffron's waist, curling herself into the curve of Saffron's body. A rush of heat swept through her, making her grin as she ground her face into Saffron's back. If you'd have told her she was going to be doing this even yesterday, she'd have called you a fool.

However, time and life had a way of working their own magic. Yesterday, she'd been down on love but keeping her chin up for Ginger's sake. Today, she was ready to embrace it with open arms. To imagine that a movie star might just be happy with little old her.

"Not so much of the old!", as Helena would say.

Kirsty smiled. Turns out, age gaps could be bridged. Misunderstandings could be ironed out. Relationships could be mended. She'd learned a lot over the past few days.

Bizarrely, Helena's website bombshell might have sped up Kirsty and Saffron's reunion. They'd been forced to confront issues neither of them were keen to talk about head-on. If Helena hadn't botched the website so spectacularly, and Saffron's agent hadn't set her up with Echo, they would have ended up in bed together again, but they'd have probably left things unsaid. After last night, nothing had been left unsaid. Or untouched.

A hand grabbing hers pulled Kirsty's attention back to the present, a world she was happy to live in. She didn't want to share Saffron with anyone else. Would anybody notice if they just shacked up in her flat, in this very bed, and didn't emerge for a week? Perhaps she could get Anton to work her shifts in the shop. Although he might struggle leading the wine tasting featuring select Italian vineyards next week.

"Morning." Saffron's voice was studded with gravel as she kissed Kirsty's fingers, before turning to face her. Kirsty sucked in a breath. Saffron was even more beautiful this morning than she had been last night, if that were possible. She reached out and smoothed Saffron's golden hair behind her left ear.

"Morning yourself." She leaned forward and kissed Saffron's lips, revelling in their sweetness and warmth.

Just like that, her libido sprang to life, her whole body purring. Kirsty had read that a woman hit her sexual peak at 36. If last night was anything to go by, she was pretty sure she had the data to contest that. She didn't recall having so many orgasms in such a short space of time ever before.

She pulled back, tracing the curve of Saffron's upturned mouth with her index finger. "What's that smile for?"

"I hope the same reason you have a massive one on your lips. Because I've woken up in your bed." She rolled onto her back and spread her legs wide. "A king size, no less."

"I like to spread out."

"I noticed that last night." Saffron rolled on top of her and pressed down.

Kirsty's mind scrambled.

She kissed her thoroughly, deeply, until Kirsty had no idea where Saffron's lips started and hers ended.

After a few minutes, Saffron pulled back, eyeing her. "Where have you been all my life?"

Kirsty snorted, and pushed Saffron off, reversing their roles and pressing herself into Saffron.

"Please. If you're serious about not being a movie star for the foreseeable future, we might have to go back to the drawing board for some of your lines. They need work. *A lot of work*. You need to cut the cheese in half at least."

Saffron gave her a grin as her phone pinged.

Kirsty gave her a look. "Leave it."

"What if it's heaven calling saying they're missing an angel?"

Kirsty sat up, her thighs squeezing Saffron below her, and let out a belly laugh. "Are you done?" She leaned forward and brought her eyes level with Saffron.

"Not nearly done with you." Saffron's tone had gone from teasing to serious.

Kirsty's heart boomed. "I'm glad to hear it."

Saffron reached up and stroked her breast. Her intent focus made Kirsty still.

"I mean it. Last night was incredible and I want to be

clear. I'm staying here. I'm getting a dog. And I want you in my plans. For the sake of clarity, I want to be your girlfriend." Saffron's cheeks glowed red. She looked adorable. "Does that sound like something you might consider?"

A grin split Kirsty's face as she shook her head. "You're seriously asking me that question? As you're lying beneath me with your perfect teeth, your golden skin, and your limbs that go on for miles?" Kirsty licked her lips, then placed a gentle kiss on Saffron's lips. "I'm totally here for this. If you're asking me to be yours, I'm in." A ticker-tape parade of happiness marched through her.

"My girlfriend owns a wine shop. What a find!" Saffron punched the air.

Kirsty kissed her again, before shuffling down Saffron, parting her thighs and placing a hand over her core. "Mine just jacked in her job and she hasn't got another one lined up. Luckily, she's hot." Kirsty slid a finger into Saffron's heat, then groaned. "Also, *seriously* wet for me."

Saffron's eyes blazed with desire. "You have *no* idea."

* * *

Kirsty waved at Danny on the top road overlooking the sea. From this vista, you could see right down to Branton Bay on the right, and way beyond Sandy Cove to your left. However, the one view Kirsty still couldn't get enough of was right in front of her.

Saffron Oliver.

Her girlfriend.

It was going to take some getting used to.

"Let me guess. Your old boyfriend?"

Danny was the fourth person Kirsty had greeted on the walk from her flat to Saffron's place.

Kirsty shook her head. "His dad used to play cricket with my dad. We were always left in the pavilion together as kids. He's very ticklish."

Saffron's phone pinged, distracting her.

"Let me guess." Kirsty gripped Saffron's hand as they walked down the diagonal path—lined with scorched grass—to the main promenade. "Ginger."

Saffron let out a light chuckle. "She's not giving up easily. She wants to meet us for lunch or a drink or dinner." Saffron kissed Kirsty's hand, before slowing down. "Can we give her something? She did get us together in a roundabout way."

Kirsty nodded. Ginger had been instrumental. They'd shared their stories of Ginger's intervention over the past couple of days, so they owed her. "Dinner later on? By then I might be ready to share you. For now, I want to walk along the beach with my girlfriend, get an ice cream, and then go back to hers for more hot sex."

Saffron gave her a grin. "I'll have to check my schedule, but I'm sure it can be arranged."

At the bottom of the hill they bought an ice cream from Nathan's Ice Cream Hut. Kirsty chatted to him for a few moments, before presenting Saffron with her 99.

She licked the ice cream, then took a bite of the chocolate flake before glancing back at Nathan. "He was your boyfriend, if I remember correctly?"

Kirsty nodded. "We went steady for at least three weeks, aged seven. Can you cope?"

Saffron raised both eyebrows. "Is it possible to get

retroactively jealous about something that happened years ago?"

Kirsty put an arm through hers as they strolled. Saffron was the model stroller, now. "Get used to it. This town is a living, breathing part of my history."

"I'm getting that."

Two teenage girls ran in front of them and shyly asked for a selfie with Saffron. She untangled herself from Kirsty, deposited her cone in Kirsty's spare hand, then posed like the pro she was, making the girls giggle uncontrollably as they walked away.

Kirsty was going to have to get used to being stopped, too.

Saffron took back her ice cream and re-threaded her arm through Kirsty's. "No matter how famous I am in the world, I'll never top your fame in this town."

As if to back up her point, Kirsty's primary school teacher walked past.

"Hi, Mrs Warton!" Kirsty trilled, like she was still eight years old.

Mrs Warton shook her head. "How many times, dear? It's Marion!"

Kirsty grinned, as she always did. It was never going to be Marion.

"But you know what?" Saffron added. "I'm perfectly okay with that. More than okay. This is your town, and I can just blend into the background. It's kind of what I've always wanted."

Kirsty reached up on tip-toes and pecked Saffron on the lips. "I know." And she did.

Kirsty put a hand in her pocket and pulled out a piece of paper. She frowned. She recalled Helena putting it in her pocket last night and saying something about opening it in the morning. She dodged more people on the path as she tried to unfurl it with one hand.

"What's that?" Saffron licked her ice cream, looking down.

There, scrawled in Helena's spidery handwriting, was a note that read: *Life can be like a Hollywood rom-com. You just have to let it happen.* Helena had added a love heart and a kiss.

Kirsty's heart boomed. She grinned, pocketing the note and glancing up at Saffron.

Helena was right.

You just had to let it.

Chapter 34

There was a knock on the front door, and Saffron glanced up from her to-do list, frazzled. That'd better be the caterer, who'd been expected thirty minutes ago.

She swung the door open to reveal Kirsty. "Why are you knocking on the door?"

"It's common etiquette when visiting."

"Yes, but… given you've sampled the goods, it seems like you should be able to walk right in. It's why I texted you that the door was unlocked." Saffron gave her a peck on the cheek.

"Such a sweet talker. But, I'll have you know, I don't even let myself into my parents' house."

Saffron slowly blew out a frustrated breath.

"What's wrong? The crease in your forehead has creases, which doesn't bode well for your recent retirement." Kirsty ran a finger over Saffron's brow.

"The caterer isn't here yet."

"Caterer?" Kirsty chuckled. "You hired someone to cook dinner for family and friends?"

"It was either that or risk poisoning everyone. Ask Ginger about the time I cooked fish pie." Saffron stuck her hands into her pockets, rocking back on her heels.

"Pretty sure I'm okay not hearing the details." She presented Saffron with a wrapped gift, that she had tucked under one arm. "Open this now because you need it."

"Is it Valium?" Saffron shook the shoe-sized box with both hands. "A lot of it."

"Easy. It's fragile," Kirsty warned.

Saffron eased a finger under a seam, not wanting to tear the paper covered in vintage wine adverts. "Where'd you get the paper?"

"An Italian supplier. You like?"

"It's pretty enough to hang on the wall." Saffron exposed one side of the box. "Aw, a decanter. It's perfect." She kissed Kirsty on the cheek again. "I can get used to you giving me gifts."

"Making a mental note of that. We need to decant the red I sent over earlier."

"That reminds me…" Saffron consulted her phone. "The guests are arriving in mere minutes and I don't have any food to offer them."

"You don't have anything in the house?"

Saffron shook her head, wiping a sweaty palm onto her jeans. "I'm still getting the hang of being domestic. This is going to be an epic failure, isn't it? Why'd I think I could handle a dinner party? My assistant used to arrange everything. You know, she's still on the payroll. Maybe she can save my bacon."

"This isn't a Hollywood gala." Kirsty motioned for Saffron to bring it down a notch. "No one will care if things are late. You have wine. Keep serving wine. Simple."

"Wine, right."

There was another knock on the door and Saffron

practically leapt for joy before running to the door, the box still pressed against her side. "You're here!"

Dolly apologised and asked directions to the kitchen, getting to work with a younger woman who worked at the restaurant.

Kirsty opened the bottle of red and after Saffron rinsed the decanter, she filled it. The two of them moved into the lounge to get out of the way.

"I feel better." She shook her body, letting the stress go. "Can I get you a glass of wine?"

"What? No Jeeves?" Kirsty waggled her brows.

"He has the night off. Let's go out into the garden." Saffron grabbed a bottle and two glasses. "Sorry, my girlfriend, who owns a wine shop only just gave me a decanter so you have to put up with wine straight from the bottle."

"How do you put up with such incompetence?"

"Luckily she has other qualities that make up for the wine faults." Saffron shot Kirsty a suggestive look, making Kirsty roll her eyes.

The sound of waves greeted them, and the waning sun left a chill in the air.

"I'm going to miss the long summer nights." Kirsty pulled her cardigan over her chest.

"I would like to point out, more darkness means more time in bed." Saffron handed Kirsty a glass of red.

"Fair point, well made." Kirsty took a sip. "Why'd you invite guests over when we're still in the early stages of shagging?"

"It seemed like the grown-up thing to do." Saffron shrugged. "Next time, I'll run my ideas by you."

"Oh, no." Kirsty shook a finger. "I won't become your assistant. It's time, Ms Oliver, for you to spread your wings."

"It's kind of exciting and terrifying all at once."

"Hello?" Ginger shouted from inside the house.

"Garden!" Saffron shouted back.

Kirsty shook her head, tsking.

"What? She has a key and as I said earlier, Jeeves has the night off." Saffron flourished her glass.

"I brought the troops." Ginger made a *ta da* motion, as Helena, Hugh, Ian, and Ruth stood behind her.

"We all stopped at the pub on the corner for half pints." Helena kissed Kirsty's cheek and then Saffron's.

After all the hugs and air kisses, Saffron pressed her palms together. "Let me get more wine glasses." Saffron winked at Kirsty.

In the kitchen she surveyed the progress. "Do you need anything?"

Dolly, chopping mint, glanced up. "We prepped almost everything earlier, so don't you worry about a thing." She turned around. "Annie, can you set out the hors d'oeuvres?"

Saffron left them to it, taking one of the olives from the platter before Annie whisked it away.

Back outside, Saffron poured more wine, unable to keep her eyes off Kirsty, who was engrossed in a conversation with her parents.

"Whoa!" Ginger tipped the bottle up. "Don't waste any."

"Sorry!" Saffron wiped the side of the bottle.

"I've never seen you this way."

"What way?"

"Giddy." Ginger's broad smile matched Saffron's.

"I am, aren't I?"

"I hear you're buying the house." Hugh munched into a new potato cup, filled with chilli spiced crab and papaya.

"Yep. It's time to settle down."

Helena's eyes followed Saffron's gaze. "You two make a lovely couple."

"Thank you."

"Again, I'm so—"

Saffron stopped Helena with a raised hand. "No. It's done."

"What are you going to do now?" Ian had descended on the platter, swooping up gin prawns with lime, cucumber, and wasabi mayo.

"Slow down, mostly." Saffron sipped her wine.

"What does that mean?" Ruth appeared by her husband's side, Kirsty right behind her parents.

"Is this a dinner party or interrogation?" Kirsty joked, angling herself between Saffron and her parents.

"It's okay. I have a feeling this is going to be a popular question for months. I've decided to rent the shop across from Wine Time. Open an art gallery."

"Will you run it?" Helena wiped a crumb off the front of Hugh's shirt.

"Not at first. I'm planning on hiring someone who actually knows what they're doing." A nervous giggle escaped her. "I want to ease into being a business owner and learn everything from the ground up."

"She's buying a beach hut so she can focus on her own creations." Kirsty cheerfully added, "She's good. Very good."

"TMI." Ginger bumped her elbow into Kirsty.

Kirsty blushed.

Everyone laughed.

"When are you bringing home your bitch?" Hugh shoved smoked mackerel pate on a potato rosti into his mouth.

"Fine way to refer to my business partner and best friend." Helena yet again wiped away crumbs from Hugh's five o'clock shadow. "You're worse than when Anton was a baby."

"Goldie's coming home tomorrow." Saffron threaded an arm around Kirsty's shoulder, and let out a squeal. "My first baby."

"She's already set up playdates with Rufus." Kirsty leaned into Saffron.

"I'm guessing from the name, she's a Golden Retriever." Ian refilled his wife's glass with the open bottle on the table.

"That she is. At first I wanted to rename her, but after spending time with her, she really does shine."

"Will she sleep in bed with you two?" Ginger asked.

Saffron tossed serious shade at her sister causing Ginger to laugh.

Dolly caught Saffron's eye.

"Hugh, I hope you still have room for dinner?" Saffron motioned to the table on the patio.

"I'm a bottomless pit." He patted his stomach.

"In every way imaginable," Helena chided.

He gnashed his teeth.

Saffron and Kirsty shared a smile, and Saffron couldn't help but wonder if they'd reach that stage. The one where they mercifully teased each other in front of their friends, without ruffling the other's feathers.

Ginger took the seat on Kirsty's right. "When do I get the keys to the castle?"

"Are you done with the town's website?" Kirsty shifted in her chair to face Ginger.

"Finished the contract this morning. I'm ready to help set up online sales for you." Ginger placed a cloth napkin in her lap.

"Excellent." Kirsty tapped her fingertips together. "And I may need a site for my side gig. I've had a slew of divorce party requests. It seems you've started a Sandy Cove trend."

"I wonder if they'll be more popular than hen parties?"

"Not sure if that's a good thing." Kirsty squeezed Saffron's hand.

"For me, I found it wonderfully freeing. For the first time since boxing up my things and moving to a new town, I feel at peace. Ready for the next stage in my life." Ginger radiated.

Saffron leaned back to allow Dolly to set down the lemon sole, spinach, courgettes, and Jersey Royal new potatoes. "This night has taught me one thing. I need to take cooking lessons."

"Whatever you do, don't ever attempt fish pie again. I've never been so sick in my life." Ginger forked a bite of potato. "What's in the salsa?"

Dolly, luckily, was still present and said, "Mint, chili, spring onions, olives, lemon juice, and olive oil."

"It's to die for." Ginger ate another bite.

"If you're serious about cooking lessons, I'd love to add you to my Wednesday night class." Dolly wiped her hands on her apron.

"That's another part of Sandy Cove life you'll have to

grow accustomed to. Many of us wear different hats, given the tourist season has a short window," Kirsty said.

"Good to know. Dolly, consider me signed up." Saffron pretended to write her name in the air. "I've got to fill my time somehow."

"Hopefully without killing anyone." Ginger pointed her fork at Saffron, pretending it was a gun. "Death by fork."

"You have zero faith in my domesticity." Saffron feigned being hurt.

"You did hire a caterer for the night," Kirsty not so helpfully pointed out.

"Look at your plate. It's divine." Saffron circled her fork over her own serving.

"Oh boy, now she thinks she's a goddess." Kirsty spoke to Ginger, not attempting to lower her voice so Saffron wouldn't overhear.

"Be careful with this one. Soon, she'll be demanding you feed her grapes, while also fanning her." Ginger fanned her own face with a napkin, displaying a devilish grin.

"Don't forget belly dancers and musicians." Kirsty laughed over the image.

Saffron beamed, not about the image, but that the banter had already started. It had to be a good sign for their future. She placed her hand on Kirsty's thigh.

"I'm thinking of hiring a trainer to see if I can star in movies." Hugh licked juice off his finger.

"Yep. That's the thing holding you back. Not having a trainer." Helena patted his cheek.

"Don't be jealous. Some of us have star quality, right Saffron?"

"Keep it up, and you'll be seeing stars." Helena gave his shoulder a light punch.

"Don't damage the goods." Hugh rubbed the spot.

Saffron wrapped one of her legs around Kirsty's under the table, needing to be as close as possible without putting on the wrong type of show for all to see.

Ian leaned forward in his seat, making eye contact with Saffron. "Thanks to you, I was able to answer a crossword clue in *The Times* I wouldn't have known three months ago."

"What was it?"

"*Girl Racer*." He puffed his chest out.

Kirsty bristled, but Saffron comforted her with a grin. "That's the best thing that came out of the franchise."

"A crossword clue?" Ian's brow furrowed.

"Meeting all of you." Saffron boosted Kirsty's hand to her lips. "You most of all."

There was much oohing and aahhing, and Saffron wanted to snap her fingers to have Dolly clear the plates to get the meal over with, and send the guests home.

"I'd like to say something." Ruth raised a glass, looking at Saffron and then to her daughter. "Not too long ago, Kirsty teased Ian and me about being adorable and I said she'd find her adorable. And now she has."

"To adorable!" Ginger clinked her glass to Ruth's and then Kirsty's, everyone else taking part.

Kirsty leaned close to Saffron and whispered, "I love you."

The three words Saffron had always wanted to hear, but never believed she would. Or believe the person who spoke them. With Kirsty, though, Saffron was only beginning to understand how deep their love was for each other. Every moment they shared brought them closer and Saffron still couldn't believe her stroke of good luck. Fleeing the life she'd hated had led Saffron to her forever place and person and she had no intention of letting go.

Epilogue

One Year Later

"Wait. Did you box up the wine orders for The Sailor Bistro already?" Kirsty frowned at the screen behind the shop counter. They'd only had it for a few weeks and she was still getting used to it. Kirsty swore at the system daily, but it was helping hugely with their online orders, which had gone bonkers since launch. She'd thought it would be mainly businesses who wanted their wine, but it was households, too, and plenty of them.

Helena reached an arm around her from behind. "This tick here?" She pointed at the green tick on the screen. "That means it's done. It's sitting by the door. Anton is coming to bike the orders round this afternoon."

Helena was on at her to get a van now their orders had stepped up, but Kirsty still loved her bike with its vintage stylings and personal touch. Saffron agreed with Helena, telling Kirsty she wasn't getting any younger. That comment had gone down like a lead balloon. Unlike the surprise weekend Saffron had whisked her away on to celebrate her 50th birthday.

There was a time when Kirsty had been dreading turning

50. However, it transpired that 50 really was just a number. Plus, when she had a hot woman on her arm, clocking up half a century didn't seem like such a big deal. *You're only as old as the woman you feel,* as the saying went. In that case, Kirsty was a cool 33. Saffron was keeping her young. She loved *everything* about that.

In the interim year since Saffron turned down *Girl Racer 3* and bedded down in Sandy Cove, so much had changed. Saffron was now renting Donald's old menswear shop opposite, turning it into an art studio where she exhibited local artists as well as her own work. More than that, Saffron had also set up a children's arts charity, putting her money to good use where the arts were concerned.

Kirsty was beyond proud at how Saffron had adapted to normal life. True to her word, she didn't seem to miss anything about her old life. The past 12 months had been a time for Saffron to stop, reassess, and pivot. That didn't mean she'd given up on the acting world totally. *Acting, yes.* But Saffron was still drawn to the industry.

Kirsty had noticed scripts lying around the house far more over the past few weeks, showing Saff was almost ready to dip a toe back in the water. She'd set up a production company with the help of her assistant, Michelle, and was keen to head down the directing route when the right queer project came along. Kirsty was all for it. Seeing Saffron doing things her way finally was something she could totally get behind. Saffron lit up every time she spoke about it.

Kirsty walked over to the shop front and opened the door. The sun hit the pavement like a slice of lemon. It was July, and the tourists were thronging the pavements of the seaside town, soaking up its charm and good looks. Give it three months and the High Street would be empty, save for the locals. Even though the summer season was what brought in the money, Kirsty far preferred the quieter months. When the beaches were empty. The streets hushed. The cafés easy to get a seat in.

Plus, it'd mean more time for her and Saffron.

It was still something she couldn't get enough of.

Saffron coming out of her studio and shaking hands with a teenager caught her eye. Her smile was a sunbeam, and Kirsty couldn't help reflect it. The teenager was there to sign up for Saffron's arts scholarship, another thing she was doing to help the local community. When Saffron glanced across the street, she gave Kirsty a wave.

A bus driving by swallowed up whatever Saffron shouted, and Kirsty cupped her ear to show she hadn't heard. "What?"

Saffron tried again and held up her phone.

Still no joy.

Saffron waited for a gap in the traffic, before bounding over the High Street and landing at Kirsty's side.

She kissed her lips before she spoke.

They were *that* couple now.

Kirsty's heart rejoiced.

"I said, have you seen my Instagram account for the studio?" Saffron pulled it up on her phone. "We just passed 50,000 followers. Amazing!" Saffron had been working on it with Michelle for the past few months, determined to build it from scratch without trading on her fame. They'd sort of managed it, but she was more excited by that than she ever had been about her old account in her old life.

Perhaps because this one was all her. From the heart.

Saffron had a huge heart and capacity for giving, something Kirsty was learning every day.

She pocketed her phone in her artfully ripped jeans. "What are you doing for lunch? I've still got some of that incredible mackerel dish I made at Dolly's cooking class last night. Plus, crème brûlée. We could go back to mine and eat on the veranda?" Saffron put her lips beside Kirsty's ear. "Then we could retire to the bedroom for an extra helping of dessert, if you get my drift."

Kirsty's clit stood to attention. She got Saffron's drift precisely. Saffron had shown her before she came to work that morning. And the night before.

"You know I can't." Kirsty nudged Saffron with her elbow. "I've got a meeting with your sister about this year's Oyster Festival."

"Cancel it."

"No."

Saffron pouted. "Spoilsport."

Up above, the seagulls squawked in the clear blue sky. Kirsty breathed in the sea air, stroking her girlfriend's arm. A year ago, a photographer would have snapped that. Now, they were pretty much left alone. It turned out, the secret to a quiet life was to not be loud. Saffron had taken to it like a duck to water.

A family with a double buggy walked towards them. Saffron edged over to stand in front of Wine Time to give them room. "Your festival window display is fabulous this year, by the way. A different level." She grinned at Kirsty before running her gaze over the impressive wine paintings gracing the window. Saffron was responsible for every single one.

"They're not bad, are they?"

She nodded. "Who's the artist?"

Kirsty shook her head. "Nobody you'd know. Some local woman. Rosemary? Thyme? Some kind of herb? A made-up name if ever I heard one." She slid a hand around Saffron's waist.

Saffron tutted. "I hate those people who are all showy. Just have a normal name."

Kirsty leaned in. "I'll let her know." She pressed her lips to Saffron's and the world around them stopped. Kirsty sank into the moment. Into *them*. The woman who'd given up on love had found it right on her doorstep.

"*Girl Racer* rocks!" shouted someone from the opposite pavement, cutting through a lull in traffic.

Saffron pulled back and punched the air, making the fan whoop. She turned back towards Kirsty, her piercing blue gaze intense.

"That's a lie, by the way." She kissed Kirsty's lips once more, making Kirsty's heart get up on tip-toes and do a pirouette. "*Girl Racer* sucks. *You* rock."

Kirsty pressed a finger to Saffron's chest. "No, *we* rock."

Saffron turned up her silver screen smile. "I'll go with that."

THE END

319

A Note From The Authors

TB here. First, thanks so much for reading *One Golden Summer*. Clare and I decided to co-write this story back in 2019, before the world got (how should I phrase this?), *so weird*. When we planned my visit to London, we set aside three days to pop over to Whitstable, which was our inspiration for Sandy Cove.

Clare has a special place in her heart for the seaside town, and when she started showing me around, I immediately understood why. It's an exceptional place overflowing with charm, panoramic vistas, culture, and oysters.

Co-writing this novel during trying times presented some difficulties, but I would like to focus on the good, not the bad. For me, the timing of this project helped keep me sane. Nearly every day, we were in some type of contact, and I think many of us are learning how important it is to have connections. I'm fortunate to call Clare Lydon a true friend and, now, my co-author.

If you enjoyed the story, we would really appreciate a review. Even short reviews help immensely.

Thanks again for reading this English seaside romance.

TB & Clare

Meet Clare Lydon

Clare Lydon is a London-based writer of contemporary lesbian romance. She's a No.1 best-seller on lesbian fiction charts around the globe. If you're a sucker for romantic comedies, prepare to fall head over heels in love. You can check out her website here.

Clare is famed for her London Romance series, as well as her much-loved standalones including *Before You Say I Do, Nothing To Lose* and *You're My Kind*. She hosts two podcasts — The Lesbian Book Club & Lesbians Who Write — and has spoken at queer festivals and prides around the country.

When she's not writing, Clare watches far too many home improvement shows, while drinking nuclear-strength coffee & eating Curly Wurlys.

If you'd like a free lesbian romance, *It Had To Be You*, sign up to her VIP Readers Club for offers, sales & updates too! Go here: www.clarelydon.co.uk/it-had-to-be-you

Meet TB Markinson

TB Markinson is an American who's recently returned to the US after a seven-year stint in the UK and Ireland. When she isn't writing, she's traveling the world, watching sports on the telly, visiting pubs in New England, or reading. Not necessarily in that order.

Her novels have hit Amazon bestseller lists for lesbian fiction and lesbian romance. For a full listing of TB's novels, head over to her Amazon page.

Feel free to visit TB's website to say hello. On the *Lesbians Who Write* weekly podcast, she and Clare Lydon dish about the good, the bad, and the ugly of writing. TB also runs I Heart Lesfic (www.iheartlesfic.com), a place for authors and fans of lesfic to come together to celebrate and chat about lesbian fiction.

Want to learn more about TB? Hop over to her *About* page on her website for the juicy bits. Okay, it won't be all that titillating, but you'll find out more.

Go here: www.lesbianromancesbytbm.com

Printed in Great Britain
by Amazon